KISS ME TWICE

Chaz woke in Kelly's arms the next morning and lay there, just drinking in the moment as he stared down at his wife. She cuddled up against him, one arm curled over his chest and one leg thrown over his thighs. Bare skin to bare skin, just the way he liked it.

He smiled in remembrance. They had spent the night getting reacquainted the best way he knew how. And between bouts of lovemaking on the bed, in the tub, on the floor, he had shared a few stories of his captivity and learned a little more about what her life had been like while he was gone.

The whole experience was enlightening. He knew now that it was too late to get his comfortable old Kelly back, but he was coming to appreciate the advantages of this new, more confident, wife of his.

Pure contentment filled him, but he had no illusions that his good fortune was due to any action of his. Kelly's presence in his arms and his bed was a miracle, a great gift. If only he didn't screw it up. . . .

BOOK YOUR PLACE ON OUR WEBSITE AND MAKE THE READING CONNECTION!

We've created a customized website just for our very special readers, where you can get the inside scoop on everything that's going on with Zebra, Pinnacle and Kensington books.

When you come online, you'll have the exciting opportunity to:

- View covers of upcoming books

- Read sample chapters

- Learn about our future publishing schedule (listed by publication month *and author*)

- Find out when your favorite authors will be visiting a city near you

- Search for and order backlist books from our online catalog

- Check out author bios and background information

- Send e-mail to your favorite authors

- Meet the Kensington staff online

- Join us in weekly chats with authors, readers and other guests

- Get writing guidelines

- AND MUCH MORE!

**Visit our website at
http://www.kensingtonbooks.com**

MY FAVORITE HUSBAND

Pam McCutcheon

ZEBRA BOOKS
Kensington Publishing Corp.
http://www.kensingtonbooks.com

ZEBRA BOOKS are published by

Kensington Publishing Corp.
850 Third Avenue
New York, NY 10022

All Kensington titles, imprints and distributed lines are available at special quantity discounts for bulk purchases for sales promotion, premiums, fund-raising, educational or institutional use.

Special book excerpts or customized printings can also be created to fit specific needs. For details, write or phone the office of the Kensington Special Sales Manager: Kensington Publishing Corp., 850 Third Avenue, New York, NY 10022. Attn. Special Sales Department. Phone: 1-800-221-2647.

Zebra and the Z logo Reg. U.S. Pat. & TM Off.

First Printing: December 2003

10 9 8 7 6 5 4 3 2 1

Printed in the United States of America

*Thanks to everyone who gave me such
wonderful input on the book and gave me support
while I wrote it: Linda Kruger, Deb Stover,
Paula Gill, Karen Fox, Angel Smits, Laura Hayden,
Maureen Webster, and Yvonne Jocks.*

*But this one is especially for Mae Boles, who is
the best support a writer could have. You
make it easy for me to write, Mom!*

One

It ought to be the happiest day of my life.
It ought to be the saddest.

It was both. It was neither. It was . . . confusing.

Kelly Richmond Vincent, soon to be Kelly Richmond Vincent Preston, sighed as she stared out the window of the small anteroom at the chapel. She just wanted to get it over with.

"What's the sigh for?" Scott asked. "The wedding or the funeral?"

Kelly gazed at her brother who lounged against the door, looking every inch the suave, careless playboy he pretended to be. She hesitated, not knowing how to answer. Finally, she said, "Yes." The answer fit her mood and the situation.

Scott grinned, then dropped his pose to sling an arm around her shoulders. "What d'ya say we skip out on both and fly to the beach?"

"What beach?"

"Any beach. Doesn't matter. We'll just go, far away from this cold Colorado winter and all this . . . stuff."

God help her. For one brief moment, she actually considered it. The idea definitely appealed to her wild side. But years of being responsible, of doing the right thing, were too much to ignore. "I can't. You know that."

Scott hugged her tighter. "Why not?"

She leaned into the hug. "Because I'm the one getting married . . . and burying a husband."

He grinned. "Better not let anyone else hear you say it that way. It sounds sinister."

"You know what I mean."

"Yes, but why on earth did you schedule them on the same day?"

"I didn't. Spencer did." She had organized the memorial service for her first husband, but her fiancé had made all the wedding arrangements, telling her all she had to do was show up and look beautiful. "It was the only time we could both get away from the office. The fact that they're on the same day is just coincidence."

"A bad one—"

He broke off and moved away from Kelly as their mother hurried into the room, beaming. Grace Richmond had no reservations. She adored Spencer and was eager to have him for a son-in-law.

But she stopped dead when she saw her children's faces. "What's wrong?"

Panic overwhelmed Kelly. *Why am I doing this? It's insane.* She couldn't handle it. "I-I'm not sure this is such a good idea."

A look of alarm crossed her mother's patrician face. "Of course it is, dear. Why would you think otherwise?"

"I don't think I'm ready yet." Not to marry again, not to say good-bye to Chaz forever, not to deal with this horrible day.

"Nonsense," her mother said bracingly. "All brides feel that way. You'll get over it."

Odd, Kelly hadn't felt that way at her first wedding. . . .

Grace Richmond patted her daughter's hand as if by doing so she could pound some sense into her. "You've promised Spencer you'll marry him. You can't back out now. He's waiting for you at the altar, for heaven's sake."

Kelly gazed down at her hand. She could sure use a hug right now, but other mothers hugged. Hers patted. "I know." But she didn't move.

"It's Charles, isn't it?" her mother asked, her exasperation plain.

Annoyance flashed through Kelly and she pulled her hand away. "Chaz, Mother. He goes by Chaz." Or rather, went.

"It's been over five years since his plane went down in the Amazon," her mother said, obviously confused as to where Kelly's problem lay.

"I know." She'd spent the five years and all her savings searching for him. Fruitlessly. "It just feels like I'm betraying him."

Scott looked sympathetic, but her mother's expression turned concerned. "You're doing the right thing, dear. He couldn't possibly be alive after all this time. And the judge declared him legally dead last week. There's no impediment to your marriage."

Intellectually, Kelly knew that, but emotionally was another thing entirely. For five long years, she had never given up, never stopped hoping she'd find some trace of Chaz. How could she just . . . quit?

"And you promised Spencer—"

"I know, Mother." She *had* promised, and Spencer

had helped see her through the tough times, both personally and professionally. She owed it to him.

Mother was right. Spencer was a kind, thoughtful man. He would make a wonderful husband.

And she really needed to start a new life, one without the constant worry she had lived with since Chaz had disappeared. He was dead. Everyone said so, even the law. She just needed to accept it so she could get on with her life.

And Spencer would never let her down, never hurt her like Chaz had—he was far too considerate. She definitely needed some stability and consideration in her life, someone who put her needs above his own. Yes, marrying Spencer was the right thing to do.

Her decision must have showed on her face, for her mother brightened. "You'll do it, then?"

"Yes. Just . . . give me a minute, okay?"

"Of course, dear."

Grace Richmond hurried away and Scott raised an eyebrow as he handed her a glass of water. "You sure about this?"

"Yes . . . no. I don't know." She gazed into the glass and shrugged helplessly. "I'm all mixed up."

"Good ol' Spence isn't helping either, is he?"

He had been a bit insistent on their marrying as soon as possible, but . . . "He means well. He just wants what's best for me."

"So long as it's him," Scott said dryly.

There was some truth in that, but she couldn't let it slide. "No, really. He's been very good to me—and very patient. He helped me get promoted, helped me search for Chaz, and—"

"Helped you right into his waiting arms."

"That's not fair, Scott. I've been faithful to Chaz the

whole time." And to Spencer's credit, he had understood. Despite the fact that he had been pursuing her for at least four of those years her husband had been missing. . . .

"Oh, I see," Scott said in an enlightened tone. "You're just marrying this guy so you can finally get some."

Kelly choked on her water. Trust Scott to say the unexpected. She slugged him in the arm. "Hardly." Though she did miss the sex she and Chaz had shared.

"Then why?" Scott asked in a puzzled tone. "He's nothing like Chaz."

Scott had always liked Chaz. Then again, Chaz had charmed everyone . . . except Mother, of course. "*Because* he's nothing like Chaz. I don't want another Indiana Jones wannabe as a husband, gallivanting all over the world and leaving me behind to wait and worry. I couldn't go through that again, and Spencer won't do that to me. He's handsome, intelligent, sophisticated—"

"Bland, boring, blah," Scott finished for her. "How can you stand to be with him after Chaz?"

Living with Chaz had always been an adventure . . . when he was home. But his search for elusive archeological finds led him to remote and dangerous parts of the world. "Life with Spencer will never be as exciting as it was with Chaz," she conceded. "But that's a good thing. He's . . . comfortable. Safe. Reliable." Everything Chaz was not. "And he thinks *I'm* exciting."

Scott hooted. "Well, that should tell you something right there."

She hit him again and grinned despite herself. "I'm not boring—I just appeared that way in comparison to

Chaz." Who wouldn't? He was so vibrant and alive. . . .
Or, at least he had been. It was still difficult to think of
him as dead.

"That's true," Scott conceded. "You've changed
since he disappeared. You managed to cast off our
mother's finishing school look and become your own
person. You look snazzy."

She grinned at him. "Thanks. A lot of that is due to
Spencer, you know." He'd taken her in hand to jazz up
her image, make her look the part of a fashion magazine editor. She owed him a great deal.

Scott sighed. "Well, if that's what you want, I hope
he makes you happy."

"Thank you," Kelly said with tears in her eyes.
"That really means a lot."

Scott gave her another hug but released her when
their mother returned.

Mother paused, obviously uncomfortable with their
display of emotion. She handed Kelly a bouquet of red
and white hothouse roses. "They're ready for you
now."

"All right, Mother. Let's go." Kelly rose and took
Scott's arm.

Spencer Preston waited for her at the front of the
small chapel, next to the minister. Tall, blond, elegant,
and very classy, he was the epitome of the *GQ* man—
and a credit to *Pizzazz*. He smiled at her and her doubts
disappeared.

This is right. This is what I need—a fresh start.

But as her mother and Scott took their places as wit-
nesses to each side of them, Kelly couldn't help but
compare this wedding to her first.

At Chaz's insistence, their wedding had been a big,
splashy affair, not to mention a great deal of fun. She'd

worn a frothy, expensive dress with miles and miles of train and had hundreds of guests. It was wonderful. She'd felt like a princess in a fairy-tale wedding, and Chaz made a wonderful Prince Charming.

Contrast that with the one this morning when she wore just a simple knee-length ivory dress with a touch of her signature red. There would be no levity in this wedding, and there were only the five of them—the minister, her mother, Scott, and the two of them plighting their troth.

Whatever the heck that meant. Just what was a troth anyway, and how did you plight it?

She shook her head at her irreverence and reminded herself to pay attention. Besides, she shouldn't complain. Since she was so newly widowed—legally, anyway—a small ceremony was infinitely more suitable.

The minister asked if she would take Spencer to be her lawfully wedded husband. She murmured the correct responses, then Spencer did the same, and she was officially Mrs. Spencer Preston.

Okay, it's done. I can't back out now.

There was relief in that thought. Now she could get on with her life.

Spencer kissed her, then smiled. "Finally, Mrs. Preston." Gathering her into a possessive embrace, he smiled while her mother took pictures, then they all went to lunch to celebrate. Later, as they left the restaurant, Spencer gazed at her tenderly and asked, "Are you sure you want to do this next part?"

How sweet of him to ask. She laid a hand against his cheek. "Yes, I'm sure. I need to get this behind me before I can start on our new life together."

He gave her a gentle kiss on the cheek. "I understand. Are you sure you want to do it alone?"

"I'm sure." It wouldn't be right to show up at Chaz's service with her beaming new husband in tow. Or her gloating mother. That's why she'd asked Scott to make sure they didn't come. "I'll be fine. And I'll meet you afterward . . . where?" She suddenly realized she had no idea where they were to spend their wedding night or their honeymoon. She had put so much time into the memorial service, she didn't know what plans Spencer had made.

"I'll have a limo pick you up afterward," he whispered. "We're staying at the Pourtales in Colorado Springs. Since Candace has only given us a week off, I thought we'd spend the whole time there."

She raised one eyebrow and smiled. "Impressive." A luxurious five-star hotel and no jet lag to worry about since the hotel was only about an hour's drive. It certainly sounded good. And it was nice of their mutual employer, Candace Everett, to give them time off from their jobs at *Pizzazz* magazine on such short notice. Especially since they were right in the middle of the search for a new *Pizzazz* Girl . . . and it was rather obvious that Candace had her eye on Spencer for herself. "Sounds wonderful. I'll meet you there."

After they left, Kelly put on a navy duster that completely concealed her light dress and drove across Denver to another chapel at a funeral parlor. She was cutting the time a little close, but she had arranged everything in advance so she wasn't worried.

Until she got there.

Prominently displayed at the front of the chapel was a beautiful polished mahogany casket with a huge spray of flowers covering the top. She pulled the funeral director, Mr. Throckmorton, aside and pointed at it accusingly. "What is that?" she demanded.

The tall, gaunt man gave her a puzzled look. "It's a casket."

"I can see that," she snapped. "Why is it here?" This was just supposed to be a memorial service. Chaz's body had never been found, so she couldn't imagine what—or who—was inside.

He looked disapproving. "In these cases, we've found it helps those left behind to have a focus for their grief. A physical object to concentrate on."

"Well, I don't want it," Kelly said. It was just too . . . creepy. "Get it out of here."

His expression turned mournful. "Your guests have already begun to arrive. If I take it away now, how will it look?" He gestured toward the chapel, inviting her to look. "See how comforting they find it?"

She glanced into the chapel and groaned. He was right. People were clustered in small groups in the pews, whispering and sniffling as they cast sad glances at the coffin.

Rent-a-body. God, how ghoulish. "Well, I didn't ask for it and I'm not going to pay for it."

"The sisters of the dearly departed requested it," Throckmorton informed her. "They have already arranged payment."

It figured. They had always butted in where they weren't wanted. Irreverently, Kelly wondered how the occupant of the casket—or rather, his loved ones—felt about it. "Well, can you at least tell me who's in it?" At his pained expression, she added, "Never mind. I don't want to know."

She had just wanted to say good-bye to Chaz with a minimum of fuss and bother, but the memorial service was going awry already and it hadn't even started yet. Her jaw clenched, Kelly stalked toward the front pew, looking neither right nor left, determined not to make eye contact. She didn't want to talk to anyone. Not about Chaz, not about anything. She had planned this as her own good-bye to him, and she didn't want to share it with anyone else.

She seated herself and stared determinedly ahead— anywhere but at the stupid casket. She wanted to grieve for Chaz, but all she could do was wonder who was inside that mahogany creation. Some starched-up businessman? Someone's grandmother? Elvis?

She stifled a grin. That last thought was a classic Chaz reaction . . . and he was probably looking down and laughing hysterically right now. Trust him to have a great time even at his own funeral.

Damn, she missed him. Missed his laughing blue eyes, his extravagant gestures, his joy of life. *Why did you have to leave me?* she cried inside.

Immediately, she tamped down the thought. She was here for closure so she could move on to a new life, not open five-year-old wounds. She heard a stir come from the front of the chapel and raised her eyes gratefully. The service ought to help.

She listened politely as his family minister said a few words, then asked Chaz's sisters and cousins each to speak. Chaz's sisters expounded on his loving attitude and his cousins on his adventurous and charming ways. Kelly tried to take their sentiments in the spirit they were intended, but couldn't help but remember how his family had complained about his careless familial attitude and how *un*charming they had found his adventurous ways.

The last cousin had just started speaking when Kelly

felt someone sit down next to her. It was Scott, with a concerned expression on his face.

"Kell, I have to tell you something," he whispered.

"Shh." This was not the time. Chaz's family didn't care much for her and she didn't want to give them any reason to criticize her deportment at Chaz's memorial service.

Unless Scott was about to tell her something that would make it worse. "Mother isn't here, is she?" she asked in horror.

"No, but—"

"Not now," she whispered fiercely. If it wasn't about Mother making a scene, it could wait.

"Kell, you really need to listen—"

"Hush." Why was he pushing this? Scott wasn't usually so insensitive. Annoyed, she whispered in a snappish tone, "If you don't be quiet, I'll tell Mother what really happened to her favorite Aubusson."

"You wouldn't." He actually sounded wounded.

"Only if you don't *be quiet*."

"But it was such an *ugly* rug," Scott murmured. "And the guys down at the pool hall think it adds such class. . . ."

No, he was not going to cajole her into smiling this time. She gave him a glance that said clearly, "Shut up or else."

He shrugged. "Okay, it's your funeral."

No, it was Chaz's. And nothing was going as she'd planned. She turned a polite face to the cousin, who finished with a maudlin statement, and then the minister asked if there was anyone else who wanted to say anything. He knew better than to look at Kelly. She'd made it very clear she wanted to say her good-byes in private.

A deep voice came from the back. "*I'd* like to say something."

Kelly glanced up and frowned as the man made his way toward the front. What kind of idiot came to a memorial service dressed in khaki? With that deep tan and full beard, he must be one of Chaz's archeologist friends. Ah, that explained it.

Scott leaned closer and whispered, "I really need to—"

She whipped around and fixed him with a killing glare that made him back off with his hands raised. What the hell was the matter with Scott? She would have understood it if he had tried to disrupt the wedding, but not the memorial service. He had liked Chaz.

With Scott now suitably cowed, Kelly turned back to face the front and gazed at the man at the podium. He did look familiar. She knew she had seen him before, but couldn't quite place him. She was sure his hair used to be brown, not sun-streaked blond like that . . . and something else wasn't quite right. The full beard? It nagged at her. She knew she ought to know him, but who was he?

The man didn't bother introducing himself. Instead, he nodded at the elaborate casket and said in a rich voice full of humor, "I just have one thing to say. If Chaz Vincent's body was never recovered, who the hell is in that box? Elvis?"

She knew that voice—intimately.

Ohmigod. Kelly shot to her feet as her mouth dropped open and shocked exclamations rippled throughout the room. Those bright blue eyes, that grin, that voice . . .

It's Chaz!

Chaz grinned at her and spread his arms wide. "Hi, honey. I'm ho-oome."

Joy filled her. Her husband was alive!

Horror filled her. Her husband was waiting in the Portales honeymoon suite.

Ohmigod, what do I do? Reaching out blindly, she found Scott there to support her.

"I tried to tell you . . ." he muttered.

The combination of emotions was too much. As a mishmash of feelings roiled through her, Kelly did the only sensible thing.

She fainted.

Two

As Kelly crumpled into her brother's arms, Chaz cursed himself. He should have broken it to her easier, but no, he had to make a grand entrance and scare her half to death.

Pandemonium broke out in the room as everyone rushed toward him. Everyone, that is, but the person he wanted most, the one whose memory had kept him sane during the five years of his captivity.

Chaz ignored the outstretched arms and exclamations of his friends and relatives and shoved past them, desperate to get to Kelly. But they all wanted a piece of him, this miracle who had come back to attend his funeral.

After hearing umpteen versions of "Chaz, is that really you?" while feeling like a salmon trying to swim upstream, Chaz finally stopped and bellowed, "Yes, it's me. And yes, I'm alive. I'll explain everything later—just let me get to my wife, please."

They finally let him through and he saw Kelly slumped in Scott's arms. Thank heavens Scott had managed to keep her out of the crush, save her from being trampled. Chaz scooped his wife up into his arms but the the bombardment of questions never stopped. "Find us someplace quiet," he told Scott.

Nodding decisively, Scott broke trail through the gaping crowd. Chaz followed him, black-clad mourners trailing in his wake.

A tall man with a discreet nametag on his jacket identifying him as Mr. Throckmorton met them at the side of the chapel. "This is most irregular," he said, scowling at Chaz.

"Whatsamatter?" Chaz asked. "Never have one of your memorial services disrupted before?"

Throckmorton's tone turned wry. "Not by the departed."

"Well, it's a new experience for you then, isn't it?" He nodded down at Kelly, still unconscious in his arms. "Can you find somewhere private for me and my wife? Then restore order out here?"

"Of course." He motioned them into an empty room.

Scott followed Chaz in, and just before the door closed, he saw Throckmorton raise his arms like a revival preacher addressing a tent full of rich sinners.

Chaz felt a momentary pang of guilt for leaving the man to clean up what he had started, but right now, his wife was more important. "That ought to keep them for a while," he said, and propped Kelly up in a nearby love seat. "Guard the door, will you, Scott?"

"Sure."

Chaz gazed down at Kelly in consternation. He hadn't thought through his miraculous resurrection scene, hadn't thought about how his wife would react. Who knew she'd pass out like that?

Not knowing what else to do, he chafed her hands and peered anxiously into her face. The one thing that had kept Chaz going the whole time he'd been gone was the thought of her, the wife he'd left behind. He'd kept a picture of her in his heart, with her homey, comfortable clothes and long, beautiful tumble of hair. She epitomized what home and family meant to him. For some reason, he hadn't expected her to change, but she had. She looked so . . . different.

He didn't know much about fashion—especially not what had been "in" for the past five years—but her clothes screamed chic, even to his untutored gaze, and so did her raven-black hair, cut short with clean lines that made her look elegant and sophisticated. And that bright red lipstick made her lips look oh, so kissable. Memory of those full, sensuous lips and her long, slender legs had haunted many a night.

She could still bowl him over, but this wasn't the Kelly he'd left behind, and he wasn't sure he liked it. What had happened to his wife?

Kelly moaned and raised one hand to her head, then opened her eyes and froze. "It *is* you," she whispered in wonder.

"Yes, it's me."

"But what . . . ? How . . . ?"

He couldn't resist an urge to tease her. "You know how I love a good joke. I just waited until you finally had a memorial service for me so I could show up and shock the world."

A tiny frown creased her forehead. "That's not funny."

Remorse filled him. "I know. I'm sorry. I just—" His warped sense of humor had a bad habit of taking over in times of stress. All he knew was that he was very glad to be home—finally—and wanted to make up for lost time with his wife. Starting now.

Repeating his earlier words, he said softly, "Hi, honey. I'm home," and gathered her into his arms.

God, she felt good. He'd missed this, missed her. Missed her soft, responsive body, her warmth and humor, her way of making a house a home. She returned his embrace, but he sensed some reserve, some holding back. What was wrong?

Dumb question. She'd just had the shock of her life, finding her supposedly dead husband had come back to life. He released her gently. "You must have a million questions."

"Yes, I do." She stared up at him, her eyes searching his face. "But I still can't believe it's you. You look so different. You hair is lighter and you're so tan, so thin, so"—she stroked his beard in wonder—"so hairy."

"Yeah, well, five years in the Manu wilderness will do that to a guy."

She sat up straighter and regarded him curiously. "What happened? We searched everywhere. We found the downed plane and all the other . . . bodies, but couldn't find a sign of you anywhere."

"Yeah," Scott said from the doorway. "I'd like to hear this, too."

Though impatient to get his life back to normal, Chaz knew he needed to take the time to explain what had happened. They deserved to know. "I wasn't on the plane when it crashed. They dropped Garcia and me off a few miles up from our landing spot at an unscheduled stop. We wanted to check out some ruins we saw from the air, then planned to meet them at the rendezvous point." He and Garcia had made the rendezvous, but the rest of them hadn't. "I didn't know what happened to them until I got back to civilization."

Kelly frowned. "Garcia? I don't remember that name."

"A last minute addition," he explained. "Garcia's a guide and knew where we could find some Inca ruins."

"That's right—you were looking for the lost city, weren't you?"

"Yeah." The legend of the safe haven where the last ruling Inca had retreated with all his gold had fascinated Chaz. "But when the plane didn't show up, we had no idea what happened to them so we decided to look for it along its planned route."

"Didn't you find it? The investigators found it right away, on the flight plan you filed."

"Unfortunately, we were captured by a local tribe before we could do so."

She gasped and covered her mouth. "So that's why you've been gone so long. Were you imprisoned the whole time? Did they . . . hurt you?"

"Yes, we were, and no, they didn't hurt us. Not physically anyway." But being deprived of freedom, the luxuries of civilization, and his adorable wife were torture enough. "At first, we went along with them, since they seemed to know the ruins pretty well. We hoped they would take us to the lost city and figured we could get away at any time." *We were wrong.*

"What happened?"

"We took sick—some tropical fever, I guess—and it lasted for months. By the time we were strong enough to understand what was going on, they'd moved far into another part of the jungle." He and Garcia had both lost their gear and had been hopelessly lost and disoriented, not to mention disappointed that their captors had no idea where the lost city might be. "They nursed us back to health, but for some reason, they seemed to consider us good luck. They wouldn't let us go."

"What did you do?"

He shrugged. "What we could. We escaped several times, but they always recaptured us. At least they treated us decently." If decent meant being imprisoned and guarded continuously. "But I'm home now and I really don't want to talk about it."

"But how did you finally escape for good?" Kelly asked, obviously enthralled by his story.

Uncomfortable with dwelling on the past when he wanted only to concentrate on the future, he donned a straight face. "Well, we found these ruby slippers, so I slipped them on and clicked my heels together, saying, 'There's no place like home. There's no place—'"

She slugged him in the arm. "Be serious. How did you get away? After searching for five years, I deserve to know."

He sighed, knowing she'd bug him until she heard the whole story. "Someone formed another expedition to search for the lost city. They came across us and ransomed us out of there."

"Ransomed?"

"Yeah, with a few bribes." Talk about humiliation. A few strings of beads, a machete, and a dented canteen had bought their way free. "If they hadn't come along, we might still be there."

"Thank heavens they did," Kelly exclaimed, then her tone turned oddly apprehensive. "But one thing still confuses me. How . . . how did you know to come to your memorial service?"

"Well, when I didn't find you at our apartment, I went by your mom's house and caught Scott just as he was leaving. He told me you were here."

"He did?" She exchanged an enigmatic glance with Scott. "Did he tell you anything else?"

"No—nothing important, anyway. Nothing matters except that I'm finally home." He tried to hold her again, but she held him at arm's length. "What's wrong?"

She bit her lip, looking uncertain and adorable. "There are . . . a couple of problems."

"Like what?"

"Well, for one thing, you're legally dead."

Chaz threw back his head and laughed. "Well, if that's all, I think I can get that judgment reversed." He leaned closer to those luscious lips of hers. "Let me prove to you just how alive I am . . ."

She backed off with such an odd look on her face that he knew there was something else wrong—and he wasn't going to get anywhere with her until she spilled it. "Okay, what else?"

She cast a pleading glance at Scott who said, "Sorry. I didn't tell him."

"Tell me what?" Chaz asked.

Kelly turned her apprehensive glance on Chaz. "I'm married."

He laughed. "I know. I was there, remember? Eight years ago this past April. Now we can take up where we left off."

He tried to kiss her again, but she shook her head and held him off, looking even more anxious. "It's not that simple. I mean I married . . . someone else."

Shock made him speechless. Someone else? Who? He glanced at Scott for confirmation. When Scott nodded sympathetically, it finally hit him. No, slammed him was more like it. All this time he had been desperately trying to get back to Kelly, and she hadn't cared. She hadn't waited. Instead, she had spent the time in the arms of another man.

Ignoring the pain and pleading in her expression, he whispered accusingly, "You betrayed me."

Kelly shook her head as guilt swamped her. She *had* betrayed him and there was no good explanation, no good reason she could give him for doing so. Only excuses.

Scott spoke up from the doorway. "No, she didn't."

Chaz's head swung in his direction. "What?"

"She didn't betray you."

"Oh, no?" Chaz said. "Even the law calls it bigamy."

"Not really," Scott said reasonably. "In the eyes of the law, you're dead. So, she was a widow when she remarried. I'm no lawyer, but it's possible her second marriage may be totally legal."

Kelly didn't know if Scott was trying to reassure Chaz or her, but whatever he was trying to do, it wasn't working.

"But I'm not dead," Chaz said, stating the obvious. "So what does that mean?"

Scott shrugged. "That you're screwed?"

"Like hell it does." Chaz swung back to Kelly and she would have given anything to take away the pain and accusation in his eyes. "When were you married?"

"This morning," Kelly said in a tentative voice.

Surprisingly, Chaz didn't comment on her getting married the same day she "buried" him. Instead, he brightened. "You mean this so-called second marriage isn't legally consummated yet?"

"That's right—"

"You're not still intending to go through with it, are you?" he asked incredulously.

"Of course not." Not now . . .

With relief in his expression, he said, "Then you can get an annulment, no problem."

"Yes, I suppose . . ." She wasn't sure exactly what the legal requirements were for annulment. But how on earth was she going to tell Spencer?

"Wait a sec," Scott protested. "Legally, that still leaves Kelly a widow . . . or married to a walking corpse."

Chaz gave a short bark of laughter, but there was little humor in his expression now. "We'll figure that out later—do whatever needs to be done. We'll either have the courts declare me legally alive, or get married again if we have to. Right, honey?"

A spark of rebellion flared deep inside her. She had forgotten how Chaz liked to take charge of everything. She had gotten used to running her own life while he was gone—liked it, even—and wasn't quite ready to relinquish that privilege to anyone. "I'm so glad you asked my opinion."

Taken aback, Chaz said, "Hey, you're the one who had me declared dead so you could play footsie with another guy while I suffered in captivity."

It did sound bad, put that way. "Not right away," she protested. "Everyone thought you were dead, and finally convinced me you must be. I waited five years."

His eyes narrowed. "Isn't that the minimum time in Colorado to have someone declared dead?"

"Well, yes, but it wasn't like that. . . ."

"Whose idea was it?"

She squirmed. "Spencer's."

"Is that the guy you married?" When she gave a reluctant nod, Chaz asked, "So who is he, anyway?"

"Spencer Preston. You remember—he's the food editor at *Pizzazz*."

"You married some twerp with two last names?" For some reason, that seemed to bother Chaz more than the marriage itself. "What kind of creep is he?"

Feeling obliged to defend Spencer, Kelly said, "He's not a creep. The whole time you were gone, he was very good to me. He helped me get promoted, helped me cope with your loss, helped me search for you."

"Helped you right into his bed, I'll bet."

Fired up now, Kelly said, "That's not fair. I was faithful to you the whole time."

Chaz raised an eyebrow. "Until today, you mean."

"Well, we all thought you were dead." Couldn't he understand that? If she'd still thought him alive, she would never have gone through with it. "There was no sign of you."

"Oh, yeah? How long did you look?"

He still sounded betrayed, but Kelly was beginning to get a little ticked. "For *five years*."

Scott chimed in, looking a little miffed himself. "She did, you know. The only reason she accepted the promotion was to have the money to keep searching for you. She spent every cent, depleted her savings, even made the supreme sacrifice of moving back home with Mother to save money." He made an impatient gesture. "Though everyone else was convinced you were dead, she kept on looking. She only stopped when even the law said you were dead."

Thank heaven for little brothers. Scott's diatribe must have worked because Chaz regarded her thoughtfully now. "Is this true?"

When she nodded, he took her into his arms and held her close. "I'm sorry," he murmured. "All I thought about was getting home to you, to where we left off." He squeezed her tighter. "God, I missed you so much."

Tears filled her eyes and spilled over. "I missed you, too." Missed his fierce hugs, his loony sense of humor, the way he made her feel as if she were the only woman in the world. She returned his embrace and then some, thinking everything would be all right if he would just hold her tight and never let her go. Maybe she could even pretend the horror of the past five years had never happened.

He released her for a moment to cuddle her in his lap as a smile played around his lips. "So, you didn't sleep with anyone else while I was gone, huh?"

"Of course not," she said indignantly. "How could you think such a thing?" Though it was rather difficult to maintain her indignation when she was curled into him like a purring kitten.

He kissed her neck, his beard tickling her ear. "Well, you *did* marry someone else," he pointed out, then continued nuzzling the sensitive spot on her neck as he slid one hand halfway up her thigh and the other cupped her breast.

Feeling a little breathless, she asked, "How many times do I have to explain that?" She tried to act annoyed, though she rather enjoyed the marvelous things he was doing with his hands and mouth. It had been so long. . . .

Ignoring her question, he squeezed her lightly and her body revived from its dormant state to respond to the remembered sensations, tightening her breasts and making her well with moisture. If she wasn't careful, she'd melt into a puddle of longing here and now. She knew her expression gave her away—she could never hide her desire from Chaz.

"Does he make you feel this way?" Chaz murmured. "Does he make you sizzle the way I do?"

"N-no," she admitted. Though, in all fairness, Spencer had respected her married status and never progressed beyond a chaste kiss, though she knew he'd wanted to. He'd never been given a chance to make her sizzle.

Chaz, on the other hand, was doing a fine job with very little encouragement. He slid his hand further up her thigh and a moan escaped her lips.

"Jeez," Scott exclaimed. "Get a room, willya?"

Embarrassed, Kelly pushed Chaz's wandering hands away and tried to straighten her clothing. Good Lord, what must they think of her? Melting in one man's arms—in a funeral parlor, of all places—while another waited in their honeymoon suite, hoping to do those same sweet things to her body.

Ohmigod, Spencer was still waiting for her, expecting her to sizzle with *him* tonight. Kelly pushed away from Chaz and struggled to her feet. She needed a clear head to decide what to do, and Chaz did nothing but cloud her senses.

"What's the matter?" he asked. "You are going to tell this guy that your real husband has returned, aren't you?"

"Yes, of course." Though she wouldn't put it quite that way. . . . "I just want to do it in my own way."

"How hard can it be?" Chaz protested.

Very, but Chaz had never had the problems Kelly did with relating bad news. "Let me tell him. I need to find a way to soften the blow." Though she had no idea how she was going to accomplish that feat. "After all, this was supposed to be his wedding night."

"Yeah, well it's supposed to be *my* reunion night,"

Chaz reminded her with a smoldering look. "And I
don't want to miss a minute of it." He drew her back
into his arms and whispered suggestive things, marvelous things he promised to do to her, pouring the
longings of five years into her ears in a matter of moments.

Kelly drew a shaky breath. This wasn't *exactly* how
she'd planned on spending the evening, but the thought
of warm oil, cool satin sheets, and a hot-cha-cha Chaz
sounded *verrry* intriguing.

But she couldn't do that to Spencer, either. Heck,
she couldn't sleep with either of them without feeling
guilty. So what should she do? To avoid answering that
question, she asked, "Where are you staying?"

He kissed her neck again. "Wherever you are,
sweet."

Well, she had planned on staying at the Pourtales
honeymoon suite, but a ménage à trois held no appeal.
And she certainly didn't want to go home. If at all possible, she wanted to avoid the scene Mother would
make when she learned about this development. At
least until after all this was resolved. "Okay, why don't
you find a hotel, and I'll call you there afterward."
After she had some time to decide what to do.

Chaz grinned at her. "Not on your life. I'm coming
with you."

"To the Pourtales? I don't think that's such a good
idea. . . ." She wanted to break this to Spencer gently,
not shove Chaz's existence in his face.

"Yes, it is," Chaz insisted. "I know how soft-hearted
you are. He's liable to look sad and you'll want to comfort him, and the next thing you know, he'll be making
whoopie with my wife on a frilly, heart-shaped bed."

She pulled away from him. "I wouldn't do that!"

"It's not you I'm worried about—it's him. And I'm going to make damned sure he doesn't take advantage of the situation. Or you."

She knew that stubborn look—Chaz wasn't going to budge an inch. She might as well go along and find a way to reduce the damages. And she could be just as stubborn. "Okay, but you're not showing your face until after I've explained it to him." When Chaz opened his mouth to protest, she said, "I mean it. He's been very good to me while you were missing, and I'm not going to toss him aside just because you've returned from the dead. What kind of person would that make me?"

Besides, she wasn't quite sure that's what she wanted to do anyway. She needed time to think this through, time to decide what was best. But time was apparently the one luxury they wouldn't allow her.

Chaz grimaced. "You're right—you couldn't do that and still be the Kelly I love. But I'm still going to be nearby to make sure you tell him."

"Fair enough. Now, how are we going to get out of here without being mobbed by all those mourners?" She didn't relish the thought of facing that crowd.

"Hold on a sec," Scott said. He opened the door a crack and nabbed the funeral director, who was still standing guard, pulling him into the room with them.

Wearing a slightly harassed air, Mr. Throckmorton tugged on his coat and straightened his tie. "I quite understand your need for solitude," he intoned. "But I have another service scheduled in an hour. Would it be possible to move this along a bit?"

Scott slapped him on the back. "Just what we had in mind. If you don't want a scene. . . ."

Throckmorton raised an eyebrow. "Is there any way to avoid it?"

Scott grinned. "There is if you have a back way out of here."

"Yes, of course," he said, then hesitated. "But what shall I tell the . . . others when you've gone?"

"The truth," Chaz suggested. "Tell them we skipped out. With us gone, there's no reason for them to stay. They'll all be so eager to spread the news of my miraculous reappearance, they'll fly out of here."

That seemed to decide him. "Very well." Throckmorton went to the other side of the room and swept aside some curtains in an alcove to reveal a door. "This goes out the side, to the parking lot." He slanted a look at Kelly. "And I believe your wife has a limousine waiting there to take her to the Pourtales."

At Chaz's questioning glance, she said, "That's right. Spencer arranged it."

"Perfect," Scott exclaimed and strode to the door. "I'll just alert the driver."

As he headed out the door, Chaz turned to the funeral director. "Thank you for making my memorial service a memorable one." He offered his hand.

Throckmorton shook it, saying gravely, "Oh no, sir. That was all your doing."

Chaz laughed. "True, but you did it up nice. I do have one question, though."

"Yes?"

"Who *is* in that pine box?"

The man's expression turned pained, though Kelly wasn't sure if it was because of the question itself or because Chaz had cast aspersions on his work of art.

"No one," Throckmorton said. "Anything else would be . . . unseemly."

Chaz's grin widened. "Well, I'm glad to hear that, anyway. Thanks again. There'll be a bonus for your assistance . . . and even more if you'll give us about twenty minutes or so to get away before you let the mob loose."

"Of course."

"Great," Chaz exclaimed. "Let's go."

He grabbed Kelly by the hand and pulled her toward the door. Thankful for the reprieve, she followed him outside to find Scott holding the limo door open for them. They slid into the plush interior and Kelly looked up at Scott with a grateful smile. "Thank you. But . . . could I ask you one more favor?"

"What's that?"

"Could you break the news to Mother?" Yet another scene she dreaded.

Scott grimaced. "Not on your life, kiddo. She can find out some other way." He paused, then added with a sudden look of alarm, "And I don't want to be around when she does. Move over—I'm coming with you."

Scott shoved into the seat beside them and shut the door. Turning to the driver, a big blond woman, he said, "Get us out of here."

As the driver complied with nothing more than a lifted eyebrow, Kelly sighed. How bizarre. First her dead husband and now her brother had joined her on what should have been her honeymoon.

How on earth was she going to explain all this to Spencer?

Three

Chaz glanced at Scott warily. He liked Kelly's brother, but he hadn't expected him to come along for the ride. In fact, Chaz had seriously considered seducing Kelly on the way to the hotel. Having an audience cramped his style.

He glanced at Kelly, who was chewing her lip, a nervous habit that drove him crazy. Her full bottom lip made him think of hot nights and even hotter sex. Now she worried at it because of her *other* husband. Why was she so concerned about this guy? She couldn't possibly love him.

Could she?

Chaz dismissed the notion. No, after the way she had responded earlier, he was absolutely certain Kelly still loved him. And since he wanted Kelly concentrating on *him*, not this twerp who had conned her into marrying him, he moved closer and slid an arm around her shoulders, then said to Scott, "Why don't you get off at the next corner so my wife and I can get . . . reacquainted?"

Scott appeared amused, but Kelly wasn't. Pushing Chaz away, she turned to her brother. "No, Scott. Stay where you are."

Uncertain, Chaz asked, "Why? I thought you wanted him to tell your mother about my miraculous return."

Kelly shrugged but kept her distance. "I changed my mind."

He tried moving closer again, but she shook her head with a warning look. "Don't."

"Why not?" Hell, he'd waited five years to see her, and she was playing coy? What was going on? Didn't she want him anymore?

"Because I can't think when you're so near," she complained.

Well *that* was a relief. "And that's a bad thing?"

"It is if you want me to figure out how to tell Spencer."

He did—the sooner, the better. But he knew how much she hated to break bad news. Chaz captured her hand and kissed it. "Hey, don't worry about that little chore. I'll be glad to do it for you."

She gave him a wry glance. "Yeah, right. Like that'll happen."

Chaz was taken aback. That's not the way the old Kelly would have reacted. The old Kelly would've been grateful for his help . . . and not quite so mouthy. "You've changed," he said softly. "Your clothes, your hair . . . your sassy attitude."

"And that's a bad thing?" she challenged, repeating his words back to him.

The jury was still out on that. He needed some more time to get to know this new version of his wife first. Hedging, he asked, "How'd it happen?"

"Well, after you were gone so long, I needed to learn to cope, so I did."

Yeah, by going totally independent on him. "But how? When I left, you were a copy editor at *Pizzazz*. Now you look like one of their models."

She looked surprised. "Not quite. And, I know you

don't want to hear this, but most of the change is Spencer's doing. . . ."

He grimaced but knew he needed to hear it anyway. He motioned for her to go on. "How, exactly?"

"He took me under his wing, taught me how to dress in the best styles and colors for me, how to wear my hair to flatter my face, and how to choose a look all my own."

"Why?" She was perfect just the way she had been when he left.

"I needed a new image."

"But I *liked* the old Kelly."

"The old Kelly didn't get anywhere," she reminded him. "The new one got promoted to associate editor, then editor. I owe him a lot."

"Well, you certainly look the part of a high-fashion editor now." He couldn't help it—a touch of disapproval colored his voice.

She gave him an odd look. "Don't you like the way I look?"

Frankly, no. He wanted his old Kelly back. "You look very . . . sophisticated."

"What's wrong with that?"

"Nothing. It's just not . . . you. Not the you I remember, anyway."

Her expression turned soft. "Oh, Chaz. Everything must seem very strange to you after all these years. The change was gradual for us, but it must look pretty drastic to you." She smiled at him, then raised an eyebrow before he could hope for too much sympathy. "But it's all your fault, you know."

How the hell did she figure *that*? "How? Because I was held captive in peril of my life?"

She gave him an admonitory look. "No, because you hared off on another expedition without me."

"It's my job." Surely she didn't blame him for that.

"No, it's your addiction. Though we were only married a few years, you were gone half that time, trotting all over the world in search of archeological treasure. You left me alone. A lot. So stop trying to make me feel guilty because I got on with my life."

What was her problem? She'd never complained before. It must be that other guy's fault. Chaz glanced at Scott for support but his frantic motions disavowed any desire to take part in this discussion.

"But you were my anchor, my roots. I needed you here," Chaz explained. Didn't she understand that?

"Well, I needed you here, too," she said in a reasonable tone.

Feeling as if he were sinking in quicksand, Chaz suspected he was losing this argument, but couldn't figure out why, so he decided to use heavier ammunition. "Well, while you were playing footsie with whatshisname, my buddy Garcia and I were held captive by a vicious band of pyg—" He broke off, knowing he'd regret it if he finished that sentence.

Confusion creased her pretty face. "Pigs?" she asked in disbelief.

Scott chuckled. "I think he meant pygmies."

Chaz slanted an annoyed glance at Scott. *Now* he chose to enter the conversation?

I don't need that kind of help.

"You were captured by little people?" Kelly asked incredulously. "And you couldn't get away? What'd they do? Bite your kneecaps? Punch you in the shins?"

Chaz shot a warning glance at Scott, who appeared to be convulsed with mirth. "It's not funny. They used deadly poison darts. And besides, we were lost. And sick. We needed to get our bearings first."

Kelly shook her head in disbelief and abruptly changed the subject on him. "So, tell me, Chaz. Did you find what you were looking for?" Her tone was mild but there was an aspect to it he didn't quite understand . . . or care for.

Warily, because he felt as if he were in quicksand again, Chaz said, "What does it matter?"

Her eyes narrowed. "A straight answer, please. Did you find what you were looking for?"

He was tempted to lie, but he'd never been able to lie to her. "Well, we didn't find the city. . . ."

"But?" she persisted.

"But we did find a few artifacts." And had received a very nice sum for them, too.

"I knew it," she exclaimed in disgust. "Tell me, was that before or after you escaped from this vicious band of pygmies?"

"After."

Uh-oh. That did it. She looked like Mount Vesuvius about to blow.

"Damn it, Chaz. Are you telling me that even after you were free, you didn't head immediately for home?"

"I had given my word to bring something back," he reminded her. Chaz Vincent never went back on his word—she knew that. "And it was only for a short while."

"How long?"

"Not very . . ."

"*How long?*" she persisted.

"A few weeks," he admitted. "I figured after five years, a little more time wouldn't matter." Not when he had an obligation to meet.

She smacked him in the arm. "And you didn't call me?"

"I couldn't," he protested. "There're no phones in the Amazon jungle. Besides, I wanted to surprise you."

"Well, you got more of a surprise than you bargained for, didn't you? Do you realize that if you had come home immediately, none of this would have happened?"

"Are you blaming *me* for the mess you got yourself in to?" he asked incredulously. "Hey, I'm the injured party, here."

"Men!" Kelly exclaimed in disgust. She leaned forward and tapped on the glass to get the driver's attention. "Could you pull over, please?"

The woman complied and Kelly slid toward the door.

"Hey, where are you going?" Chaz asked.

"To the front seat. There's too much testosterone back here."

"But—"

"Keep your mouth shut, Chaz," she warned him. "Or you'll just dig yourself in deeper." She got out of the limo and glared back in at him. "Don't talk to me again until we get to the hotel. I need to think."

Alarmed, Chaz asked, "You are still gonna get rid of that other guy, aren't you?"

His only answer was to have the door slammed in his face, then she had the driver roll up the privacy glass separating the back seat from the front.

Hell, now what? Turning to Scott, he asked, "What did I do wrong?"

Scott's expression was half amused, half sympathetic. "What didn't you? Did your attitude ever strike you as say, a tad selfish?"

"No," he said bluntly. "It was a matter of honor. I gave my word that I would search for the lost city. I couldn't just return home empty-handed. You know that."

"I understand," Scott said sympathetically. "But to Kelly, it looks like selfishness."

He knew that. He just didn't understand why. But since Scott was her brother, maybe he had some more insight into her convoluted female mind. "Do you think she'll tell that other guy to take a hike?" Chaz asked. Then he answered his own question. "Of course she will—she's always been loyal." It was one of the things he loved about her.

But sudden doubt assailed him. "Unless that's changed, too?"

"No, that hasn't changed," Scott said softly. "But the question is, who will she be loyal *to?* The man who left her to her own devices while he had adventures all over the world . . . or the man who stayed here by her side?"

Good Lord, was there any question?

From the look on Scott's face, maybe there was. . . . Suddenly, Chaz wasn't quite as sure of Kelly as he had been.

Kelly stewed the rest of the drive to Colorado Springs. She was sorry for his captivity and all he had suffered, but Chaz hadn't changed. He was still a thrill-seeker, still focused more on his wants and needs than hers, still irresponsible when it came to matters of the heart. She doubted he would ever grow up.

Spencer, on the other hand, was totally grown-up—loyal, responsible, caring, and very attentive. Instead of getting rid of Spencer, maybe she should ditch Chaz.

Then again, though Chaz had his faults, he was also charming, boyish, and adorable . . . most of the time. More like a playmate than a husband.

Or a child?

She shook her head, now totally confused. She wasn't sure how the courts would rule on her marital status, but she doubted they would think her marriage to Spencer legal. Chaz was her husband. Legally, Spencer was . . . extraneous. At least, that's how she thought the law would view it.

But is that the way I want it?

She had no idea, but she had to get one soon, because they had already pulled up to the hotel. Nestled at the bottom of Pikes Peak and surrounded by the grandeur of the Rocky Mountains, the Pourtales was covered with local peachblow sandstone and dotted with ornate white wrought-iron balconies. It looked like a classy, understated wedding cake.

The setting was perfect, too. Though normally lush and green during spring and summer, it glittered in pristine white splendor with yesterday's snowfall, lending it the air of a picture-perfect postcard. Kelly sighed. Too bad she couldn't enjoy the scenery.

The chauffeur, who had, thankfully, been silent throughout the trip, brought the limo to a halt outside the Pourtales and cast Kelly a questioning look. Though the woman didn't say a word, Kelly had the feeling that she was prepared to do whatever Kelly wanted, including ditching the men and taking off for parts unknown.

It was tempting. . . .

But that was Chaz's modus operandi, not hers. Sighing, Kelly exited the car. Reluctantly.

The driver opened the trunk and Scott and Chaz each grabbed one of Kelly's small suitcases—in her favorite shade of lipstick red—and followed her to the registration desk inside the plush gold and white lobby.

But once she got there, flanked by the two men, Kelly

wasn't quite sure what to say. She stared in consternation at the tall, thin man behind the counter, whose nametag read "Bernard Billings, Assistant Manager."

When she remained silent, he smiled with a mouth full of perfect white teeth and prompted her with, "May I help you?"

She supposed she had to say *some*thing. "Uh, yes. Has my—Has Spencer Preston checked in?"

With any luck, he'd taken off to the Amazon jungle as well.

"Oh, yes." No such luck. "You're Mrs. Preston?"

She said, "Yes," Chaz said, "No," and Scott said, "Sort of."

Mr. Billings raised both eyebrows, and Kelly shot Chaz and Scott warning looks. This snooty gentleman didn't need to know the sordid details of her private life and she certainly didn't want to explain them. It was easier just to let him assume what he wanted. "Yes," she said firmly. "I'm Mrs. Preston."

Billings gave her a tight smile, his gaze flicking in silent question to the men beside her. "Very good. I had the privilege of checking Mr. Preston into the honeymoon suite earlier today." He handed her the key. "I wish you every happiness in your married life."

Chaz snorted but Kelly ignored him, saying only, "Thank you."

Still smiling fixedly, Mr. Billings asked, "Shall I tell him you're on your way up?"

Kelly said, "No," Scott said, "Yes," and Chaz said, "Oh, let me . . ." with a gleam in his eye.

The assistant manager turned to Kelly with a questioning look.

"No," Kelly said firmly with another warning glance at the men beside her. "I want to . . . surprise him."

That must have satisfied Billings for he nodded, but stared at Chaz and Scott, obviously wondering where they fit into this situation. "May I help you, gentlemen?"

"No, that's all right," Chaz said carelessly. "I'm with her. I'm her husband."

Billings frowned as he took in Chaz's khakis and beard. "And the gentleman in the suite would be . . . ?"

"This is my *first* husband," Kelly said with a quelling look at Chaz. "Mr. Preston is my second husband."

"I . . . see."

Ignoring him, Kelly turned to Chaz. "Didn't you want a room?"

"Oh, yes," Chaz exclaimed. "A room for *two*, please."

Scott grinned at him. "Say, that's good of you, Chaz."

"Not you," Chaz said. "For me and my wife." Then he draped a proprietary arm around Kelly's shoulders.

Billings paused in his typing to give Kelly another look full of attitude.

"He means his *other* wife," Kelly explained, surreptitiously stomping on Chaz's instep.

Chaz winced. "Huh?"

"Yes," she said, putting as much ice into the single word as she could. "You know—the one who usually stays home like a good little homemaker."

"Oh." Chaz dropped his arm. "Yeah. Her."

"She'll be along later," Kelly explained to Billings.

"Guess I'll need a room of my own, then," Scott said.

"You're staying, too?" Kelly asked.

Scott grinned. "Wouldn't miss it for the world."

"Very good," Billings said. "And you are?"

"Her other husband," Scott said, and draped *his* arm around Kelly.

Billings' poker face slipped and Kelly suppressed an urge to chuckle. It really wasn't funny. Quickly, she said, "He's just kidding. He's my brother—the family clown." And his sense of humor looked like it was about to get the three of them thrown out of there. Annoyed, she elbowed Scott in the ribs.

"Oof," he exclaimed, but grinned at her. "Sorry, Sis." Turning to Billings, who regarded him as if he were a particularly loathsome specimen, Scott added, "Can we all have rooms on the same floor?" At the manager's questioning look, he confided, "We're a very close-knit family."

Billings's gaze skidded across Scott, Kelly, and Chaz, who must have looked rather cozy clumped there together at the registration desk. He raised another expressive eyebrow but said nothing. Kelly was tempted to refute Scott's suggestion, but didn't want to cause any more of a scene. Besides, if she argued for different floors, Chaz was liable to loiter out in the hallway on her floor and heaven knew what would happen then. Better to leave it this way.

Soon, they all had keys, but the ordeal wasn't over yet. Billings turned to them once more. "May I have your luggage sent to your room?"

Kelly glanced down at her cases. Yes, but to which room? Never mind—she didn't want to deal with that right now. "Could you store mine until I call for it?"

Once again, Billings managed to radiate disapproval, but he said nothing as he summoned a bellman and had her suitcases checked. "And you gentlemen?" he asked, pointedly not noticing their lack of luggage.

"It's coming later," Scott explained.

But irrepressible Chaz said only, "Oh, I won't need any."

Quickly, before Chaz could expand on his outrageous remark, Kelly grabbed their arms and steered them toward the elevator. She glanced back over her shoulder to see Billings staring after them with a frown, and resolved to avoid him at all costs.

They took the elevator to the third floor and found that the honeymoon suite was on one end of the hall and Chaz's room was toward the other end, across from Scott's. All in full view of each other. Great—just what she needed. To keep them from accompanying her, she followed them to their rooms.

It was no use chastising them—it wouldn't do any good. As Scott opened his door, she said, "I want you both to stay here while I . . . break the news to Spencer."

Chaz looked like he wanted to protest, but Kelly wasn't going to budge on this one. "I mean it," she told both men. "No more games, understand?"

Scott looked contrite. "Sorry, Kell. I promise—no more games." He glanced at Chaz. "And Chaz won't play any either. That would be selfish. Right, pal?"

He gave Chaz a significant look that Kelly couldn't interpret, but apparently Chaz could, for he just muttered, "Yeah. I guess."

"Your word, Chaz," she insisted. If he gave his word, she could trust him to do exactly as he said.

He hesitated and his eyes flashed annoyance, but he said, "Okay, you have my word on it. No more games." Pushing his way into Scott's room, he said, "I'll just wait here with your brother." Then, making a show of checking out what was in the little refrigerator, he asked, "How long will it take to break the news?"

Kelly followed him in, closing the door behind her for fear that Spencer might step out into the hall and see them. "I don't know . . ."

Chaz slanted a glance at her. "Well, it better not take too long or I'll come after you."

That brought her chin up. "I'm going to have dinner with him first, *then* I'll tell him." Maybe a good meal would soften the blow . . . and help her figure out which husband to keep.

Chaz looked like he was about to protest, but a warning glance from Scott stopped him. Instead, he abandoned the refrigerator to cross to her side with a peculiarly intent expression.

Alarmed, Kelly stepped back and found herself flat against the door. Chaz planted both arms on either side of her and leaned in until she felt breathless. Lean and hard, with a musky male scent that made her dizzy, Chaz was all man.

"Well, just remember one thing while you're having dinner with Spence," Chaz whispered, his breath mingling with hers as he stared intently into her eyes.

"Wha—what's that?"

"Remember what's waiting for you afterward. . . ." He captured her lips with his in a lingering, steamy kiss that made her heart zing and her blood sizzle all the way to her toes.

Ohmigod, how could she possibly forget? "O-okay," she stammered once he released her lips, then she somehow managed to fumble the door open. Regaining some of her composure after leaving Chaz's intoxicating nearness, she said shakily, "And don't you forget to stay here."

Apparently satisfied with the havoc he had wreaked on her senses, Chaz merely gave her a smug smile. "All right. Hurry back." Then he closed the door.

Whew! Kelly straightened her clothes and checked her reflection in the hall mirror. Good Lord, her lipstick was smeared and her hair was disheveled. It wouldn't do to go to her new husband looking as if she'd just been thoroughly kissed by another man, even if she had been.

Especially if she had been.

Quickly, she opened her purse and repaired the damage then headed toward the honeymoon suite . . . and Spencer.

She walked slowly, hoping inspiration would strike and she would find the perfect way to tell him. Unfortunately, nothing struck but an attack of cold feet. For one wild moment, she considered bolting for freedom to that beach Scott had mentioned earlier, but her innate sense of justice refused to allow that. Just imagining the scene when Chaz told Spencer exactly what had happened made her shudder.

Besides, she'd still have to deal with it all when she got back. No, she owed Spencer more than that. But not until *after* dinner. . . .

Steeling her resolve, she knocked softly on the door to the honeymoon suite.

Spencer opened it immediately, looking suave, handsome, and very blond. Beaming, he drew her inside. "Finally . . ." He gathered her gently into his arms and kissed her.

He made her feel safe and cherished, but though his kiss was very nice, it had nowhere near the sizzle quotient of Chaz's. *Damn.* If only she could combine

Chaz's zing with Spencer's dependability, she'd have the perfect man.

Her disappointment must have showed, for he released her with a puzzled, "What's wrong?"

"I just feel a little . . ." *Guilty.* ". . . nervous."

With a compassionate smile, he drew her farther into the room. "There's no reason to be," he said softly.

She avoided answering by looking around the elegant suite. He had certainly done it up right. The lights were low, romantic music played in the background, the tables were filled with bouquets of roses, and a magnum of champagne sat chilling by the bed—which was neither frilly nor heart-shaped, though it *was* covered in satin.

The bed . . .

She averted her eyes quickly as she worried her lower lip. "My stomach just feels a little . . . queasy," she said haltingly. "Can we have dinner now?"

"Of course," Spencer said, his smile flashing in that smooth, handsome face of his. "I'll call room service."

"No," she said quickly. If she stayed too long in this room, she might have an unwelcome visitor in the form of Chaz . . . or end up on that bed before she could explain matters.

When Spencer turned to her with a puzzled expression, she added, "You're always talking about how wonderful the dining room is here. I'd really like to see it."

His expression softened. "You really *are* nervous, aren't you?"

Kelly gave him only a sickly smile in answer. It must have been enough, for he shrugged on his jacket and escorted her to the door. "All right. We'll have dinner downstairs, then."

As he closed the door behind them, Kelly darted a glance down the hallway and saw Chaz and Scott spying on them from their partially opened doorway. With a fierce scowl, she made swatting motions at them to get out of sight before Spencer could see them.

They closed the door, but not all the way. They still peeked out at her, though Spencer wouldn't be able to see them. At least, not if she distracted him.

She turned to Spencer with a bright smile and tucked her arm in his, willing him not to look in that direction. Luckily, he didn't. All his attention was for her as he led her toward the elevator. Once they made it there, she released her breath in a relieved sigh. She was safe. For now, anyway.

When they arrived downstairs, the genteel beauty of the dining room with its apricot and cream decor, shining crystal chandeliers, and hushed tones helped her relax. As did the wonderful chateaubriand and the wine Spencer chose to accompany it. She drank more than she'd intended, hoping the spirits would give her enough courage to tell him what had happened.

But the meal was over all too soon, and Spencer led her back upstairs, all consideration. It immediately made her feel guilty. But as the door closed behind them, Spencer drew her into his arms again.

Not wanting a repeat of the kiss that had left her comparing Spencer to Chaz—to Spencer's detriment—Kelly backed away from him. She couldn't do this.

Spencer dropped his arms to his side with a puzzled expression. "What's wrong now?"

She twisted her fingers together and avoided his eyes. "It's just that something . . . unexpected came up today."

"At the memorial service?"

She nodded. Instead of giving her courage, the wine she'd imbibed just made her thoughts confused and muddy. She didn't know what to say.

"I knew it was a bad idea for you to go there."

He had no idea *how* bad.

"What happened? Are you feeling sad because of Chaz?" he asked in sympathetic tones.

Sad? No, that was one emotion she *wasn't* feeling. "No, it's just that—" She broke off, not knowing how to say it. "He's . . . he's . . ." She couldn't say it.

"Is it because you finally realized he's dead?"

"Noooo . . ."

"Then what's the problem?" He reached over to take her in his arms. "Whatever it is, you can tell me."

"I just—"

The phone rang and she sighed in relief. Saved by the bell.

Then she froze, wondering who it could be. Her mother, calling to find out what happened? His friends, calling to spread the news of Chaz's miraculous return? Chaz himself?

Suddenly sober, she lurched toward the phone, hoping to catch it first, but Spencer had already answered it.

"Hello, Scott. Yes, I'm fine. What can I do for you?"

She relaxed a little, but not much. With Chaz's corrupting influence, who knew what Scott would take it in his mind to do? Or say?

She waited breathlessly as Spencer listened for a minute, then handed the phone to her. "It's for you."

Releasing her breath in relief, she said, "Hello, Scott? What's going on?"

"Chaz is chomping at the bit here," Scott said. "Have you told Spencer yet?"

She gave Spencer a sickly smile. "No . . ."

"Well, do it soon," Scott said. "Before Chaz does something we'll all regret."

"Okay."

Scott hung up, but Kelly held onto the phone a while longer, not willing to give up the security it represented. But she could think of nothing else to say, so she carefully placed the receiver in its cradle.

"What's wrong?" Spencer asked with concern. "Did something happen to Scott?"

"No." But Chaz would happen to Spencer if she didn't do something, quick.

"Your mother?"

She started to say no, then caught herself. What a great excuse. Given a little more time, she might even be able to find the perfect way to explain everything to Spencer without hurting his feelings. And decide what to do afterward. "There's been . . . an emergency."

"What kind of emergency?"

"I-I'm not sure," Kelly said. The truth was, she was a very bad liar. At times like this she wished she was as glib as Chaz. Gathering up her purse, she said, "I have to meet Scott."

"Where is he?"

"Here," she said without thinking.

"Here? In the hotel?"

Thinking rapidly, she said, "Yeees . . ."

"Why?"

"Because . . . because he has to tell me something and didn't want to do it on the phone." There, that should work. "I'll just . . . meet him down in the lobby, okay?"

"I'll come with you."

She put out a hand to stop him. "No." That wouldn't do at all.

"Why not?"

"I-I just want to do this myself, okay? I'll let you know what's going on right away."

He looked doubtful, but she knew he wouldn't argue further. Giving him a kiss on the cheek, she opened the door and called out, "I'll be right back."

Closing the door behind her, she cast a swift glance down the hallway. Good, no Peeping Toms. Quickly, she hurried to the elevator before they could open the door again and spot her. She just needed a little space to think, unencumbered by walking testosterone in any form.

Once she was downstairs, she realized if she didn't do something, Chaz might charge in on Spencer, so she called Scott's room. Luckily, Scott answered. "I'm downstairs," she said in a rush. "I haven't told Spencer yet, but I need some time to think about how to do this without hurting him." Like she hadn't already done that by acting like a crazy woman.

"What are you going to do?"

"I-I'm going to get a room by myself. Once I figure out what to do, I'll call you. Wait a little while until I'm in a new room, then tell Chaz so he doesn't do anything dumb, okay?"

"Okay, if you're sure. . . ."

"I am. I just need a little more time."

"All right, Kell. Take care, and call me if you need anything."

"Thank you," she said in real relief. It was so much easier dealing with him than Chaz.

With a sigh, she turned toward the registration desk, then stopped. Damn. The only person on duty was that same Mr. Billings. Well, there was nothing else to do but brave it out—she couldn't lurk here forever waiting for the shift to change. So, she marched up to the desk.

He smiled warily and asked, "How may I help you?"

"I'd like a room, please." She fixed him with a glare, hoping it would deter him from asking questions.

"Is there something wrong with the honeymoon suite?"

"No. I'd just like a different room." She handed him a credit card.

"And your husband?"

"He'll stay in the honeymoon suite," she said with another glare, daring him to say anything else.

Unfortunately, he took that dare. "I . . . see. And your *other* husband?"

Smart-ass.

"He has a room of his own." And before he could ask about Scott, she said, "And so does my brother." Raising her chin and letting the temperature drop in her voice, she said, "I want a room of *my* own. Do you think you can manage that? Or do you have a problem with women staying alone in your hotel?"

That made him lower his insolent gaze. "Of course not, ma'am." Without any more ado, he passed over a key and her credit card. Thank heavens it was the off-season, or she might not have been able to get a room.

But as she turned to leave, she suddenly realized she needed his help. "Oh," she said airily. "Just one more thing. You won't tell anyone where I am, will you?"

He raised a supercilious eyebrow again. "No one?"

"No one," she repeated. Then knowing that she really did need to get this man on her side, she added confidingly, "It's just that I have the jitters and need someplace—alone—to work through them. You understand, don't you?"

"Yes, ma'am. Of course," he said with a fake toothy smile.

Well, that was the best she could hope for, for now.

She just had one more unpleasant duty to do, then she could relax. She decided to call Spencer from the lobby before he came after her. Once she got him on the phone, she blurted out, "There's something I have to tell you, but I don't know how to do it, so I'm going to spend some time alone until I figure out how to do it right."

"But—"

"I'll call you again in the morning, if not before." Then she hung up before he could say anything more and headed toward the elevator once more. But once she reached the elevator bank, she caught sight of a familiar female figure coming in the door. Oh no, it was Candace—their boss. What was *she* doing here?

Kelly hid behind a tall potted palm and peered out. Sure enough, it looked like she was registering to stay. Since two of her senior editors were taking their honeymoon, Candace had decided to close the office and let everyone have a holiday for a week, saying she was going away to pamper herself . . . but Kelly had no idea they'd end up in the same hotel!

And she certainly didn't want to call attention to herself or answer questions at this point. So, she darted for the open elevator, hoping Candace wouldn't notice her. Once inside, Kelly held her fingers to aching temples.

Ohmigod, what else can go wrong? So far, she had one husband in the honeymoon suite, one at the other end of the hall with her brother, a boss down below, and she was about to spend her wedding night alone. Could it get any worse?

She glanced down at the key and groaned. Apparently, it could. The oh-so-helpful Mr. Billings had given her another room all right . . . on the third floor along with the rest of them.

Four

Chaz paced around Scott's room, anxious to get out, to do something—anything. On one pass, Chaz caught sight of Scott's expression and scowled. Damn it, the man was amused at his expense.

Chaz stopped dead, his voice oozing sarcasm. "I'm soooo glad you're being entertained."

Scott just grinned. "Does pacing help?"

"It doesn't hurt." And he had to work off this excess energy somehow. Especially since it appeared Kelly wasn't going to let him take care of it the way he had planned. "Tell me again what she said."

"She said she was going to get a room. By herself."

Chaz wanted to hit something to relieve his frustration, but contented himself with raking his hands through his hair. "And she didn't say what room she was in?"

Scott gave him a sympathetic look. "No—I think she wants to be alone for awhile."

This wasn't going at all as Chaz had planned. And it was all that food editor's fault. "Damn it, why can't she just tell him?"

"Oh, I don't know," Scott drawled. "You think it might be just a tad difficult?"

Chaz dropped into the other chair. "All she has to do

is say 'I can't sleep with you because my *real* husband is alive.' "

When Scott just raised an eyebrow, Chaz waved away his silent objection. "I know, I know. It's not that easy. I'm just—" He broke off, unwilling to say it aloud for fear the actual words would give his apprehension more weight.

"You're afraid she's having second thoughts and won't pick *you*," Scott said softly.

Shit. It sounded just as bad as he thought. Fear, anxiety, and frustration all roiled through him in one big seething nauseous wave. Chaz dropped his head into his hands to keep Scott from seeing the raw emotions on his face. "Yes," he whispered, laying his soul bare with that one simple word.

Everyone else in his entire family had always tried to change him, make him into something he was not, something he could never be—normal, boring. Kelly was his touchstone, the one person who understood him, the one person who loved him for himself. Or so he had always assumed. Had he lost that? Had he lost *her*?

"She always put me first," he murmured. And that was one thing he desperately needed. No one else had—he always came in a poor second or tenth, his needs and desires rendered unimportant in the noisy chaos that was his family, their love forever hedged with conditions and qualifiers.

When Scott made a small sound, Chaz glanced up. "I know what you're going to say, and you're wrong. It's not selfish. I put her first, too."

"Do you." It was more of a statement than a question.

"She's the most important person in my life," Chaz declared. "She comes first with me, always." Everyone deserved to have someone who felt that way about them, no one more so than Kelly.

"Except when you're leaving her. . . ."

"But that's my *job*. That's what I do."

"No—that's your choice, and it doesn't give Kelly much of one, does it?"

Don't tell me even Scott is trying to change me now. "What the hell do you want me to do?"

"I want you to do what's best for my sister."

"And what's that?" Chaz demanded. "Or should I ask, *who's* that? Are you saying that other guy is best for her?" God, he hated to ask the question, hated to sound so damned needy. But he really wanted to know the answer.

Scott shrugged. "I don't know. That's her decision. And it sounds like that's what she's trying to do right now—make that decision."

Chaz couldn't stand it. How could she make such a huge choice without talking to him, without letting him explain how much he loved her? Hell, if he had to bare his soul to keep her, he'd do it. "If only I could *talk* to her."

Scott gave him an odd look. "What's stopping you?"

"The small fact that I don't know where she is?"

"Well, I know you've been out of touch for five years," Scott said with a half grin, "but there's this new invention called the telephone. . . ."

I'm an idiot.

No, in his own defense, Chaz had to admit that his years in the jungle had left him out of practice with modern amenities. Without a word, he dashed out of Scott's room and fumbled with the key to his own until the door finally opened. He didn't want to talk to Kelly in front of her brother.

Grabbing the phone, he dialed the hotel operator. "Hello, may I speak to Kelly Vincent?"

There was a pause, then the woman said, "I'm sorry, but we have no one registered by that name."

Annoyed, Chaz realized she must be registered under that other man's name. Did that mean she considered herself married to him and not Chaz? Suddenly insecure, he said, "Try Kelly—" He broke off, sinking onto the bed as he tried to remember the man's last name. Presley? Spencer? Reston? No, it was Preston. "Try Kelly Preston."

"Yes, sir. Just a moment, please, I'll connect you."

Chaz didn't realize he was holding his breath until Kelly answered on the third ring with an apprehensive, "Hello?"

"Hi, honey," Chaz said softly. He panicked, wondering what he should do now. With no plan, he wasn't sure exactly what to do or say, but he knew attacking her wasn't a good idea.

"Chaz?"

Damn, didn't she know her own husband's voice? But he didn't allow his annoyance to show in his tone. "Yes, it's me. How are you?"

She paused, then said, "Confused." Before he could ask anything else, she added in a rush, "I'm sorry, I just couldn't tell him."

"I knew you were too softhearted."

"What are you saying, Chaz? That you told me so?"

"No, no," he protested, trying to dispel the irritation in her tone. "It's one of the things I love about you."

When she said nothing, he added in a softer tone, "I just want to see you, touch you, hold you."

"Oh, Chaz," she breathed.

Encouraged by this sign she might be relenting, he

said, "It's been a long time. I was faithful to you, too, you know." And that was despite some very determined temptation.

"That's good to hear."

"Can I come to your room so we can talk?"

"No, I don't think that's such a good idea."

Chaz scowled and punched the pillow. He wanted to demand to know why not, but knew it would get him nowhere. "I just wondered—" He broke off, discarded several other frustrated questions, then finally blurted out the one at the forefront of his mind. "Will you pick me?"

God, that sounds pitiful. What woman in her right mind would choose such a pansy ass?

"Oh, Chaz . . ." she said again, this time with a sigh.

In desperation, he tried to understand her tone. Was that love and melting he heard . . . or sorrow laced with pity? Who knew? Why didn't women and feelings come with manuals, fergawdsakes?

Not knowing what else to do, he chose a neutral response. "Yeah?" Then hit himself in the thigh. Great, just great. She wouldn't choose him for his intellectual brilliance, that was for sure.

"I . . . I don't know."

So he was wrong on both counts. That was definitely indecision mixed with helplessness. He felt for her, he really did, but there was no time to coddle her feelings right now. First she had to make the right decision, *then* he'd let her wallow in any feelings she wanted. "Is there anything I can do to help? A hug, maybe? A little loving?"

A whole lotta down and dirty sex?

"No, no," she said hastily. "That would be too distracting."

Well, yeah. That was the *point*. "Well, what if—"

"No," she said, interrupting with the word he was getting tired of hearing. "I need to figure this out by myself. With no interference from you or Spencer."

"But—"

"No buts, Chaz. You're not helping your case any. I'll call you in the morning. And don't call me again tonight—I'm going to tell the switchboard to refuse all calls."

He had to try one last time. "But—" It was too late. She had already hung up.

Now what? Accepting failure was not an option. What could he do to change her mind, to let her know he'd do anything to get her back? He needed to think.

He stood up to pace again, and caught a glimpse of himself in the mirror over the dresser. Good Lord, he looked like an utter barbarian, especially in this re-fined setting. No wonder she was apprehensive.

Chaz ran a hand over his beard thoughtfully. Well, the first thing he could do was get rid of this rat's nest. Kelly didn't like it, and to tell the truth, he was rather tired of it himself. Yes, that would help.

Jazzed by the thought of taking positive action, Chaz made a quick trip to the gift shop and picked up a range of toiletries as well as some clothes. He even made a stab at trying to pry Kelly's whereabouts out of Billings, but the guy managed to somehow sneer his contempt and disapproval without losing his polite fa-cade. Worse, he wouldn't reveal a damned thing—he was about as helpful and responsive as a slab of gran-ite. No, that was giving granite a bad name. Even granite had some character.

Chaz returned to his room and made short work of shaving off his beard. It made the lower half of his face look a little paler than the rest, but he could live with that, now that Kelly wouldn't have to worry about whisker burn.

Okay, now what? He tried to call her again, but she'd made good on her promise to have the switchboard refuse all calls. So, that option was out. If he could only *see* her. . . .

But how could he find out where she was? He couldn't exactly go around knocking on every door in the place. And, without knowing what floor she was on, hanging out in the hallways was bound to be fruitless.

Unfortunately, that snob Billings was still on duty at the desk, so learning anything that way was out, too. But he *could* wait until Billings went off shift and hope for a more affable desk clerk. Okay, when did the shift change? It didn't matter—he'd just go downstairs and wait them out.

As Chaz passed the registration desk, Billings gave Chaz the once-over, obviously not impressed by his fresh, clean-shaven look. Concerned Billings might call hotel security if he lingered in the lobby, Chaz veered toward the hotel's bar across the way. Perfect. No one would question the amount of time he spent there.

The only problem was, there was only one table where he could see the front desk, and it was already occupied by a classy-looking blonde who toyed with a glass of white wine. Chaz ordered a beer at the bar, then debated his options. It looked like the blonde had settled in for the duration.

Shrugging, he decided there was only one thing to do. He walked over to her table and gave her his most charming smile, hoping he looked harmless. "Mind if I join you?"

She hesitated and he quickly tried to remember

some persuasive remarks from his dating days, but she finally smiled and said, "Sure, why not?"

But her eyes were red and puffy, probably from crying, and she looked like she was about to burst out again at any moment. Sheesh, just his luck. To head off the waterworks, he said, "Hi, I'm Chaz."

"Candace."

He searched for an innocuous conversation opener, keeping one apprehensive eye on her and one on the front desk. "So, you like it here?" Lame, really lame. But who cared? It wasn't like he was really trying to pick her up. He preferred warm, cuddly brunettes, like Kelly.

She shrugged. "Usually, it's my favorite place to relax. But the man I love married another woman today."

Yeah, there was a lot of that going around.

"I'm sorry," he said. Then, not knowing how to go on after that conversation killer, he asked, "You want to talk about it?"

"Not really."

Ooookay. He swigged from his bottle and glanced at the desk again, hoping Billings would be gone. No such luck.

Candace caught him this time and glanced behind her. "What are you looking at?"

He smiled sheepishly. "The front desk. I'm waiting for someone." Anyone but Billings.

She glanced around. "I . . . see. And this is the only place you can see them come in, isn't it?"

He felt another sheepish smile form on his face and decided to own up. "I'm sorry. I'll just go—"

He half-rose from his chair, but she motioned him back. "No, sit."

He raised his eyebrows but decided not to quibble at being allowed to do exactly what he wanted. "You sure?"

She shrugged. "Why not? I could use the company. Why don't you tell me your story while you're waiting?"

"Story?"

"Yes, story. Don't bother to deny it. I'm in journalism, and you just reek of a man with a story to tell."

Yeah, one hell of a story—if you read the tabloids—but he wasn't going to reveal it to a reporter.

She smiled sympathetically and added, "Don't worry, I won't tell anyone. I'm a publisher, not a reporter, and besides, I'm off-duty here."

Maybe, but he wasn't taking any chances. Then again, Candace might be able to shed some light on the female mind. "My wife is trying to choose between me and another man." No need to go into details that might produce unwanted headlines.

Candace raised an elegant eyebrow. "My, that *is* a story. So, what went wrong?"

"What did I do wrong, you mean?" Women always assumed it was the man's fault. When she only shrugged, he added, "You wouldn't understand." Only another man would.

"Try me."

He shook his head and took a swallow of beer, then decided, why not? "She's mad at me because I came home later than she thought I should."

"How much later?"

"A few weeks," he admitted. "But it wasn't as bad as it sounds—I'd been gone a long time."

"Leaving her alone?"

"I had no choice."

"So, why didn't you come home when she thought you should?"

"Because I'd made a promise I had to keep. It was a matter of honor." Didn't anyone understand that concept anymore?

"A man's honor is so important to him," she said, sounding condescending.

"What's wrong with that?"

"Nothing. But what most men don't realize is that women have honor, too. We just show it differently."

Kelly was one of the most honorable women he knew, by his standards. But what about hers? How did she account honor? "How is it different?"

"Well, I'm no expert, but it seems to me that men are more concerned about keeping their word to strangers. Women care more about keeping faith with people they care about."

"But I did keep faith with her," he protested. "Just . . . later. And I didn't *want* to do it—I had to, to keep my word."

Candace shook her head. "It doesn't matter how you felt about it, especially if you didn't tell her—only your actions matter."

Hmmm.

"And what your actions apparently showed," she continued inexorably, "was that she came in second to someone or something else. No woman likes that."

Ah, hell. Is that what he'd done? No wonder she was upset. But there was no sense crying over what he couldn't change. "How can I fix it?"

"Go to her. Don't let her stew for long. If you love her, show her that she comes first."

He grimaced. "That's what I've been trying to do, but I can't. She's holed up somewhere in this hotel and she won't answer the phone. I don't even know where she is."

"Is that why you're watching the front desk?"

"Sort of." He glanced past her, but Billings was still there. Then a splash of color in the bellman's hands caught his eye. *I recognize those red suitcases.* He grinned.

"Never mind—I just figured out how I can find her. . . ."

Candace watched Chaz go, feeling a little guilty. She'd been a little hard on him. Too hard, maybe?

Maybe not. She wished someone had pushed her years ago to declare her feelings to the man she loved. But she'd been too proud to approach him, too afraid to show her true feelings. Afraid he'd cry sexual harassment, afraid he'd feel sorry for her, afraid he'd reject her.

After all, the man worked for her . . . and was obviously infatuated with another woman. There was nothing more Candace could have done. Was there?

It didn't matter anymore. It was too late. Spencer had married Kelly . . . and tonight was their wedding night.

Candace closed her eyes in anguish. She would have to watch their happiness every workday for the rest of her life. Somehow, she had to summon the strength to deal with this, to find a way to get beyond the pain and pretend everything was all right.

She glanced down at the wine glass in her hand. Alcohol wasn't the answer, but talking to Chaz had made her feel a little better, especially if she could help him find the love she had lost through her own foolish pride. She lifted the glass in a silent toast. *I wish you better luck than I had.*

* * *

Kelly stretched out on the bed, staring up at the ceiling, still clothed in the dress she'd worn to one husband's wedding and the other husband's funeral.

Obviously, she couldn't be married to both men, and she was fairly certain Chaz was her legal husband . . . but was that what she wanted? Spencer was very good to her, putting her needs above his, but he didn't make her feel the way Chaz did. After all these years, Chaz still had what it took to make her feel like a breathless teenager. But she wasn't a teenager anymore, and Chaz never seemed to be around when she needed him the most, never considered her wants and feelings.

True, it wasn't his fault that he'd been missing for five years . . . not entirely. Then again, he hadn't come home immediately. Instead, he stayed and played in his own little world a little longer—a world that didn't include her. Would it always be like that with him?

With an exclamation, she tried to wipe the thoughts away. This was ridiculous. She kept going around in the same old circles in her mind. If she wasn't careful, she'd wear a rut in there.

She usually wasn't so wishy-washy. She usually knew exactly what she wanted. But everything "usual" had been turned upside down today and she didn't know what she wanted anymore. No, that wasn't true. She wanted the best of both men—Spencer's reliability and Chaz's sizzle. But unless she made a choice, she'd have neither.

For one brief moment, that seemed like the solution—leave them both—but that was worse. She'd put relationships on hold for far too long. She deserved a chance to be happy, and she was going to take it, damn it.

She just wasn't sure who to take it *with*. . . .

Well, maybe it would be clearer in the morning. For now, she'd get some sleep. Suddenly remembering her suitcases were still downstairs, she called the bell captain to have them sent up, and in a very short time she heard a knock on the door.

"Bellman," a voice called out.

He brought in the bags, but just as she closed the door behind him, there was another knock on the door. She'd tipped him, and had both of her suitcases. What had he forgotten? Puzzled, she opened the door and found Chaz, sans beard, grinning at her.

All she could do was stare in shock at his freshly shaven face. The well-remembered contours and his flashing dimple were so endearingly familiar, they caught her off guard.

He took advantage of her daze to saunter past and enter the room. "Hey, it's nice in here."

Regaining some of her senses, she said, "It's a room just like yours, Chaz. Why don't you go there?"

He cast her a reproachful glance as he dropped into a chair. "Now is that nice? And when all I want to do is talk to you?"

In resignation, she closed the door. "How'd you find me?" If Billings had told him, she'd have the man's job—and assorted body parts to boot.

Chaz grinned, flashing his dimple again. "Easy—I followed your suitcases."

Yeah, Chaz had always been resourceful.

"And imagine my surprise when I found out your room is only a few doors down from mine."

More evidence of Billings's warped sense of humor.

"But why are you here? I told you I'd call you in the morning."

"I know, but Spencer has been seeing you every day for the past five years." He rose to stand in front of her. "Would you begrudge me just a few minutes?" he asked with a beseeching smile.

Damn, Chaz did beseeching very well. And without that beard, he looked much more like the Chaz she had loved . . . well and often.

She took a step back, not trusting him or herself. "If I know you, you're looking for far more than just a few minutes."

"Well, of course," he said, moving nearer, "but I'll take what I can get."

"Well, you're not getting any." He was too close—she couldn't think straight. She moved back another step, and came to a halt when she bumped up against the bed. *Uh-oh.* Wrong direction.

As if stalking her, Chaz moved in for the kill, but she put both hands on his chest. "Stop right there."

It didn't deter him in the least. He leaned in closer, a half-smile on his intent face.

"Stop or I'll scream," she warned.

He grinned. "Sounds like fun." He drew her in close to his body.

"I mean it, Chaz. I have a knee and I know how to use it."

"You wouldn't do that. . . ." He moved in closer, his lips just a breath away.

Unfortunately, he was right. "You've been drinking," she accused. She could smell beer on his breath.

"Just one beer, while I waited for you to call for the bellman."

He leaned forward, and she leaned backward until

they were practically bent horizontal above the bed. Any moment now, his lips would touch hers, and she'd be lost. Desperately, she searched for another way to stop him. "I-I'll choose Spencer."

That worked. He backed off and regarded her incredulously. "What?"

"If you don't stop this determined seduction, I'll choose Spencer." She would, too. Chaz had to learn to take no for an answer.

"That's a low blow."

But it worked—he let her go. Shrugging, she straightened her dress and stepped away from the bed and Chaz. "So what do you call what you were doing?"

"That wasn't low, that was . . . heaven," Chaz said softly.

Damn, did he have to sound so sexy when he said that? "You'd better leave," she said unsteadily. "It's late and I'm tired."

"Too tired to talk?"

"Too tired to fight you off," she corrected.

He held his hands up in surrender. "Okay, no more touching, I promise. I just want to talk to you."

Did the man never give up? "Does it have to be now?"

"This won't take long," he promised. "Please, sit."

With a sigh, Kelly sat in one chair and he seated himself opposite her. She might as well hear him out. He certainly wasn't going to leave until she did. "Okay, what is it?"

He gave her an earnest look. "I'm afraid all you remember are the bad times, and the time you spent searching for me."

There might be some truth in that. For years, thoughts of Chaz had been all bound up with concern for his safety, and fear of what might have happened to him. "Maybe."

"Well, before you make your decision, I just wanted to remind you of the good times we had. The times *I* remember."

She glanced at him curiously. "You say that as if I choose to recall only the bad."

"No, that's not what I meant. But you've been focused on finding me, whereas my memories of you were all that kept me going."

Curious now, she asked, "What memories?"

He smiled. "Remember when we were dating and went hiking in the mountains and got caught in that rainstorm?"

"I remember we were drenched, muddy, and absolutely filthy by the time we got back to the car."

"Yes, and you were trying so hard to maintain your mother's impossible standards and keep clean . . . until you slipped in the mud and fell in that huge puddle. I could tell the moment you gave it up. You looked so . . . free, so full of life and laughter."

She chuckled. "I think I went slightly insane." She had splashed around in the puddle, and made mud pies and threw them at him when he laughed at her.

"No, not insane. Carefree. Adorable. That's the moment I fell in love with you."

"Lord, what a horrible image of me to carry around with you." But despite her words, the memory left a warm glow in her heart. If he could love her while she looked like that . . . Well, he must be the insane one.

He shook his head. "Remember watching old movies in front of the VCR on Saturday nights? We'd bundle up under your grandmother's quilt and eat popcorn and snuggle."

She smiled. "I remember." She had always felt warm and cherished in his arms.

"How about the parties we threw? I loved playing games with you. We were the best charades team in the world."

She nodded. It had felt good to loosen up and be as silly as Chaz. They had had some good times.

"But the best times of all were Sunday mornings. We'd lay in bed, make slow, lazy love, read the comics, and talk about our hopes and dreams."

Tears suddenly pricked her eyes. They had seemed to have so much promise, so much potential then. When Chaz was home, life had been perfect.

"Don't throw all that away," he begged softly.

"But it wasn't always like that." It had been fun and exciting when he was with her, but when he was gone, she missed him terribly and worried every moment about his safety. It was hard to live like that.

He captured her hands in his. "Don't dwell on that, please. Remember the good times—it can be like that again."

"I don't know, Chaz. It couldn't be the same. We aren't the same two people who married eight years ago. I've changed—I had to, with everything that happened." And she had learned to suppress the wild tendencies Chaz roused in her.

"So, he's made you a stick-in-the-mud?"

That hurt. She pulled her hands away. "If that's true, why would you want me?"

"Oh, honey, I didn't love you for just the good times. I love you because . . ." He paused, gesturing impatiently. "Because you're you. You're warm, homey, comfortable—"

"You make me sound like a sack of old clothes," she protested.

"No, no. That's not what I meant at all. Look, you know I'm not as good with words as you are."

That wasn't quite true—he'd been doing quite well up until now.

"Can you give me the benefit of the doubt here?" he pleaded.

Okay, he was trying, and she had to admit that his reminiscences had touched her. "All right. But I'm not making any promises."

He must have seen some softening on her face, for he asked, "Does that mean I can stay?"

"Don't push it."

He grinned, unrepentant. "Hey, you can't blame a guy for trying."

"No, I guess not. But you'd better leave now. I really do need to get some rest." She went to the door to give him the hint.

To her surprise, he took it. Rising, he said, "All right, I'll go for now. But don't forget, I'm just down the hall if you should need anything." He wiggled his eyebrows at her. "Anything at all."

He looked so guileless she couldn't help but laugh. "I won't, but thanks."

She opened the door and Chaz walked out into the hallway. "And don't forget," he said, lowering his voice. "It's always been you I loved. Only you."

Her resolve started to melt and she took a step toward him. "Oh, Chaz—"

"Chaz, *mi querido*," a husky voice exclaimed, interrupting them. "There you are. I haf been looking everywhere for you." The lightly accented voice belonged to a tall, dark Latin beauty with masses of luxurious dark hair and creamy brown skin. That's about all Kelly was able to register before the woman was in Chaz's arms, covering his face with tiny kisses.

What the—? Planting her hands on her hips, Kelly said, "So it's been only me, huh?"

Chaz peeled the woman away from him and gave Kelly a desperate look. "It's not the way it looks, honest."

The woman's eyes narrowed as she stared at Kelly and asked, "Who are you?"

"I'm his *wife,*" Kelly said, but it didn't seem to faze the woman at all. "Who are *you?*"

The woman cast a surprised glance at Chaz. "Did he not tell you? I am Amalia Garcia. We spend the last five years together."

"*You're* his buddy Garcia?" Why, that lousy, cheating scum.

"Yes," the woman declared. "Though I will soon be Amalia Vincent." She tucked a hand into Chaz's arm and beamed up at him. "We are to be married."

Five

Chaz closed his eyes and swore silently. *I'm dead meat*. The hurt and confusion on Kelly's face was almost too much to bear. And it was all Amalia's fault. He had never hit a woman in his life, but he came awfully close to it then.

He backed away from Amalia before he did her bodily harm. "We're *not* getting married. I'm already married—*happily* married. I told you that." Over and over again. Damn it, he'd thought he was free of the woman. How the hell had she found him?

"Not for long," Kelly declared. The hurt had disappeared from her expression, now replaced by anger.

"Good," Amalia said and moved to take his arm again. "Then nothing will stop our wedding."

Chaz peeled her off with an annoyed glance, and turned his attention to the woman who really mattered. "It's not how it looks, honey, honest." She had to believe him—Amalia meant nothing to him.

"Really?" Kelly asked with her arms crossed and a closed-off expression on her face. "It looks like you lied to me about your *buddy* Garcia."

"I didn't lie," he protested and suddenly realized he was back in that shifting quicksand once more. In response to Kelly's raised eyebrow, he squirmed a little. "I just didn't tell the whole truth."

"Why not?"

"Because I wanted to explain it to you slowly." *After* they had reunited and everything was all right between them. "I knew you wouldn't be rational about this." Besides, to be honest, he wanted to put off the scene as long as possible.

"Rational? You expect me to be rational about the fact that my husband lived with another woman for five years and couldn't be bothered to tell me about it?"

Damn it, he'd used the wrong words again. How could he make her understand? "I know it looks bad, but you make it sound like we were living in sin or something."

"Weren't you?"

"No, no, of course not. Let me explain—"

"Why you talking to this woman?" Amalia pouted and stuck to him like a blood-sucking leech. "Now we can be married. You must leaf her."

Leaf her? Chaz had a sudden bizarre vision of festooning his wife with foliage, but shook his head. Familiarity with Amalia's accent made him realize what she had really meant.

Down the hall, a door opened, and Scott popped his head out. When he spotted Amalia clinging to Chaz, his eyebrows rose. "What's this?"

Good—reinforcements. "Could you help me out, here?" Chaz asked. He definitely needed it. Without knowing how, he was somehow sinking deeper every moment.

Scott moved out into the hall and glanced curiously at the woman attached to Chaz. In a bemused tone, he asked, "Just what kind of help do you need?"

Chaz tried to pry Amalia's fingers from his arm. "Get her out of here, would you?"

Scott glanced at the tight grouping they made. "Which one?"

Giving Scott a glare at his obtuseness, Chaz said, "Not Kelly, of course. I need to talk to her." Alone, so he could explain everything—make her understand how little this woman meant to him, how much Kelly mattered.

"Don't bother removing her, Scott," Kelly said in a scathing tone. "It's obvious he's been used to having her around—for the past *five years.*"

Comprehension dawned on Scott's face. "Ah, this must be Garcia." He shook his head sadly at Chaz. "Bad move."

"Yes, I am Amalia Garcia," his barnacle confirmed. "And I am not a bad moof. We are to be married."

"Stop *saying* that," Chaz exclaimed. How could he make Kelly understand if Amalia insisted on spewing her inane fantasies to everyone who would listen?

"But we must marry. We haf been together for many years."

Lord, the woman had a one-track mind. It had taken him about a week to tire of it and a month to be totally sick of it. And after five years, he'd thought seriously about slitting his wrists—or hers—to be rid of her.

Unfortunately, the expression on Kelly's face showed she felt the same way—about both of them. To erase that impression, he protested, "But nothing *happened* between us. Besides, I'm already married."

"Well, that's debatable," Scott said.

Amalia's face lit up. "Yes?"

Chaz glared at Scott, but Kelly's ever-helpful brother explained, "The law thinks he's dead."

"Ah yes, I read about his funeral, so I meet his family."

"You met my family?" Chaz repeated in a faint voice. He groaned to himself, wondering what she had said and how much damage control he had to do.

Ah hell, who cared? They always thought the worst of him anyway. It was Kelly who mattered now.

"Yes—should I not know my husband's family? But I get there after you leaf." She pouted at Chaz again, obviously trying to appear sexy but only succeeded in looking childish. "They were upset with you for not saying where you go."

"Then how did you find me?" he asked, wondering what gods he had pissed off to deserve this.

"That nice Mr. Throckmorton told me."

Well, Throckmorton could kiss his bonus good-bye. *In fact, he can kiss my—*

"So, if you are dead, does that not mean you are . . . free?" Amalia asked.

Ignoring her strange logic, Chaz stated the obvious. "I'm not dead." But Amalia was going to be if she didn't shut up. "And I'm *not* free. I'm very much married—to Kelly."

That is, if she didn't kill him after this mess. Turning to his wife, he pleaded, "Give me a chance to explain."

"Why, Chaz? So you can lie some more?" She paused, adding sarcastically, "No, wait. I mean so you can 'leave out' more vital information?"

The quicksand was up to his waist now. "I won't leave anything else out, I promise." He'd already learned that lesson. "And I won't lie. Nothing happened, I swear. I never touched her."

Not that Amalia hadn't tried. And after the first cou-

ple of weeks, he hadn't even been tempted by her too
obvious charms. Her clumsy advances and aimless,
self-centered prattling were the worst of the tortures he
had endured. That's why he called her Garcia, to maintain some distance, treat her like one of the guys.

Amalia moved closer to rub up against him like a
cat in heat. "Why do you lie? We were as man and
wife. We luff each other."

"No, you don't love me—you just think you do."
Desperately, Chaz turned to Kelly. "She's the one
who's lying. Can't you see that?" The woman was a
jealous fiend and would lie, cheat, and steal to get
what she wanted.

But Kelly looked like she was buying this fishy
story, hook, line, sinker . . . and half the rod and reel as
well. The quicksand was about to close over his head.

He turned to Scott, hoping for support. *Throw me a
rope, please!*

But Scott merely frowned at him, obviously not
knowing who to believe. "Do you luff her, too?"

He was making jokes at a time like this? "No, I love
Kelly."

This was just too surreal. Why had Amalia tracked
him down . . . and why on earth did she assume he
would marry her? He had never implied any such
thing. In fact, he thought he'd made it rather plain he
hated the sight of her. What the hell could he do? Frantically, Chaz cast his gaze around, searching for a way
out.

That's when he noticed that other doors along the
hall had opened, the rooms' occupants peering out at
them with varying degrees of annoyance and curiosity.
Damn it, he didn't need an audience—having Scott
and Amalia there was bad enough.

Turning to face the Peeping Toms, he raised his voice. "What is this? A damn movie set? You want to be an extra? I can arrange it."

Hastily, they all closed their doors. Feeling satisfied that something had gone as he planned, Chaz returned his attention to Kelly. "Can we do this somewhere else?"

"Good idea," Amalia said brightly and grabbed Chaz's arm. "My room is this way. . . ."

He shook her loose again, wishing he had some kind of repellant to keep her from lighting on him again. "Then go to it—I need to talk to my wife. Alone."

Kelly shook her head, looking cold as ice. "There's no need. I wouldn't think of standing in the way of true luff."

Sheesh, her too? He rolled his eyes, but Kelly continued implacably, saying, "You can have a divorce."

Chaz felt as if he'd been sucker-punched. Oh, no—not the "D" word. He opened his mouth to protest, but the only thing that came out was a moan.

The quicksand had just closed over his head.

Kelly hadn't expected the shaft of pain that speared through her at her own words. The same pain showed on Chaz's face, but that's what she'd wanted, wasn't it? To hurt him as much as he'd hurt her?

Unfortunately, his *buddy* looked like a self-satisfied feline who'd just rolled in a bed of catnip. Kelly felt an overpowering urge to slap her, but managed to control herself. She wouldn't give Chaz the satisfaction—he'd probably love a catfight.

"No," Chaz exclaimed in horror. "Not a divorce. You don't want that."

Kelly regarded him with disdain. "You have no idea what I want. You never did."

"That's not true—"

"Can we do this somewhere more private?" Scott asked, interrupting him. "Before they kick us out of the hotel?"

"No!" Kelly and Chaz declared together. Immediately, Kelly wished she could take it back, not wanting to be in agreement with Chaz on anything. But being in a confined space with him and his "buddy" would be worse.

The question was, why did Chaz say no? No doubt he wanted a clear line of retreat.

Though right now, Chaz was advancing—toward her. "Please, honey. You're not being reasonable."

Kelly had started to back away, but this just ticked her off more. She stood her ground, even took a step toward him as her voice rose uncontrollably. "*I'm* not being reasonable?" She ignored Scott's shushing motions—the hurt and anger needed an outlet. "What did you expect? You betrayed me, you lied to me, and you want me to be *reasonable* about it?"

"But I didn't betray you—"

"Yes, you did," his bimbo interrupted.

Chaz whirled on her, fury in his eyes. "Stop it."

"What's the matter, Chaz?" Kelly taunted. "Having a lover's spat?"

Chaz turned back to her and wheedled, "Come on, honey. Don't be like this—"

"I'll be any damned way I please, and you have nothing to say about it." Feeling safe from Chaz's charm in her anger, she took another step closer and jabbed her finger in his chest. "In fact, you have nothing to say about anything. I want nothing more to do with you."

Chaz just gaped at her wordlessly but unfortunately, Amalia seemed to have no problems with *her* mouth. "Good—then he is mine. Come with me, Chaz. You need a *real* woman."

Like I'm fake?

For the first time, Kelly took a good look at Chaz's buddy, wondering what he saw in her, searching for flaws. Amalia's nose was too thin, her mouth too wide, her hair too shiny, and she looked unbalanced with those large breasts on that skinny frame.

Damn it, she was beautiful. And sexy.

Jealousy roiled through Kelly. She suddenly felt too short, too chubby, too plain. If Chaz had to be imprisoned with a woman, why couldn't it have been an ugly one?

The thought aroused a fierce competitive edge that Kelly hadn't known she possessed. *Hell, lady, you might be a knock-out, but can you make mud pies?*

Suddenly, Kelly realized she was going about this all wrong. By dumping Chaz, she was leaving the field wide open for this bimbo. They might deserve each other, but they didn't deserve happiness after all Kelly had been through.

Wait a minute. Seeing how Chaz was trying to get as far away from his clinging vine as possible, maybe Amalia wasn't as irresistible—or as much of a woman—as she thought.

So I'm not a real woman, huh? "What do you mean by that?" Kelly demanded.

Amalia shrugged with style and elegance which just ratcheted up Kelly's anger even more. Wriggling a body that would give most men wet dreams, the woman asked, "Do I haf to explain it?"

"Yes, I think you do." Go ahead, let her show her true feelings to the world. Then Chaz would see just how conceited and self-centered she really was.

Stroking Chaz's arm, Amalia gave her a calculated smile and said, "Well, you were not able to keep him at home, but I will not haf any trouble."

Anger exploded within Kelly, more so because that shaft hit the bull's eye. She *hadn't* been able to persuade Chaz to stay home with her. And this woman knew far too much about their personal lives for Kelly's peace of mind. Ignoring Scott's frantic motions once more, Kelly said, "Well, Chaz made it quite clear he doesn't want you. He wants *me.*"

Amalia scowled and Kelly hurried to follow up on her advantage. Grabbing a double fistful of Chaz's shirt, she yanked him up against her chest and said fiercely, "He's my husband and you can't have him." Then, to pound home the point, she gave him a long, hot, angry kiss.

But before the kiss could turn her knees weak, she broke off to gauge her opponent's reaction. Amalia appeared supremely annoyed, Chaz was delighted, and Scott looked . . . odd. Kind of sick and horrified at the same time as he gazed at something over her shoulder.

Kelly twisted around to see what he was gawking at and her knees almost buckled as the blood drained from her head.

Ohmigod, it's Spencer.

A tiny voice wailed inside her mind. This wasn't how she wanted him to find out. . . .

"Your *what?*" Spencer asked, looking as pale as she felt.

"She said he is her husband," Amalia explained helpfully. "Though perhaps he is not." Then, looking back and forth between Spencer and the others and evidently sensing undercurrents she didn't understand, the woman asked bluntly, "Who are you?"

Spencer's expression turned stony. "I'm her other husband."

Six

Kelly closed her eyes against the pain and bewilderment on Spencer's face. Could he have possibly learned the truth in a worse way?

She wished the floor would open up and swallow her right then and there, but no such luck. Fainting sounded like a good idea, too—anything to get her out of this mess—but she didn't know how to do it on purpose, much less realistically. She'd probably end up hurting herself anyway, so she was just going to have to deal with it.

The only one who seemed happy about Spencer's statement was Amalia. "Ah, good," the bimbo exclaimed. "Then Chaz is mine."

Chaz scowled at her. "Now cut that out. How many times do I have to tell you? I'm not going to marry you. I'm married to Kelly. She's the one I want. You're . . . irrelevant."

Amalia pouted again. "What is this word? Is it a bad thing?"

Chaz just rolled his eyes in disgust, so Scott filled her in. "It's not bad," he said soothingly. "It means you're . . ." He paused, searching for the right word, ending up with, ". . . extraneous." At her puzzled look, he added, "Superfluous?" She frowned and he added, "Uh, not needed."

Her expression cleared. "Ah, I see. But Chaz does need me. We are to be married."

Now Scott appeared as exasperated as Chaz looked and Kelly felt.

Unfortunately, Spencer still appeared confused. Feeling bad for him, Kelly took a step in his direction, but Chaz blocked her way.

"So *this* is the guy you married?" he asked disapprovingly, looking Spencer up and down as if he were some unwashed homeless junkie.

Spencer stiffened, and waves of frost rolled off him as he glared at Chaz. But, ever polite, he said, "I'm afraid I haven't had the pleasure . . . "

Animosity choked the air, threatening to suck up all the available oxygen, but, true to her upbringing, Kelly wanted to avoid a scene at all costs.

It's a little late for that.

Okay, avoid making a *worse* scene, then.

Stepping between her two husbands—and didn't *that* thought make her senses reel?—Kelly said, "Chaz, this is Spencer Preston, my—" She broke off, fearing that finishing that statement would only make things worse. Ignoring her brother's knowing grin, she turned determinedly to Spencer. "Spencer, this is Chaz Vincent, my . . . first husband."

"*Only* husband," Chaz said firmly.

Ignoring him, Spencer gazed at her with a frown creasing his brow. "But how did this happen? And why are all these people here?"

Kelly hesitated, wondering how best to explain.

In the pause, her helpful brother jumped in with his version of events. "It's really quite simple," he told

Spencer with an engaging smile. "You two had Chaz declared legally dead so you could get married. But Chaz wasn't dead—he was just held captive with Garcia. He showed up very much alive at his own funeral, so he decided to come along on your honeymoon. I thought it sounded like a good idea, so I came, too."

Spencer nodded, though he still looked perplexed as his gaze swung toward Amalia.

"Oh, her?" Scott said. "She's Garcia—Amalia Garcia—and she wants to marry Chaz, but she's irrelevant."

Amalia stamped her foot. "I am not irrev—irrel— That thing you said. I am *not* not needed."

Kelly glared at Scott's levity.

Misunderstanding her, he said blithely, "Well, she's irrelevant to Chaz, anyway. Kelly thinks she's very much relevant since Amalia spent the last five cozy years with him."

"Thanks so much for the rundown," Kelly said, hoping she could stop the revelations pouring from her brother's mouth.

Scott grinned. "No problem. Any time."

Spencer appeared thoughtful. "So this is why you left me alone in the honeymoon suite? Because your first husband rose from the dead?"

Kelly sagged in relief. Trust Spencer to cut through Scott's obfuscation to what was truly important.

"He makes me sound like a zombie," Chaz protested.

Ignoring him, Kelly turned to Spencer. "Yes. I-I didn't know quite how to explain, so I wanted to be alone for awhile, to figure out how to break it to you." Only this wasn't how she'd planned to do it.

Some of the tension left his face. Relief, perhaps, that she hadn't left him alone on their wedding night for another reason?

"Then the solution is quite simple," Spencer said. "Kelly will just have to divorce both of us and remarry one."

Spencer and Amalia looked cheered by this idea, but Chaz wasn't having any of it. "And I suppose you think you're the one she should marry?" he challenged.

Spencer's urbane shrug managed to convey the thought that naturally Kelly would choose him.

Chaz must have read it the same way, for his expression turned belligerent as he clenched his fists and said, "That won't be necessary. All she has to do is annul her marriage to you. Then it will be as if it never existed."

Could it be that simple? Kelly frowned. Her head was beginning to hurt.

Spencer stiffened, apparently annoyed at this reminder that he had never had a chance to consummate the marriage. "I can offer Kelly the best. An elegant lifestyle, peace of mind, and freedom from any worries. What can you offer her?" Spencer let his gaze sweep over Chaz in disdain. "Dysentery?"

"He is right," Amalia said in a cooing tone to Chaz as she stroked his arm. "Let him take care of *her*. I will take care of you."

Chaz shrugged her off, his gaze boring into Spencer. "I can offer her a hell of a lot more than you, pal. The important things—like passion, excitement, adventure. Ever heard of them? Or are you too busy being *elegant?*" he said with a sneer.

Kelly watched in consternation as her husbands faced off, their civilized veneer stripped away. Oh, she knew Chaz had all that heat simmering just below the surface, but to see Spencer angry enough to be rude was quite shocking. She didn't think he had it in him.

She ought to be angry with both of them, but there was something exhilarating about having two men fight over her. Especially when they were both ignoring the bimbo. It was kind of nice to be the center of attention for a change.

"Well," Spencer said, shooting his cuffs and meticulously straightening them, "I'd rather be elegant than obstreperous."

"Obstreperous?" Chaz repeated in disbelief. "Who uses words like that?"

"I not know what it means," Amalia said in puzzlement. Turning to Scott, she asked, "What does it mean?"

Ever helpful, Scott explained, "It means . . . unruly, belligerent. I think Spencer is calling Chaz a bully."

"Oh," Amalia said, then narrowed her eyes at Spencer. "Chaz is no bully—he is mine."

As if *that* made any sense. Annoyed, Kelly snapped, "This is none of your business. You're irrelevant, remember?"

"Ha," Amalia exclaimed, jerking her chin up. "If I am irrev— That, that thing, you are . . ." She paused as if searching for the right English word, then broke into a stream of Spanish, punctuating her words with a stamping foot, flashing eyes, and waving arms.

Kelly watched in awe—she'd never seen anyone lose their temper with their whole body before. It was just as well she didn't understand a word of it. If she had, she surely would have been offended. As it was, Amalia's display reminded Kelly she needed to maintain her temper to ensure her husbands didn't lose theirs.

Unfortunately, they seemed to have forgotten her in watching Amalia's little fit. Chaz looked apprehensive, but Spencer's expression was oddly admiring. Scott, naturally, was amused.

Disgusted with the lot of them, Kelly turned to leave, but Chaz caught her arm. "No, wait."

"Why?" she asked.

"You haven't told him yet," Chaz said patiently.

"Told who what?"

"You haven't told that guy," he nodded toward Spencer, "that you're my wife. Legally, it's the only thing that makes sense."

"Nonsense," Spencer declared. "At least I didn't jaunt off on archaeological expeditions all over the world and abandon her. I was here for her when you weren't."

Chaz stared at him in disbelief. "You think I *wanted* to be held prisoner for five years?"

"Hold on," Scott said, interrupting them both. "What you two want isn't at issue—we all know what that is . . . *who* that is. The question is, what does Kelly want?"

"I'm sooo glad someone realizes that," Kelly said sarcastically.

Then wished she hadn't. All eyes turned toward her, waiting for her to answer the question and end this. Unfortunately, she couldn't. How could she choose one man and leave the other dangling in the wind? In the middle of a hotel hallway, no less? She couldn't, not publicly like this.

"So, who's it gonna be?" Scott asked. "Mr. Elegance or Mr. Excitement?"

They all looked at her expectantly, but it was too much. Pain speared through her head and Kelly rubbed her temples. "I-I don't know. I'm tired and I have a headache. I can't think. I need to rest."

Chaz scowled. "But—"

She held up a hand to stop him. "Not another word, or I'll say to hell with both of you."

Spencer looked offended. "But *I* didn't say anything," he protested.

"You just did," Scott said with a grin. "Come on, is it too much to ask to leave her alone to think for awhile? After all, it's the rest of your lives she's deciding. Would you want to be rushed into such a decision?"

Scott could be useful on occasion. "He's right," she said. "I just need some time."

"How much time?" Chaz asked.

"I don't know." Her temples were really throbbing now. And she wouldn't put it past Chaz to continue bugging her with the same question until she answered to his satisfaction. "But don't even think of bothering me. The first one to disturb me is out of the running."

Chaz looked guilty, but Spencer appeared surprised. Obviously, he had never even thought of intruding upon her until she announced she was ready.

So which was better? The man who was considerate of her feelings? Or the one who was so anxious to be with her that he ignored all the rules?

If she followed her heart, the answer was clear. After her reaction to Amalia's possessiveness, it was obvious Kelly still loved Chaz as much as she ever had. But loving him had caused her so much pain. Could she live with that again?

Could she live without him? Kelly massaged her temples, wishing the pain and pressure would go away.

"No," Amalia exclaimed with a stamp of her foot. "It is cruel of you to leaf us like this. You must choose. Now."

Darn it, Amalia was right. And from the expression on everyone else's faces, they thought so, too.

The quandary warred within Kelly, creating a maelstrom of contradictory emotions.

I need to make a decision. I can't make a decision. I want Chaz. I want Spencer.

I just want out! she screamed inside her head. That did it. The pressure that had built up inside her burst open, letting loose an explosion of emotion—she covered her face and sobbed.

Chaz stared in consternation at his wife as she bawled in big gulping sobs. He couldn't ever remember seeing her cry before and it tore him up inside, especially the thought that he might be the cause of her misery. He took a step toward her, but so did the other guy, and Chaz realized she hadn't given either one of them the right to comfort her. Yet. He almost growled in frustration.

Kelly turned blindly toward her brother and Scott did what Chaz only wished he could—he took Kelly in his arms and made soothing noises as she sobbed into his shoulder.

"Look, guys," Scott said with a scathing glance. "I don't think she's going to make any decisions tonight."

Chaz took another step toward her, but Scott scowled at them both. "Let her get some rest now. Don't worry, you can continue harassing her tomorrow."

Though Chaz didn't care for Scott's attitude, he couldn't fault the man's concern for his sister. He nodded and watched as Scott led Kelly back to her room. She was still weeping, though more quietly now, and it made him feel like a brute.

As the door closed behind them, Chaz realized he was now alone in the hallway with Amalia and that other man.

"Good," Amalia declared. "She is gone. Come with me."

Good Lord, did she never give up? Glaring at her, Chaz said, "I'm not going with you. Anywhere. Anytime. Got that? You might as well give up and leave."

Amalia shrugged. "We will be married. You will see. For now, I get my beauty sleep." Apparently thinking Kelly wasn't going to be a threat for the rest of the night, Amalia sauntered off, swinging her hips and her hair as if she were a model on the runway and the world's eyes were upon her.

It didn't impress Chaz one iota, but he caught the other guy eyeing her with speculation.

The other guy? Chaz scowled as he realized what he'd been doing. Unwilling to give the man reality by naming him, Chaz couldn't bring himself to call him Spencer or Preston, even in his mind—they were just too wimpy for words. And he wasn't about to think of him as Kelly's other husband. But he couldn't just keep calling him the other guy. What should he call him then?

Asshole leapt to mind.

Naw, he might let it slip in Kelly's presence and she wouldn't appreciate the little nickname. But Chaz couldn't let the asshole get the upper hand—Mr. Elegance would just have to realize he would always be in second place.

That was it—he'd think of him as Number Two. Chaz grinned. He rather liked all the connotations associated with that. Deuce was even easier. Good, Deuce it was.

But a suitable nickname didn't solve any real problems. Chaz tried to ignore Deuce's presence in the hallway, but it ate away at him, like an itch he couldn't scratch, an inkblot in his peripheral vision. Chaz twitched in frustration, wanting to punch the guy for taking advantage of Kelly while she was in a vulnerable state and for having the gall to marry Chaz's wife. But Kelly wouldn't like it if they brawled in the hallway of this fancy hotel, so Chaz kept his fists balled in his pockets and willed Deuce to leave.

Unfortunately, the blot remained. At this point, Chaz would have gone to his own room to give Kelly a chance to recuperate, but there was no way in hell he was going to leave Deuce with a clear playing field right outside Kelly's door.

The SOB moved closer and Chaz bristled. The time he had spent in captivity had left him with a very thin veneer of civilization and if the twerp with two last names started anything, Chaz wouldn't be responsible for his actions.

But Deuce halted about four feet away, as if to make sure he was as close to Kelly as Chaz was.

Chaz snorted derisively and leaned against the wall just to the side of her door, casually crossing his arms. Deuce just as nonchalantly leaned against the other side and crossed *his* arms, until they looked like a pair of eunuchs guarding the sultan's harem.

Hell, wrong image. Chaz was definitely no eunuch, though he couldn't speak for Deuce. And this was no secluded harem—this was his wife's bedroom. Deuce had no right to be anywhere near it.

Chaz felt a sudden primal urge to claim the territory as his own in unmistakable terms, but he didn't know how to go about it, short of whizzing on the carpet.

Not a good idea—Kelly and the hotel management probably wouldn't like it. It wasn't civilized.

His lips quirked into a wry grin at the thought. The grin seemed to make Deuce uneasy, so Chaz let it widen into a sneer. *Mess with my woman, willya? As soon as I can find a way to win her back, you're outta here.*

But though he retained his civilized ways, Chaz still felt the need to claim Kelly as his own, to be with her in her time of need. She was upset and he should be with her, holding her, comforting her, telling her everything would be all right. Damn it, it should be Chaz in there with her—not her brother, and certainly not the *elegant* man she'd chosen as her second husband.

Sudden doubt assailed Chaz as he wondered why she had chosen a second husband so unlike her first. If she had married another man like Chaz, he could have understood it, at least. But to choose one who was his polar opposite in every way . . . what did that say about their marriage? Had it been that bad?

No, it couldn't have been. He remembered nothing but good times, wonderful companionship, and hot, sweaty sex. Oh, there had been a few fights, sure, but that was the sign of a healthy marriage, wasn't it? Or had he idealized his marriage during those five years, making it out to be much more than it really was?

He mulled that over in his mind for a moment, then decided he hadn't exaggerated it. When he and Kelly had reminisced earlier, she had responded to the shared memories as warmly as he. Had she changed that much, then, that a future with a wimp like Deuce seemed desirable? He couldn't imagine it.

The door opened then and both he and Deuce leapt to attention, but only Scott emerged. He closed the door behind him, smiling slightly when he saw the "guard" positions they had taken.

"How is she?" Chaz demanded, only to be immediately echoed by Deuce.

"She's fine," Scott reassured them, making a calming gesture. "She's just worn out. It's been a long day."

Yes, it had. Chaz realized with a start that the day had started out with her marrying one husband and finding another was alive, then had been packed full of events since. "She must be exhausted," Chaz murmured.

Scott nodded. "I'm sure you both understand she's too tired to make a decision right now."

"Of course," Deuce said in that smarmy tone of his.

Not to be outdone, Chaz added, "It can't be easy for her." *Or us.* But he left that unsaid.

"It isn't," Scott said with a sigh. "I'm not sure it will ever be."

Fear spiked through Chaz. At first, he had been so certain Kelly would choose him, so utterly confident in her love for him, that he hadn't even considered any other outcome. Now, however, he wasn't so sure. Would she blame Chaz for making her cry? Would she believe Amalia's skewed version of events?

Would she do the unthinkable and choose Deuce?

Chaz couldn't stand the idea of her making a decision without giving him a fair hearing, without giving him the chance to show her how much he loved her, needed her. "I have an idea," Chaz blurted out.

Both men looked at him in surprise, though Deuce's expression also held a healthy dose of suspicion.

Now, how to make this palatable to everyone? "Why don't we give her more time to decide . . . and give her more information on which to base that decision?"

"What did you have in mind?" Deuce asked with narrowed eyes.

Ignoring him, Chaz spoke directly to Scott. "I figure I—I mean we—could each have a day with her, alone. It would give her a chance to see each of us at our best and maybe help her figure out who she wants to be with for the rest of her life."

It galled Chaz that he would have to give Spencer a full day alone with Kelly, too, but it was the only way they would all go along with it.

"What's the catch?" Spencer asked in a suspicious tone.

"No catch," Chaz said. Except that when the stakes were this high, he played to win.

Scott nodded slowly. "I think she'll go for it, but she's sleeping now. I'll ask her in the morning."

Chaz felt himself relax a little. At least this way he'd have a chance with her. "Good."

"So," Scott said, "the next question is, who goes first?"

Chaz and Deuce eyed each other, unsmiling. Which was better, to go first and set the standard, or to go last and clinch the deal? Apparently, Deuce was having the same problem deciding, for he didn't say anything either.

"Never mind," Scott said. "We'll flip a coin. Heads, it's Chaz. Tails, it's Spencer."

Scott flipped the coin and peered down at it, showing it to both men. "Tails it is—Spencer goes first."

Deuce smirked and Chaz tensed. Maybe this wasn't such a good idea after all. . . .

Seven

Kelly woke, feeling disoriented for a moment or two in the strange room. Stretching in the bright morning light, she realized she had worn an oversized T-shirt to bed . . . which seemed wrong somehow.

She struggled to clear the sleep from her brain and the world slowly came back into focus. Oh, yeah. Kelly couldn't bring herself to wear the negligee Mother had given her for her honeymoon, so accommodating Scott had scrounged up a shirt for her to wear.

Her mind cleared even more and the events of the previous day came into full clarity. The wedding, the funeral, the scene in the hallway . . . and Chaz, Spencer, and Amalia. Kelly moaned and pulled the bedspread over her head, wishing the world would just go away. It worked for ostriches, didn't it?

A knock came at the door and she burrowed even deeper, pretending she hadn't heard it.

A moment later, it sounded again. This time, she heard Scott saying, "It's me, Kelly. Open up."

Well, Scott was safe. Kelly uncovered her head and dragged herself out of bed to let him in.

"Good morning," he said in a disgustingly cheerful tone as he breezed in holding a breakfast tray with a newspaper tucked under one arm.

He looked so crisp and clean, it made her feel grungy. She grunted a greeting.

Setting the tray and paper on the dresser, he added, "Well, aren't you a little ray of sunshine." At her glare, he said, "Yeah, I know. You're not a morning person. Go on, clean up a bit while I set up breakfast."

Gratefully, Kelly did just that. Brushing her teeth, splashing some water on her face, and brushing her hair into some semblance of order made her feel a little more human. And when she emerged from the bathroom, the smell of fresh-brewed coffee made her inhale gratefully. "Hmm, what did I do to deserve this?" she asked, taking in the pot of coffee and assortment of pastries he had brought.

Scott smiled and handed her a cup of coffee. "I figured you wouldn't want to brave the hallway and the Great White Hunters lying in ambush for you without some sort of nourishment."

She took an appreciative sip and said, "You make it sound like I'm some sort of game."

Waggling his eyebrows, Scott said, "Well, they certainly want to play."

"Not funny." But in a strange way, Scott's quirky sense of humor made her feel better. She selected a croissant and smiled at him. "You're always rescuing someone, aren't you?" And she was his latest project.

Scott blinked at her in surprise. "Me?"

"Don't deny it. You may pretend to be a playboy, but I know who managed the family finances over the years, and how close Mother came to ruin until you helped her put the pieces back together."

He shrugged. "I'm just lucky."

No, shrewd. But if he wanted the world to think he was a carefree fool, that was his business. Since it seemed to make him uncomfortable, she dropped it. "Thanks for breakfast, anyway. I do appreciate not having to brave the husband gauntlet." The thought of having to deal with Chaz or Spencer and their inevitable questions this early in the morning made her cringe.

Grinning, Scott selected a cinnamon roll for himself. "No problem."

She took a bite of the flaky pastry, then when Scott didn't volunteer any further information, she asked, "So, how are they?"

"The Great White Hunters?"

She grimaced at the description but nodded.

"About like you'd expect. Worried about you, wanting you to choose between them."

She made a face, knowing she had to do that today, but wanting to put off the confrontation as long as possible. Scott gave her a sympathetic look. "I know—it's tough."

She sighed, feeling embarrassed as she remembered her crying jag. "I sort of lost it last night."

"You were entitled." Scott grinned. "And it was very effective, too. I'll have to remember that next time I need out of a bad situation."

Oh, yeah—she could just see Scott bursting into tears and acting hysterical. "I didn't do it on purpose."

"I know," Scott said, more gently. "Do you feel better now?"

"Yes, just a little foolish." Not to mention headachy from all the crying.

"Are you up to facing them, knowing what they want?"

She sighed. "I'll have to be." What other choice did she have? Then, in a burst of confidence, she blurted out, "It would be easier if it weren't for Amalia." The

Latin beauty's presence complicated things, made it more difficult to concentrate on the real issues.

Scott nodded slowly. "Yes, I see that."

Gazing wistfully at her brother, Kelly asked, "Do you think he was telling the truth?"

"Chaz, you mean?"

"Yes. Do you think he was telling the truth about Amalia?" She desperately wanted to believe that Chaz hadn't been tempted by her.

Scott considered for a moment, taking a sip of his coffee. "Yes, I think so. She's a man-eater. The only way to survive with a woman like that is to keep your distance."

"But she's so beautiful." How could Chaz resist such loveliness, especially since they had been in such close proximity?

"No," Scott said, correcting her. "*You* are beautiful. She's bold, striking, dramatic. Probably high maintenance. Exotic women can be very wearing on a man."

Kelly felt herself soften. What had she done to deserve such a wonderful brother? "Thanks." But did Chaz feel the same way?

"So," he said with the lift of an eyebrow. "What is it *you* want? Don't think—just blurt out the first thing that comes into your mind."

"Mind-blowing sex," she said instantly. Then covered her mouth in chagrin. She should know better than to rise to Scott's bait.

He threw back his head and laughed. "Sorry, I can't give you that."

She waved her hand in negation. "Forget I said that." But she knew better. Sometime, somewhere, Scott would find a way to remind her. Probably in the most embarrassing way.

Scott's grin widened, but he didn't make any promises. "So, have you made your decision yet?"

"Yes, I think so. But at this point, I'm tempted to divorce both of them and head for the Amazon myself." Getting lost in the jungle far from civilization and having her own adventure with the male version of Amalia was very appealing at the moment.

"Well, I'll support you no matter who you choose," Scott said.

"I know," Kelly said softly. Scott had been her rock over the past five years. But there was an odd note in his voice. "But you think I'll make the wrong decision, don't you?" Wrong according to Scott, anyway.

He shrugged. "It doesn't matter what I think."

That was a yes.

But he was wrong. "Yes, it does matter."

Ignoring that, Scott said, "You've made a decision, haven't you?"

"Yes, I—"

Scott held up a hand. "Wait. Whatever it is—*who*ever it is—keep it to yourself."

"Why?" Hadn't they all been pestering her to make this choice?

"Make him wait. Make them both wait."

"What do you mean?"

Scott frowned. "I don't really care for the way either of them has treated you. Chaz is too cocky and sure of himself, and Spencer is haughty and condescending."

"Well, maybe," Kelly said, feeling the urge to defend both men. "But we saw them at their worst yesterday." It was understandable, given the situation.

"Exactly my point," Scott exclaimed. "You shouldn't have to make a decision based on which husband is least objectionable. That's no way to start a new life together. You need to see them at their best, not their worst."

He had a point, but Kelly wasn't exactly sure how she would go about doing that. "I take it you have a plan in mind?"

He grinned. "Yes. Or, rather, they came up with the idea last night and I think it's a good one."

"What is it?"

"The plan is for each one of them to have a date with you—one today and one tomorrow—to show themselves at their best advantage. The theory is that it will make it easier for you to choose once they've wined and dined you."

"They came up with this?" Kelly asked in surprise.

"Yes—it was Chaz's idea, actually."

That surprised her even more. "I can't believe Chaz would propose something that might give Spencer an edge."

"I think he's afraid you've already chosen Spencer, and this is his way of making sure he gets one last chance to woo you and change your mind."

That made sense. And the thought of Chaz being anxious and uncertain made her soften. She sure wished she could have seen it, though. Chaz Vincent didn't often let his vulnerabilities show. "I see."

Scott raised an eyebrow. "So, you agree?"

"I don't know. It seems a little . . ." She trailed off and gestured helplessly.

"Devious? Dishonest?"

"Well, yes." Especially since she was pretty sure about who she was going to choose.

He grinned. "All the better, Sis. Take it from me, they deserve it after what they put you through yesterday." He must have read the uncertainty on her face, for he added, "Besides, whoever comes out on the losing end will at least have the consolation of knowing he gave it his best shot before you made your choice. You really owe it to them to let them try."

Kelly considered that for a moment. Scott made a lot of sense. And letting them cater to her for a change held a lot of appeal. It would give her the upper hand and at least the illusion of control. Not to mention delaying the moment when she had to choose one man and hurt the other.

Coward.

Yes, it was the coward's way out, but if everyone else thought it was the way to go, who was she to quibble? "Okay, I'll do it," she said, then realized that left her with another choice to make. "But who should go first?"

"Don't worry," Scott said. "I took care of that. Just in case you agreed, we flipped a coin last night and Spencer won the toss. Shall I tell him he can take you out this afternoon so you can plan?"

"Yes, but . . . what shall I do until then?" Staying confined to her hotel room didn't sound like much fun.

Scott set down his coffee cup and headed toward the door. "Well, maybe you can figure out what to say when Mother sees the *Denver Post*." He tossed her the paper. "Must be a slow news day. Congratulations—you made the front page."

She shook open the paper and glanced at it. Sure enough, there at the bottom right blared the headline *Explorer Attends Own Funeral*.

"Oh, no. What if the other hotel guests see this?" she wailed. There was an old picture of Chaz on the front page, and he was bound to be recognized.

"Don't worry. I bought up all the papers in the hotel.

You just have to worry about those in the rest of the state." And with that parting shot, he left.

As the door closed behind Scott, Kelly crumpled the paper and groaned, unwilling to see her messed-up life paraded for all the world to see. She should have expected it—with all those mourners at the memorial service, at least a dozen were bound to share the juicy news with the world.

She was just surprised the reporters weren't beating down her door already. After all, Amalia had managed to track Chaz down fairly quickly. It was only a matter of time before the press followed her example and found them here.

She buried her head in her hands and groaned. Could it possibly get any worse?

After he woke and dressed, Chaz puttered around his room for awhile, uncertain what to do and reluctant to leave until he knew exactly where everyone was. Knowing he'd eventually have to leave this hotel, he made a few phone calls to get in touch with his old contacts to see if they'd heard of any work for him. They gave him a few leads, but he was too antsy to follow up on them right now. Between calls, he had left his door open a crack and peered out into the hallway whenever he heard a noise.

Finally, when Deuce had room service delivered and Scott entered Kelly's room with a tray, Chaz figured it was safe to leave his room for a little while and go in search of food himself. The thought of staying confined in this space to order room service made his skin crawl, so he made his way down to the restaurant.

Perusing the menu, Chaz grinned. The old Chaz

would protest at spending this much money on eating out, but food—real American food—was right up there in the top five things he missed the most during his time in captivity. Hell, he deserved it.

Feeling righteous in his gluttony, Chaz ordered a huge breakfast, then settled in for a serious bout of thinking.

But before he could even get started, he heard a feminine voice ask, "Mind if I join you?"

He glanced up to see the classy blonde from the bar the night before. What was her name again? Oh, yeah—Candace.

He wanted to blow her off, but there was something in her expression that reflected a kindred pain. So he swallowed his rebuff and said, "Sure. Why not?"

As soon as she was seated, the waiter returned to take her order—a substantially smaller breakfast than the one Chaz had just chosen. Once the waiter had gone, Chaz said, "Bad night, huh?"

Candace's eyes widened in surprise. "You mean it shows? And here I thought I had been so careful with my make-up."

"Oh, it's not your make-up," Chaz assured her. "There's just some strain in your face." Not to mention the pain in her eyes. Though he normally didn't get involved in other people's problems, anything was preferable to dwelling on his own. "You really love that guy, huh?"

"Yes." She stared down at the table, pleating the napkin between her fingers. "Last night was his wedding night."

"No wonder you couldn't sleep."

She acknowledged that with a wry grin, then studied his face. "You don't look much better."

He shrugged and was saved from answering by the waiter who delivered their breakfast. Feeling a little guilty about ordering so much food, Chaz glanced down at the spread in front of him and said defensively, "I was hungry."

Candace just smiled as she buttered her toast. "Then please, enjoy it."

They ate in companionable silence, Chaz savoring every bite, until he had had enough and was sipping his coffee.

Candace smiled at him. "You didn't answer me earlier."

"About what?" He had been so absorbed in the food, he had lost the thread of their conversation.

"I mentioned that you didn't look like you had much sleep, either. Did your wife choose the other man over you?"

He grimaced. "She hasn't made a decision yet. She's going to have one date with each of us, then make a choice." He took another sip of coffee. "He goes first, today."

"I'm sorry to hear that."

He acknowledged her sympathy with a nod, but at least he still had a chance with Kelly. Poor Candace had lost out already. Remembering their previous conversation, Chaz said, "You said something last night that made me think."

"I did?" She looked surprised. "What was that?"

"You pointed out that I was treating my wife like she was second best, that I let other things come first."

Candace looked dismayed. "Did I say that? I must have been more upset than I remember. I'm sorry, I had no right—"

"It's okay," Chaz said, soothing her. "In hindsight, I

can see that's exactly what I was doing. I thought I was being honorable in keeping my promise to the men who had funded my expedition, but in doing so, I compromised my honor with my wife." And she certainly meant more to him than any job. "But . . . how can I make it right?"

Candace shook her head with pity in her eyes. "You can't do anything to change the past. All you can do is apologize, show her that you've changed your ways, and prove that you love her. But if you've hurt her very badly, it might take some time for her to forgive you."

But he didn't have time, especially since Deuce was going to have a clear field this afternoon to make time with her. "So what happens when this other guy tries to make love to her? I'm just supposed to let him?"

"Absolutely not," Candace said firmly.

She had managed to surprise him. It must have showed on his face, for she added, "I made that mistake. I fell in love with a man who works for me and did nothing about it."

Her voice was full of regret and Chaz got the feeling she needed to talk about it. "What happened?"

She shrugged and dropped her gaze, toying with her coffee spoon. "I was afraid to let my feelings show, afraid it would seem like sexual harassment." She sighed, then added, "He pursued another employee who never gave him any encouragement. I thought he would eventually give up on her and see me waiting in the background."

She paused, seemingly unable to say the words, so Chaz said them for her. "But he didn't."

She shook her head. "No, he didn't. Instead, she finally gave in." Candace glanced up at him, tears shimmering in her eyes and said, "So don't you dare give up. If you love her, fight for her . . . before it's too late."

"All's fair in love or war, eh?" he asked with a smile.

Candace considered that for a moment, then back-tracked. "Well, maybe not *all*. But anything within reason, certainly."

That would narrow his options a little, but Chaz didn't care. Candace's encouragement had merely confirmed what Chaz already knew—he would do whatever was necessary to win Kelly back. Within reason or not.

And he'd better get back upstairs to see if the situation had changed. They paid their bills and exited the restaurant together, only to run into Scott.

"Oh, there you are," Scott exclaimed. "Whatever you do, don't go toward the lobby."

"Why not?" Chaz asked, his eyes narrowed. If this involved Kelly, there was no way Scott was going to keep him from it.

"There are reporters waiting for you."

Chaz glanced at Candace, who said, "It wasn't me. I told you—I'm a publisher, not a reporter. Besides, I didn't know you were news."

"Who's this?" Scott asked, looking from Chaz to Candace.

"A fellow sufferer in the game of love," Chaz explained. "Candace, this is Scott. Scott, Candace." He grimaced. "And I didn't know I was news, either."

"Oh, come on," Scott said, rolling his eyes. "You return from the dead to attend your own funeral and you think that's not news? You made the front page."

Candace raised an eyebrow at Chaz. "There's a little more to your story than you let on, I think."

He shrugged. "Yeah, well, it was too complicated to

go into." Turning to Scott, he asked, "What should I do?"

"First, let's get out of the public eye." Scott grabbed Chaz's arm and turned him the other way. "They've been bullying Billings, trying to get him to give them your room number or my sister's. So far, Billings has been holding out."

"Who is Billings?" Candace asked.

Scott and Chaz glanced back at her, and Chaz only now realized she had been following them. "He's the assistant manager," Chaz explained. "The snooty one."

"Oh."

Scott stared at her for a moment, then must have come to a decision, for he said, "Are you willing to help us?"

She looked a little taken aback. Chaz didn't know what Scott had in mind, but he rushed in to reassure Candace. "We haven't done anything wrong. They just want my story."

"All right, I suppose I can help," she said slowly. "But I'll want to hear this story, myself."

"Sure, no problem," Chaz said. "But later, when we have more time."

"All right," Candace said and some of the tightness disappeared from her face as she seemed to get caught up in the excitement of the moment. "What do you want me to do?"

Scott paused, thinking. "We need to get rid of them without letting them find Chaz, so I guess we need to make them think he's somewhere else."

"Good," Chaz said. "How?"

"We'll go on upstairs, and have Candace ask for you at the desk—loud enough so the reporters can hear you."

"I'll need to know your full name then," Candace said.

"Chaz Vincent."

She frowned. "That sounds familiar. Do I know you from somewhere?"

Chaz shrugged. "Probably just the papers." Scott had told him his disappearance had made headlines for several days after the plane had gone down. But he didn't want to get into all that now. "What then?" he asked Scott.

"Because of the reporters lying in wait in the lobby, Billings will refuse to give her your room number. Candace should just say something like, 'He must have left for Denver already,' then head up to room three-oh-six. Make sure the reporters know what the room number is."

Kelly's room? "Why there?"

Scott grimaced impatiently. "Because I need to make sure your wife doesn't leave her room—they'll be looking for her, too. But they'll think it's Candace's room. And, just in case they don't believe Candace, we'll have another little playlet concocted to convince them." He turned to Candace. "You up for this?"

"Of course," she said. Smoothing the wrinkles out of her slim slacks, she looked resolute and determined.

Chaz suspected she liked the thought of having something to distract her from her own problems. "Okay. Just give us ten minutes to get up the back stairs, all right?" Chaz said.

Glancing at her watch, Candace said, "Ten minutes. I can do that."

"Good," Scott exclaimed. "Now, let's go."

It took them awhile to locate the stairs without calling attention to themselves, then they hurried up and knocked on Kelly's door.

"It's me," Scott said. "Let me in, quick."

Kelly opened the door and they darted inside. Damn, she looked good. She smelled like she had just come from the shower and looked crisp and clean in a long dark skirt over leather boots and a fuzzy red sweater that looked incredibly touchable. Chaz clenched his fists by his side, curbing his instinct to reach out and touch all that sweet softness.

Oblivious to his dilemma, Kelly glanced from Scott to Chaz. "What's this all about? I thought I was seeing Spencer first."

"You are, you are," Scott assured her. "But there are some reporters we need to get rid of first."

She closed her eyes briefly and shook her head. "I should have known. Where are they?"

"Downstairs in the lobby, putting Billings under siege." When she grimaced, Scott said, "Don't worry. I have a plan . . . and I'd better let Spencer in on his part of this."

He quickly called Deuce and filled him in, adding, "We have a friend downstairs trying to put them off the scent. If that doesn't work, they're liable to follow her up here. Do me a favor and keep an eye out in the hallway. If you see a bunch of guys outside, call me right away in Kelly's room. I'll take it from there, and just ignore anything I say."

Deuce must have agreed to do as Scott asked, for Scott hung up.

"What are you planning?" Kelly asked.

A knock came at the door. "It's me, Candace. I don't think they fell for it."

"Candace?" Kelly exclaimed in surprise. "How—?"

"Never mind," Scott said. "Too late now. Just hide in here and don't come out until I call you."

He shoved Kelly and Chaz both in the closet and closed the doors. As darkness enfolded him and he fought through clinging material to the back of the closet, Chaz heard Scott open the door and close it quickly. Then the phone rang, but the closed doors and clothing muffled the sound so that Chaz couldn't make out Scott's words.

He felt Kelly move next to him and with both their backs against the wall, she whispered, "Can you hear what's going on?"

"No, not a thing," he whispered back.

And frankly, he didn't care. The entire closet was filled with Kelly's scent—a familiar combination of herbal shampoo and the light scent of baby powder. It wasn't particularly exotic or alluring, but it was all Kelly, and that was seductive enough for Chaz.

He inhaled, savoring her fragrance. Hell, if he'd been a dog, he'd have wallowed in it. All he wanted to do was sink his nose into the curve of her neck and breathe her in.

Kelly's arm brushed his and her nearness, combined with the closeness of the closet, made him realize how small this space was. Scott could have hidden them in the bathroom and achieved the same objective, but maybe he intended to do Chaz a favor by confining him in such close proximity with his wife.

The only problem was, Chaz had spent far too much time in cramped quarters like this over the past five years, planning escape, desperately wanting a way out.

God, he wanted out now, too.

His breathing turned loud in the stillness, and he couldn't seem to stop it from becoming more labored.

Suddenly, he felt as if he were back in his prison and the dense foliage, persistent humidity, and the threat of savage beasts lurking in the undergrowth seemed to close in around him.

"What's wrong?" Kelly whispered.

"Nothing," Chaz said, then realized his unwillingness to share his fears with her would only push her away even more.

She edged away, and Chaz cursed himself, then forcibly calmed his breathing. As the jungle retreated from his imagination, he said, "It's just that I don't like small spaces . . . I occupied far too many of them during my imprisonment."

"Oh, Chaz, I'm sorry," Kelly murmured. "Is there anything I can do to help?"

"Just . . . let me touch you." Without waiting for permission, Chaz turned and placed the front of his body full-length against hers, pressing her against the back wall of the closet. Though he longed to hold her, to let his hands roam her body until she screamed out his name, he held himself in check, firmly planting his hands flat against the wall.

"I'm sorry," he whispered as he felt Kelly stiffen. "I just need human contact."

He concentrated solely on his wife and though he couldn't see a blessed thing, he let his other senses take her in as he inhaled her special scent, heard the soft sound of her breathing, and felt her soften and relax against him when she realized he didn't intend to take advantage. It helped him slow his breathing and bring it under control.

Tentatively, Kelly raised her arms, and held him, stroking his back. Not as a lover, but in comfort.

Hell, he didn't care. He'd take anything he could get.

And now that his panic attack was under control, Chaz's body reminded him just how much he had missed his wife. Longing filled him, sensual remembrance flaring at every point of contact. He sighed and kissed her hair, the only place that seemed safe at the moment. Her embrace tightened and turned into a caress, causing another sort of adrenaline to sizzle through him. God, did she want him as much as he wanted her?

The inevitable hardness occurred and, wishing he could see her face to gauge her reaction, Chaz rubbed up against her, holding himself just short of grinding into her. The delicious friction sent waves of pleasure through him. Damn, what he wouldn't give for the power to make their clothes vanish right now.

Kelly gasped and he froze for a moment until he realized her hips were thrusting against his just as much as his were against hers. He let his arms slide around her and he sought her lips with his in the darkness.

They clung together in what seemed like desperation, a primal need to connect with a human being on the most basic of levels. His head swam and he retreated for a moment, only to dive back into the sweetness that was Kelly, caressing one soft breast in his hand as he licked and nipped his way down her neck.

Her whimper of desire only encouraged him, and he raised her sweater, yanked up her bra, and took her breast into his mouth.

Sudden light flooded the closet, disorienting him, and Kelly yanked down her sweater and pushed him away. Damn. Scott sure had lousy timing.

Surrendering to the inevitable, Chaz shoved aside the hanging clothes and abandoned the warm, sensual atmosphere of the closet for the cool room beyond. Kelly came out right behind him, tugging her sweater into place and fussing with her hair.

Chaz glared at Scott, daring him to say something, but Scott kept his mouth shut. Of course, he couldn't hide the amusement in his eyes.

Candace blinked in obvious surprise. "Kelly?"

Kelly nodded, nowhere near as surprised as Candace. "Hello, Candace," she said dully.

Chaz glanced back and forth between them. "You know each other?"

Kelly smoothed her hair. "Yes—Candace is my publisher."

"Your boss?" A sudden suspicion entered Chaz's mind and he glanced swiftly at the older woman.

Dawning comprehension showed on her face, too. "You two . . . know each other?" Candace asked, a myriad of expressions warring for dominance on her face.

"You might say that," Chaz drawled. "She's my wife."

His suspicion was confirmed when delight filled Candace's face. Aha. She must be in love with Deuce.

"But how do you know Candace?" Kelly asked with a frown.

"We met downstairs last night when I was trying to find out where you went," he explained. Then, before Kelly could ask any more questions, he added, "Small world, isn't it?"

A knock came at the door and Scott went to answer it, saying, "And I suspect it's about to get much smaller."

There, on the other side, was Deuce. Scott waved him into the room, but he came to a halt two steps inside. "Candace? What are you doing here? Is there something wrong at the office? Did you find a *Pizzazz Girl*?"

Good Lord, is that all Deuce could think of at a time like this—business? He deserved to lose Kelly.

Candace smiled at him. "No, it's pure coincidence that we showed up at the same hotel. I decided to give myself a treat for a week and didn't realize you'd chosen the same hotel for your . . ." She glanced questioningly at Kelly and Chaz. "Honeymoon?"

But she must have anticipated the answer, for her face relaxed and she looked years younger.

"That remains to be seen," Chaz said firmly.

But Kelly evidently didn't want Candace to know what was going on, for she quickly interjected, "What happened here, Scott? Did you get rid of the reporters? We couldn't hear a thing in the closet."

At the word "closet," Deuce gave them a quick appraising glance and Chaz grinned, hoping the imaginary canary feathers showed around his mouth.

"Yes, we got rid of them. Once Spencer told me they were outside the door, I had a loud telephone conversation with you, Chaz, telling you to get the hell out of Denver before the reporters got there. They must have heard me, because they didn't knock on the door until after I hung up." Scott grinned, rocking on his heels. "I tried to convince them you two had gone to Bermuda, but for some reason, they didn't buy it."

"Very clever," Chaz said. "I owe you one, buddy."

Scott nodded. "Maybe. I don't know how long it will keep them off the scent, but it should buy you some time."

The phone rang, but though they all gave it a wary glance, no one made a move to answer it. "I don't think

I want to talk to anyone who might be calling," Kelly murmured. "It could be Mother."

"Good," Deuce said and moved toward her. "Then perhaps we should start on our date now?"

Before Chaz could protest, Scott said, "Good idea. Get out while they're still on their way to Denver."

And Chaz had to keep his mouth shut. After all, he was the one who came up with this date idea in the first place. He consoled himself with the thought that Deuce couldn't possibly top the moments Chaz and Kelly had shared in the closet. That made it a little easier to keep his clenched fists in his pockets—even when the asshole shot him a triumphant glance and carried Kelly off with him.

As the door closed behind them, Chaz turned to Candace. "Is that the guy you're in love with?"

She darted a furtive glance at Scott, but said with a lift of her chin, "Yes. And is she the wife who is trying to choose between you?"

"Yes."

"Then the marriage isn't . . . valid? There's still hope?"

"We don't know about the validity," Scott said, "since Chaz was declared dead."

"But there *is* hope," Chaz said with a grin. "Especially if we join forces." As Scott watched with a fascinated expression, Chaz added, "It seems we have the same objective."

A slow smile spread across her face. "Indeed we do. Hmm. Remember what I said earlier about all being fair in love and war . . . within reason?"

Chaz nodded.

Candace's eyes blazed with purpose. "Well, forget

the reasonable part. As far as I'm concerned, anything goes."

"Really?"

"Yes. Let's follow them and see if we can sabotage this date."

Chaz laughed. "Hell, I'm game, but . . ." He glanced at Scott. "Are you gonna try and stop us?"

"Me?" Scott repeated, surprised. "Not on your life. I'm coming along. I wouldn't miss this for the world."

Eight

Chaz led the way out the door, then paused in the hallway. "Where'd they go?"

Scott grinned at him, closing the door behind Candace. "It shouldn't be difficult to find out. Spencer used the limo to come here before he sent it to pick up Kelly, which means he has no more transportation until the week is up."

Chaz did a slow burn as the implications of that seeped in. No doubt Deuce had intended to spend the entire time in their honeymoon suite. "So he can't leave?" Chaz asked as they hurried toward the elevator.

"He can if he hires a cab," Candace reminded him.

Oh yeah. It was the small things that constantly tripped him up, as if his time in the jungle had erased selected portions of his memory. Luckily, things seemed to come back quickly enough with just a hint. "We'd better hurry, then, in case there's one waiting." At a popular spot like this, the cabs might be lined up, waiting for passengers.

As they rode the elevator down, Chaz thought, *Why am I doing this?*

Because Candace had given him permission? Because Scott egged him on?

No, because he couldn't stand the thought of Deuce touching Kelly. It made him feel twitchy all over. Besides, he needed to scope out his competition, didn't he? To know what he was up against? Hell, if he thought of it that way, it was a moral imperative.

Feeling virtuous, Chaz headed purposefully toward the bell captain's stand, pleased that he had remembered the name for it. But Scott stopped him with a hand on his arm.

"No need," Scott said, nodding toward the other side of the lobby.

Chaz looked in that direction. Good grief, was Deuce taking her to lunch in the hotel restaurant? Obviously, the man had no imagination. Well, Chaz couldn't complain, especially since it made it easy to follow them. "That's convenient. Let's go."

"Where are we going?" came an accented voice behind him.

Chaz groaned. Garcia. He'd hoped she'd given up, but his luck was holding true—all bad. The woman clung like a burr and had as much sense.

"You're going nowhere—" Chaz began, only to be interrupted by Scott.

"We're going to lunch," Scott said. "Would you like to join us?"

Chaz stared at him in disgust, but Scott just shrugged. "Hey, you're not getting rid of her anyway, and this way we avoid a scene in the lobby."

Very true. "All right," Chaz said grudgingly.

But Amalia was already giving Candace the evil eye, probably assuming she had her sights set on Chaz as well. "Who is this?" Amalia asked bluntly.

"My wife's boss," Chaz said just as baldly. "Candace, Amalia." Feeling he had done his duty as far as the amenities went, he repeated, "Let's go." He didn't want to lose track of Kelly and her idiot suitor.

Candace merely raised her eyebrows at him. Heck, another thing he had to explain. But not now.

They were seated across the room from Kelly and Spencer, which suited Chaz just fine. He could see them easily, but they didn't know he was watching them. At least, not yet.

Pain speared through him. They both looked so refined, so sophisticated . . . as if they belonged here. Oh, he knew Kelly came from this kind of background, but he thought she'd given it up, left it gratefully behind with her mother and all of Grace's pretensions when they were married. Maybe she hadn't after all. Was this her true preference? Was this how she really wanted to go through life? If so, Chaz didn't think he could stand it.

He watched as Spencer ordered for both of them. Something froufrou and incredibly elegant, no doubt, Chaz thought with a grimace.

In silent rebellion, he gave his own order to the waiter—a plain burger and fries. Besides, it had been one of the meals he'd fantasized about during his captivity. He'd missed good old American food almost as much as he had Kelly.

"Uh-oh," Scott said.

"What?" Chaz glanced in Kelly's direction and found her staring back with a frown. "Oh, they've spotted us."

Scott nodded. "I'd better do a little damage control. Hold on."

He walked across to Kelly's table, had a few words with her, and strolled back.

"What happened?" Chaz asked, wondering how ticked off Kelly was.

"I just explained that we had to eat somewhere and didn't know they'd choose the hotel. I told her just to ignore us."

Good—Scott hadn't blown their cover. Chaz sneaked a peek at Kelly again. She seemed absorbed in something Deuce was saying, though her interest had to be mere courtesy. The guy couldn't be that fascinating, for heaven's sake—he was a fashion magazine editor. Chaz was surprised he even liked girls.

Well, Chaz might not be able to overhear what was going on over there, but he did have some control over what happened at this table. Glancing at the others, Chaz said, "Let's pretend we're having a really good time."

"What does that mean?" Amalia asked.

Rather than tell her, Chaz decided to show her. Throwing back his head, he let out a guffaw he knew would be heard all over the restaurant. Candace and Scott got the idea and joined him in laughter, but Amalia wasn't so quick on the uptake.

Scowling, she asked, "What is funny?"

Still chuckling, Scott, her self-appointed interpreter, said, "This situation. Don't you find it amusing?"

Amalia looked confused. Candace must have taken pity on her, for she changed the subject. "You have a very striking face. Are you a model?"

"No, I was a guide. But soon I will be Mrs. Vincent."

It was Candace's turn to be confused. "Mrs. Vincent?" she repeated with a questioning look at Chaz.

He shrugged. "She thinks she's my mother."

Scott laughed, but Amalia scowled again. "Not your mother. Your wife."

"I thought you already had a wife," Candace said.

Chaz shrugged, unwilling to go into the whole sordid mess again. "Scott will explain while I make a phone call."

"To who?" Scott asked.

"Who knows what he has planned for the day? I figure we'll have more flexibility if we follow them in our own car, so I'd better rent one." Besides, making Kelly think they were having loads of fun didn't seem to be working anyway.

"I have a car here," Candace said eagerly. "We can use it."

Chaz considered that for a moment. "Do they know your car?"

Her shoulders slumped. "Yes, I'm afraid they do."

"Then it would probably be better to rent one. We want to be as inconspicuous as possible."

Scott took out his wallet, pulled out a couple of cards, and handed them to Chaz. "Here, rent it in my name."

"That's not necessary—I have plenty of cash."

"But do you have a credit card? Or a driver's license?"

Scott had him there. Once again, it was the little things that tripped him up. "No, everything expired while I was gone and I haven't had a chance to renew them yet."

"Well, you can't rent a car without them, so just use mine. Don't worry," Scott said, grinning, "I'll let you pay for it."

"Good." To Amalia, Chaz said, "I'll be right back," to keep the woman from following him, then he left Scott to explain the whole mess to Candace while he found a phone.

* * *

As Chaz left, Candace felt more confused than ever. "You're Kelly's brother?" she asked Scott.

"That's the rumor."

"But why are you going along with . . . this?" She gestured vaguely, wondering why he had joined them in trying to ruin Spencer's day with Kelly.

"For the same reason you are. I don't think they're right for each other."

"I see." She couldn't agree more, but she hadn't expected Kelly's family to feel the same way. For the second time that day, hope swelled within her. Maybe this marriage wasn't as set in stone as she had thought. She needed to know more. "Can you tell me what the situation *is*?"

Her hopes rose even more as he explained that Kelly might not be legally married to Spencer. Even if the marriage was legal, Candace now had a fifty-fifty chance that Kelly would choose her first husband instead of Spencer. Those were certainly better odds than Candace had ever had before.

She glanced at Spencer and Kelly. Unfortunately, they looked very comfortable together. And Spencer was so handsome, so urbane, so sophisticated, how could any woman not choose him?

Stop thinking negatively, she admonished herself. Kelly had chosen Chaz once. Maybe she would again. After all, it wasn't totally out of the realm of possibility that she still loved her first husband.

Renewed determination surged through Candace. She was being given a second chance, and it was up to her to take advantage of it. But how?

As the waiter delivered their meals, Amalia suddenly spoke up, asking, "Where is Chaz? Why is he not back yet?" She looked around suspiciously, as if she suspected someone of making off with him.

"He'll be back soon," Scott said. "Don't worry—he's not likely to miss a meal."

Amalia looked as if she wasn't sure she believed him.

Why was this woman so determined to have Chaz? And what could Candace do to deter her? To distract Amalia, Candace asked, "You spent the last five years in the jungle?"

"Yes. With Chaz. I must marry him."

Not if Candace could help it. Chaz had to be free for Kelly. "But how did you keep your skin so flawless and your hair so shiny?" Amalia couldn't have repaired the damage that the jungle must have inflicted in such a short time.

Amalia shrugged. "The little ones find things for me."

"Little ones?"

"The pygmies who captured them," Scott clarified for her, with amusement in his eyes.

"I see. What . . . things?"

Amalia elaborated, explaining how she had sent the little ones out to fetch different flowers and plants so she could experiment until she found just the right combination to make sure she remained beautiful. The picture that emerged was of a vain, selfish woman who had been spoiled and indulged much of her life because of her beauty.

Candace smiled to herself. She knew the type only too well—she had dealt with many of them in her career as a fashion magazine editor. And she knew how to handle them. Perhaps she could find a way to help

Chaz rid himself of Amalia . . . and get Spencer to take another look at Candace while she was at it.

Satisfied that something had finally gone right, Chaz returned to the table to discover their meals had been served. "It's all arranged," he told them. "The car should be here when we're ready to leave."

Candace put her fork down and gave Chaz a half smile. "That's quite a story Scott just told me. No wonder you want to avoid the reporters."

Chaz nodded, and dug into his meal, savoring the hearty burger and crisp, salty fries. Damn, he'd forgotten how good a burger could be—almost as good as sex. He didn't even pretend to join in the conversation around the table as he concentrated on eating. And on watching Kelly.

Just as Chaz suspected, her lunch was definitely of the froufrou persuasion, with lots of finicky little courses and glasses of wine. Worse, Kelly seemed to be impressed by it. Was this the type of thing she liked? If so, Chaz certainly couldn't compete. Hell, he'd considered it classy when he used mayo instead of ketchup on his burger.

Depressed, he signaled the waiter and asked for their check. Candace and Amalia weren't finished yet, so as Chaz charged the meal to his room, he explained, "I just want to be ready when they make their move." He paused for a moment. "In fact, it wouldn't hurt to check on the car, too. Scott, why don't you come with me? Candace, can you sort of hang around and eavesdrop to see where they're going? I figure they'll be more worried about me overhearing and won't notice you."

"Of course," Candace said.

"What about me?" Amalia asked. "What do I do?"

"Go home," Chaz said bluntly, then turned and left.

Scott grinned at him. "Tsk, tsk. Now that wasn't very nice, was it?"

Chaz shrugged. "It doesn't matter what I say. She'll do what she wants anyway." Maybe if he ignored her long enough, she'd go away.

Hearing the determined clicking of heels behind him, Chaz glanced backward. Sure enough, there was Amalia, closing in for the kill. "See?"

Trying to ignore her, he found the rental car agent in the lobby and passed over enough cash to rent the car for the rest of the week. He handed the keys to Scott and said, "The car's out front. Since I don't have a license, you drive."

Luckily, he had rented a car big enough to hold four. Scott got into the driver's side and put the key in the ignition. "Now what?" he asked.

"Now, we wait," Chaz said. "Candace will tell us what to do next."

Sure enough, Candace came hurrying out, her head turning both ways as she searched for them.

Chaz gestured her over and she settled in the back seat with Amalia.

"Did you find out where they're going?" Chaz asked.

"Yes—Spencer made reservations at The Cliff House for dinner, and he asked the desk clerk for suggestions on local sights. It sounds like they're going downtown to see some museums and do some shopping. They're getting a cab now—all we have to do is follow them."

Sure enough, they headed downtown. Scott stayed far enough back that Kelly and Deuce wouldn't be suspicious, and parked a block away when the cab let them off on Dale Street. They spent the rest of the afternoon following them around the Fine Arts Museum, the Pioneers Museum, a horde of antique shops, and every hoity-toity and artsy shop in Old Colorado City and Manitou Springs.

For the most part, Chaz and his hangers-on just stayed in the car and watched, though Candace and Amalia really seemed to enjoy the shops. Chaz even spent a little time in some of them himself, picking up a few things for his date with Kelly. But Amalia didn't seem to get the concept of not being seen, and they were constantly ducking down under displays and pulling her around corners to avoid being spotted.

As evening approached, Kelly and Deuce finally seemed done with shopping and headed toward the restaurant.

"Is this all we're going to do?" Candace finally asked. "Just follow them around all day?"

"I guess," Chaz said. He had had vague plans of sabotaging their outing, but thought better of it as the day progressed. "I'm not sure what we *can* do without coming across as . . ." He paused, searching for suitable words.

"Cretins? Fools?" Scott supplied helpfully.

"Yeah," Chaz agreed, though he would've chosen a different description. Besides, he was sure they'd been spotted more than once, thanks to Amalia. Deuce was probably just waiting for him to pull something so he could look good in comparison, trying to be the better man.It would work, too. Damn it.

Chaz hated it when he had to play nice, especially when the stakes were so high. "I'm just checking out the competition, to see what I have to do to win."

As they pulled up to The Cliff House and got a good gander at the Victorian elegance, Candace shook her head. "I'm not sure you can. This will be very hard to top."

Really? Chaz thought but didn't say it aloud. Today had to be one of the most boring of his existence. Did women really like this kind of stuff?

As they walked into The Cliff House dining room, Candace and Amalia sighed over the decor. Chaz couldn't see anything special about it—just another expensive, ritzy place designed to part a man from his money. He sighed too, wondering how much this would set him back. "Uh, maybe we should skip this one, huh? They're bound to notice us. There's a Mc-Donald's just up the street. . . ."

He trailed off as Candace and Amalia gave him glances full of disgust.

"What?" Didn't everyone like Big Macs?

"It's okay," Scott said. "I don't think they'll notice us. The waiter seated them in that secluded alcove by the fireplace."

"Oh great," Chaz muttered. "Rub it in even more."

Grinning, Scott said, "Don't worry, it's my treat. I'm tired of driving and a gourmet meal sounds very good right about now."

"Yes," Candace said. "Let's stay."

Amalia chimed in, saying, "I like it here."

Chaz allowed himself to be persuaded, and even let Scott choose his meal. Scott probably didn't want to be embarrassed by Chaz's plebeian food choices.

The meal was excellent and the wine superb. But it left Chaz with a mellow glow that just depressed him more. If *he* enjoyed it, imagine what Kelly was thinking right now. Maybe Candace was right. Maybe he didn't have a chance of competing with all this. But he sure planned to try. He would just have to play to his own strengths.

Finally, the meal was over and they followed the couple back to the hotel. *Ah, good.* The evening was finally ending. Maybe now Chaz could find something interesting to do, especially since Amalia had apparently tired of the game and went off to bed. The other three followed Kelly and her escort to the elevators, not caring if the two knew they were there or not.

But as the elevator doors closed behind the couple, Kelly cast Chaz an annoyed glance and took Deuce's arm. Worse, the man had the nerve to look smug about it.

What the hell did that look mean? Was Deuce planning on romancing her in the honeymoon suite?

Over my dead body.

Though Scott had already hit the button to call the elevator, Chaz punched it again, urging it to hurry up. His imagination worked overtime as he thought about what Deuce was doing to Kelly in the elevator. Probably the same thing Chaz would do if they were alone together. Damn it.

Finally, another one arrived. When it opened on the third floor, Chaz hurried down the hall, only to see Deuce and Kelly vanish into her room without a backward glance.

No way. This was *not* going to happen. Chaz barreled forward, ready to break down the door if necessary, but Scott grabbed his arm.

"Wait a minute, Chaz. Think about this."

"Think, hell. I'm gonna kill him."

"No, you're not," Scott said in a reasonable tone, though Candace looked as unhappy as Chaz felt.

Chaz glared at him. "Give me one good reason why not."

"Because then Spencer would win."

Chaz pulled his arm free of Scott's hold, but put off smashing the door down while he thought about it. Scott had a point, but . . . "Who knows what he's doing in there, to *my* wife?"

"Probably nothing," Scott said soothingly.

"Yeah, right."

"No, really. Think about it," Scott urged. "They know you're out here. Kelly wouldn't dare let Spencer try anything for fear you'll burst in at any minute."

"So why disappoint her?"

"Because you'll only confirm her low opinion of you," Scott said with a long-suffering sigh.

"He has a point," Candace said. "I-I think he's right. If you break down that door, Spencer will look much better by default. I think you have to trust your wife."

Chaz swore under his breath. Oh, he trusted Kelly all right. It was Deuce he was worried about.

Before Chaz could get any more worried, the door opened and Spencer emerged. He ignored the lot of them and headed toward his room, looking both smug and frustrated.

Okay, so he probably got a kiss, but no nookie. *I can live with that.*

But not for long. Kelly had better make a decision real quick before Chaz lost his temper and did something Deuce would regret for the rest of his life.

Nine

When a knock came on Kelly's door the next morning, it wasn't Scott this time, but a hotel employee. He carried in a tray and a large shopping bag and waved away her tip, insisting it was taken care of.

How sweet. Scott was so thoughtful.

She lifted the lid from the plate and realized it wasn't from Scott at all—this breakfast could only have come from Chaz. A stack of light, fluffy pancakes topped with fresh strawberries and whipped cream lay on a plate, accompanied only by cranberry juice and coffee. It smelled heavenly.

As she sank into a chair, memories flooded back . . . memories of their honeymoon when they'd had this same breakfast seven days in a row. Her throat closed up and unshed tears stung against her eyelids. It had been one of the best times of her life.

She took a sip of cranberry juice to clear her suddenly clogged throat then impulsively swiped her finger through the whipped cream and tasted it. Yummy . . . decadent. It reminded her of all the creative uses to which Chaz had put that whipped cream. She couldn't savor the flavor without remembering the taste of Chaz as well.

Warmth flooded through her, and moisture pooled in places that had been dry as a desert for years.

Incredulously, Kelly stared at her finger. *I can't believe I'm aroused by the taste of whipped cream.*

But she could believe that's exactly what Chaz had intended. Shaking her head, she dug into the pancakes and tried to think of them as merely fuel, not an aphrodisiac. She was only partially successful in that, but at least she sated her hunger. For food, anyway.

No more of that, now.

The breakfast he had sent her was romantic and sweet, but his actions yesterday hadn't been. She couldn't believe he'd followed them—along with Scott, Candace, and Amalia no less. What was that all about?

Then again, it was one of the most amusing days she'd spent in a long time. Spencer had done his best to give her a relaxing time, but it had been unintentionally interspersed with comic moments as their followers popped up in the oddest places and disappeared just as fast, trying not to be seen.

All but Amalia, of course. She didn't care whether she was seen or not, and wasn't exactly inconspicuous no matter where she went.

To tell the truth, Kelly had rather enjoyed all the attention. Spencer had been most attentive and Chaz flatteringly jealous. Not to mention that kiss they had shared in the closet the day before.

Whew! Kelly used the napkin to fan her suddenly heated skin.

In comparison, Spencer's enthusiastic goodnight kiss had been rather tepid, though she had to admit he had tried hard. At least he had succeeded in giving her a very nice time yesterday.

She wondered what Chaz had in mind for today. Hmm, maybe there was a clue in the bag.

She glanced at it warily, speculating about what he'd sent. Was it a romantic gift to go along with the breakfast? Her jaw tightened. If he had sent her a negligee, it was going right back to him. She wasn't about to let him get away with that.

But it was far from being a negligee. Instead, he had sent her jeans, a long-sleeved T-shirt, sturdy cross-trainers, and a down vest. What . . . ?

Wait—there was a note attached.

You'll need these today. Pick you up at 11:00. Love, Chaz.

Evidently, he thought she wouldn't have the correct clothes for whatever he had in mind. And he was right. She had packed her luggage with a honeymoon with Spencer in mind . . . and that most definitely did not include jeans.

She grinned, wondering what Chaz had planned. Whatever it was, she was pretty sure it would be nothing like yesterday's outing with Spencer.

She showered and dressed in the clothes Chaz had sent. To his credit, he'd gotten her sizes right. And he'd even bought the down vest in her favorite shade of red. He got points for paying attention, at least.

But did he realize why she wore red? She doubted it, or he would have never chosen it.

She grimaced. *This is Chaz, remember?* The color was probably just coincidence. He would have no way of knowing it was the only zing she had allowed in herself since he disappeared. In Spencer's guiding hands, she had quashed the wild tendencies Chaz brought out in her to appear the very image of a polished, professional editor. It had gotten her noticed . . . and promoted.

As she waited, the phone rang several times but she ignored it. The only person she cared to talk to right now was Scott, and he knew where she was.

After another such phone call, the message light flashed. Kelly retrieved the voice mail, frowning when she heard her mother's cultured tones.

"It's your mother," Grace Richmond said with a hint of steel in her voice. "I've been calling you for hours. Where are you? Call me immediately."

Kelly shook her head. These two days with Spencer and Chaz belonged to her and she wasn't about to spoil them by talking to her mother. Mother could just wait.

To keep her mind off her problems and her upcoming date with Chaz, Kelly filled the time until he picked her up with a little reading and a little television. At precisely eleven o'clock, a knock came at the door. Chaz was there as promised, dressed much like she was.

"You ready?" he asked.

She nodded, then saw the crowd of people behind him. It appeared Spencer, Candace, Scott and Amalia were going along on this date as well. Chaz rolled his eyes in their direction, but Kelly could only laugh. "It serves you right after what you did yesterday."

He shrugged. "Let's see if they can keep up."

She wondered what he meant until she realized the others hadn't received the dress code. The women were in heels and the men were dressed for a nice party. They glanced at her outfit with chagrin and some looked as though they'd like to change clothes, but Chaz wasn't about to give them the opportunity.

"Let's go," he said.

Placing a hand possessively at the small of her back,

he steered her toward the elevator. And his glare kept the others from sharing. Once they were alone, Kelly gestured at her jeans. "So, what's up for today?"

He smiled down at her and placed an arm around her shoulders. "You'll see."

She stood still within his embrace, trying not to let him sense how much his nearness affected her, how the very scent of him brought back memories she'd thought long forgotten. "I see. You don't want me telling anyone else where we're going, huh?"

"Something like that," he said with an unapologetic shrug. "It's a surprise."

And when the elevator opened, he led her to a waiting cab, then opened the door for her. "I thought you rented a car," she said in surprise.

"I did, but it's in Scott's name, and my driver's license expired a few years back."

That left the others free to follow them in the rental car. Which they did, Kelly noted with a smile. Spencer drove, obviously not trusting Scott to keep up with them.

The arrangement also left Chaz free to snuggle with her in the back seat of the cab as the driver took off, apparently having already received instructions about where to go.

"How . . . resourceful of you," she said with a smile as Chaz cuddled close.

"I thought so."

But he wisely confined his amorous advances to just holding her close against his side. When she realized he wasn't going to try to make love to her in the back of the taxi, she relaxed and even began to enjoy it. It had been a long time since she had allowed a man to put his arms around her, to let herself relax into the warmth of his presence. It was really rather nice.

But all too brief. She had expected him to take her to the Garden of the Gods, but they bypassed that and went to Palmer Park, almost in the middle of Colorado Springs. "A park?" she asked in confusion.

"It's not the type of park you're thinking of," he said with confidence. Grabbing a backpack from the trunk, he paid off the driver and said, "You ready to go?"

"Sure." And so was everyone else, it seemed. The other four piled out of the rental car and didn't even make a pretense of not following them.

But Chaz didn't seem worried. "Then let's do it."

He was right—it wasn't the kind of park she'd expected. Instead of wide expanses of green grass dotted with trees and ponds, this park looked like it should be up in the mountains, with lots of huge red rocks and plenty of wild shrubbery and trees set in a small mountain of its own.

Several trails were marked and, after consulting a map, Chaz headed for one.

So, they were going to hike, were they? Okay, that sounded different. She'd enjoyed hiking with Chaz in the past. Why not now? The air was a little chilly, but not unbearable, and most of the snow had melted, so if they kept moving, they would probably be warm enough.

Kelly followed Chaz as he set a brisk pace. The trail started out fairly level but soon snaked its way up the mountainside, weaving a narrow path around scrubby trees and over large rocks.

The others tried to maintain the same pace, but when Kelly glanced back, she saw that Candace and Amalia had fallen behind, hampered by their high heels. Scott and Spencer were helping them solicitously, but Spencer looked very frustrated.

He also looked uncomfortable in his sports jacket and

stiff, polished shoes. He certainly wouldn't be able to keep up at this rate.

Chaz glanced back. "Don't worry," he said. "They'll give up soon." Holding his hand out to help her over a rock, he grinned. "Besides, we have a date with a picnic basket."

Unaccustomed as she was to climbing, Kelly had to save all her breath for the hike so she just nodded and kept following him. The exercise was exhilarating, though she knew she'd be sore tomorrow—this climb was using muscles she hadn't tested in years. She smiled to herself. The last time she had used those muscles was that wonderful day with Chaz. Would today be as memorable?

After about half an hour, they emerged into a picnic area. Chaz glanced behind her and smiled. "I think we lost them over that last set of rocks. You ready for lunch?"

Kelly nodded, knowing she'd gasp for breath if she tried to speak. Sinking gratefully onto a bench, she stretched her legs out in front of her and winced at the soreness in her calves. She would regret this tomorrow.

"Good," Chaz said, looking as if the climb had been nothing more than a leisurely stroll.

He unzipped the backpack and pulled out a veritable feast. Then again, anything would seem like a feast about now. She was so hungry that the fried chicken, pasta salad with mixed vegetables, fresh fruit, and cold soda tasted like the ambrosia of the gods.

"This is wonderful," she said after swallowing a bite of delicious fried chicken. "You certainly came prepared."

He shrugged. "I just asked the kitchen to make up a lunch for two."

"So you knew no one else would make it this far?"

Grinning around a chicken leg, he said, "Well, I hoped not, anyway. I wanted you all to myself today."

Once they finished eating, Chaz helped her up and continued to hold her hand as they took off on another trail, this one a little easier than the one before. With no one behind them to spur him on, Chaz set a more leisurely pace.

Continuing to keep his fingers laced with hers, he kept her close and pointed out shy rabbits, unusual rock formations, and the occasional tree decked out in autumn colors. It was surprisingly relaxing.

Just when she was about to beg for a break, they came to the top of the trail. Here, high above Colorado Springs, the city was spread out before them, from snow-capped Pikes Peak and the Rocky Mountains to the west, all the way to the plains to the east. She stared around, amazed. Who knew this spot of wilderness could exist in the center of the city?

They rested there companionably for a few minutes as they took in the panoramic view, Chaz's arm comfortably around Kelly's waist.

"Does this remind you of anything?" he asked.

"Not really."

"Hmm. Add in a thunderstorm and a mud puddle . . ."

"Oh. Of course." He had tried to recreate that day in the rain, the day he said he had fallen in love with her. Kelly's heart clenched. First the breakfast and now this. Damn, he was being so sweet, so romantic. She didn't remember seeing this side of Chaz before. Had it been there all along, or had this competition brought out the best in him?

She didn't know, but she was sure enjoying it, no matter the cause.

After she felt rested, Chaz asked, "You ready to go now?"

Kelly couldn't help but moan. "I don't know if I can walk all that way down again and still be alive tomorrow. Besides, you know they'll only be waiting for us at the bottom."

He grinned. "Not quite. And don't worry about walking down—you won't have to. Come on, I'll show you."

There was a parking lot at the top of the mountain, and Kelly watched in disbelief as Chaz headed purposefully toward one of the cars parked there—a Lexus. "You're not going to steal a car, are you?"

He gave a bark of laughter. "No, someone loaned me this one. I brought it up here this morning before I met you."

Impressed by his forethought, Kelly sank gratefully into the luxurious front seat. The winding drive down the small mountain was a lot faster than their walk up, and Chaz managed to totally bypass the parking lot where they had originally been dropped off, to come out a different exit.

"Wait a minute," Kelly said. "Hasn't your license expired?" Not to mention the fact that he hadn't driven in many years.

He shrugged and grinned. "Hey, why not live dangerously?"

But he was anything but dangerous as he drove leisurely through the streets of Colorado Springs.

The interior of the car suddenly seemed familiar. "This is Candace's car, isn't it?" Kelly asked.

"Yes."

"And she loaned it to you?"

"Sure, why not?"

"But she was following us up the mountain like she wanted to stop us."

"No," Chaz corrected gently. "She wasn't following *us*."

"Oh." The light dawned. Of course. Kelly knew her boss had nursed a crush on Spencer for a long time.

Hmm. If Candace had loaned Chaz her car and been willing to sacrifice expensive pumps just to keep Spencer from following Kelly, perhaps Candace's feelings were more serious than Kelly had realized. The question was, were Kelly's?

Candace leaned against the rental car in the parking lot at the park, wishing she were back in her room so she could soak her aching feet and get something to eat. Scott and Amalia were resting in the car, and Spencer paced the length of parking lot impatiently. Unfortunately, none of them had had the foresight to bring any food.

But even though Candace was tired and hungry and had ruined her best pumps, it was worth it. She was just glad Chaz had advised her of the day's activities ahead of time so she could be of some assistance, in a hampering sort of way.

Though Spencer had obviously been irritated by his inability to keep up with Chaz, he had proven to be a perfect gentleman. Hiding his frustration, he had considerately helped Candace climb as far as she was able in her shoes. At least until she convinced him to give it up.

But now they had been waiting for hours, and everyone was bored. Having a pretty good suspicion that Kelly and Chaz were long gone by now, Candace said, "I don't think they're coming back this way."

Spencer stopped pacing to regard her with a frown. "Is there another way out of here?"

"There must be," she said. Or she would have seen her car by now. But she certainly wasn't going to explain that to Spencer.

"I'll ask," Scott said, and got out of the car to approach some hikers. After a short discussion, he came back. "She's right. There are several other exits from the park. How much you want to bet they took one of them already?"

Frustration crossed Spencer's face, but he managed to control his temper like the gentleman he was. "Where have they gone?"

Scott shrugged. "They could be anywhere."

Amalia stuck her face out of the open window of the car. "This is *estúpido*. They are gone. We go back to the hotel."

"She's right," Candace said, feeling sorry for Spencer's obvious disappointment. But not *too* sorry. "They're obviously not coming back here."

Spencer sighed. "Yes, I suppose you're right." Then he muttered, "But I hate to let him win this way."

Candace patted his arm. "Well, there's nothing you can do about it, so you might as well concede this small skirmish to him." And the whole war, too, if she had any say in it. "Come on, let's go."

With amazingly good grace, Spencer agreed and they headed back to the hotel.

* * *

Kelly looked around in interest as Chaz pulled the car to a stop in front of a restaurant downtown.

"You in the mood to eat?" he asked.

Surprisingly, she was famished. She nodded, and he helped her out of the car and into a Moroccan restaurant. Rich, unfamiliar spices filled her senses as exotic Mediterranean music played softly in the background. Kelly glanced around in delight. This was certainly different.

The hostess encouraged them to take off their shoes and seated them on cushions around a low table in a secluded alcove. Ah, it seemed they were expected here, too.

Kelly was unfamiliar with the cuisine, so she let Chaz order for her, then he showed her how to eat the couscous appetizer "properly"—with their fingers.

"It's a good thing the others aren't here," Kelly said. At the surprised flicker in Chaz's eyes, she clarified, "I can't see Candace or Spencer sitting on the floor or eating with their fingers, can you?"

It was so different from her meal the evening before, it was almost as if she were in a different world. An earthier, more colorful world. Chaz's world.

He grinned and shook his head. "Or Garcia either. Not unless she has to."

Why did he have to bring *her* up? "Scott would have liked it, though."

Chaz trailed one finger along her arm with a lazy, sexy look. "Ah, yes, but then, Scott is willing to try just about anything. I'm glad his sister is just as open-minded."

Kelly flushed and looked away, unwilling to let Chaz ruin this wonderful day by deepening their rapport into further intimacy.

He took the hint and removed his hand, changing the subject to tell a humorous story about one of his colleagues. The rest of the evening, he kept up the light banter, trying to amuse her instead of seducing her.

She appreciated it greatly, and so she was very pleased with him as they returned to the hotel. They rode up in the elevator and Chaz leaned close to ask, "Am I going to get a goodnight kiss, too?"

Flush with wine and a good meal, Kelly felt very mellow. And she couldn't deny Chaz the same privilege she had bestowed on Spencer the night before. "Of course," she said, and wondered why she felt so shy all of a sudden.

Maybe it was the fact that she hadn't really seen Chaz in five years. Or because she suddenly wanted more, much more, than a kiss from him. Maybe if no one was lying in wait for her in the hall, she could allow him to stay a little longer. . . .

Amazingly enough, no one was around, so Kelly quickly let Chaz into her room, unable to believe their good fortune.

But Chaz came to an abrupt stop, muttering, "Ah, hell."

Following him in, Kelly felt like uttering the same sentiments. Instead, she controlled the urge and murmured, "Hello, Mother."

Chaz groaned inwardly. *Gee, great timing, Grace.* Why couldn't she have waited until *after* he'd said goodnight to Kelly before showing up to ruin everything? No wonder no one else was around—no one else was willing to face Grace's disdain.

Chaz would rather have wrestled a river full of piranhas than stay in the same room with Kelly's mother, but his protective instincts surged to the fore.

This was the woman who had given Kelly such insecurities, who had never let her feel good enough, who had constantly criticized her daughter and tried to make Kelly into a carbon copy of herself.

Hell, Grace even had Scott cowed. Or he avoided her, which amounted to the same thing. Well, she didn't intimidate Chaz, and he wasn't going to let her bully Kelly now that he was back. He crossed his arms belligerently and gave her a hard smile, putting her on notice that he wouldn't be so easy to intimidate. "Hello, Grace."

Ignoring Chaz, she said to Kelly, "I would like to speak to you alone."

It figured. No how are you, son-in-law? What happened? Glad to see you're not dead. . . . Obviously, this woman was *not* on his side. It just strengthened his resolve to protect Kelly from her.

Kelly glanced at him, pleading for him to stay. Chaz nodded—nothing would tear him from her side now.

Sighing, Kelly sank down on to the bed. "Sorry, Mother. Whatever you have to say to me, you can say in front of Chaz." Then, in a more sarcastic tone, "You remember Chaz, don't you? My first husband? Perhaps you hadn't noticed he's come back from the dead?"

From the expression on her face, Grace had one hell of a mad on—and it was all directed at her daughter. "Don't be ridiculous. Of course I noticed. And I'm perfectly aware he is alive, though my own daughter didn't see fit to tell me. I had to learn it from the press."

"I'm sorry about that, but—"

"Imagine how I felt. All my friends, calling me for the sordid little details. And I knew absolutely nothing. I couldn't even make something up."

So that's what she was so ticked about. Hell, didn't she even care about Kelly and what she was going through? No, all she cared about was how it reflected on her. "Your concern for your daughter is touching," Chaz drawled.

Grace leveled a searing glance at him. "More than yours. I understand *you* waited until the most dramatic moment to reveal yourself at the memorial service."

Chaz winced. He still felt bad about that, too. "Well, at least I care—"

"Stop it," Kelly said firmly. "That's enough from both of you. Mother, why are you here?"

Grace looked surprised. "I'm here to help you clean up this mess, of course."

Yeah, right. Getting in a jibe or two at Chaz was just a bonus.

Kelly looked startled. "Can you? Clean up this mess, I mean."

Grace relaxed a little. "I know a judge or two. I'm sure we can get this straightened out easily enough so you and Spencer can get on with your lives."

Damn, he had to admire the woman's gall. She didn't even hesitate about weighing in on Deuce's side. Chaz grimaced. "You don't think a small thing like, oh, our eight-year marriage might make that a bit difficult?"

"Stop it," Kelly said again. "I am not a bone for you two to fight over."

She made them sound like dogs. Then again, that would make Gracie here a bitch. Yeah, that was just about right. Chaz slanted a glare at Grace. "Well, I'm not going to let her bully you into making the wrong decision."

Grace sniffed. "And I'm not going to let him convince you to ruin your life."

"It's *my* life," Kelly said, rising to glare down at her mother. "And I'll do what I damned well please."

Go, Kelly! Now this was a change he definitely liked.

Grace tried to get a word in, but Kelly cut her off with a savage gesture. "You cannot make this go away by wishing it so or throwing money at it. Once I make a decision, then we can figure out what action to take. But until then, it's my decision to make, not yours."

Grace sneered. Oh so elegantly, of course. "Scott told me about your silly dates. I don't know why you feel the need to go through with this. The solution is obvious. You should choose Spencer, and Charles can have that . . . that woman he spent the last five years with. After all, she insists they are to be married."

Chaz rolled his eyes. "Don't believe anything Amalia says. She lives in a different universe from the rest of us. I intend to stay with Kelly."

Kelly rubbed her temples, looking as though she had the start of a horrendous headache. "It's not that simple, Mother. Again, it's not your decision. It's mine. And I'd appreciate it if you'd leave me alone so I can make it."

Grace crossed her arms and glared at Chaz. "You want me to leave you alone with *him?*"

"What do you think he's going to do?" Kelly asked in an exasperated tone. "Murder me? He was my husband, remember?"

"I still am," Chaz interjected.

"That remains to be seen," Grace said with a glare.

Kelly closed her eyes and rubbed her temples harder. "I've spent all day with him, just like I did with Spencer yesterday, and he hasn't molested me yet. I think I'm safe."

"But what will Spencer think?"

Who cared what Deuce thought? Kelly was Chaz's
wife.

Continuing to speak reasonably, Kelly said, "I spent
some time alone with Spencer last night. I owe it to Chaz
to give him the same opportunity." When Grace started
to protest again, Kelly cut her off with, "And the longer
you stay here, the more time I'll spend with Chaz."

Chaz grinned as Kelly crossed her arms in a distinct
challenge. He moved toward her to underscore the fact
that Kelly had a protector now, one Grace couldn't brow-
beat.

"Oh, all right," Grace said, rather *un*gracefully, Chaz
thought. She gathered up her things and went toward the
door. "But don't think this is the last of our conversation.
I'm getting a room here, and I'm going to stay until you
come to your senses."

With that, she swept out the door. As always, making
a grand exit.

Once the door closed behind her, Kelly seemed to col-
lapse in on herself, her face crumpling and her shoulders
sagging as she leaned into Chaz for comfort.

Chaz wished he could do something to make it easier
on her, to take the pain away, but all he could do was pat
her on the back and make soothing noises. "I'm sorry,
honey. You didn't need to go through that."

Kelly raised a tear-stained face to his. "It just makes
it even more difficult."

"I know." Grace had always complicated things. He
wiped Kelly's tears away. "Just don't let her get to you."

She sighed and leaned her head into his shoulder. "I
can't help it. She knows me too well—she knows just
what buttons to push."

Kelly's simple act of trust—her head on his
shoulder—almost unmanned him. He laid his hand gen-

tly on her head, holding her to him, love and longing making it difficult for him to speak. "Then don't let her push them," he said thickly. But he knew that was hopeless. Grace had been getting away with it for years.

"She does love me, you know. In her own way. She just wants what *she* thinks is best for me."

Chaz gritted his teeth, but managed to keep his voice mild. "No matter what you think?"

"Well, of course she thinks she knows best." Kelly raised her head to look at him. "But let's not talk about her any more."

"Fine with me." As far as he was concerned, Grace Richmond could take a flying leap off a tall cliff. Splat Mama, that was the ticket.

"I really enjoyed our day today. Thank you." Kelly smiled softly and his heart zinged into overdrive.

"So did I," he whispered. It had been difficult to keep his hands off her, difficult to go slow, but winning his wife back was worth it.

He had hoped to share much more with her this evening, and rather thought Kelly had felt the same, but the timing was no longer right. Nor could he ask what her decision was after her mother's harassment, and Chaz had no doubt Grace was outside the door waiting for Chaz to emerge. It kind of killed any amorous feelings.

But, damn it, Deuce had gotten a kiss and Chaz was going to get one, too, come hell or high water. Now.

He only had to lean down a little way to capture Kelly's mouth with his, and he tried to put all his longing, love, and passion into that simple meeting of lips.

When he raised his head, Kelly looked so warm and inviting, he just wanted to sink into her and stay all night, to hold her close and take the hurt away. Leaving her was one of the hardest things he would ever do, but he had to do it, for her sake. Giving her one last squeeze, he said, "I'll see you tomorrow."

"All right," Kelly whispered.

When he pulled away, Kelly's fingers lingered on his arm, as if she didn't quite want to let him go. He wanted to dive back into her, but somehow managed to keep his cool. With one last, brief kiss, he slipped out the door.

And came face to face with the Ice Bitch.

Smiling grimly, he crossed his arms and leaned back against his wife's door. "You're not thinking about going back in there, are you, Grace?"

"My actions are none of your concern," she said, frost rolling off her in waves.

"They are when they concern my *wife*. She needs her rest and neither you nor anyone else is going to bother her further tonight. Is that clear?"

"Perfectly." Grace gave him a tight little smile. "But this isn't over. She and Spencer are perfect for each other, and I intend to see them together. Is *that* clear?"

No, Deuce and *Grace* were perfect for each other. "You can try," Chaz drawled.

"And, mark my words, I will succeed." With that parting shot, Grace turned her back on him and walked away.

Unwilling to let her have the last word, Chaz called out, " 'Night, Mom."

Chaz grinned when he saw her back stiffen, but she didn't respond. Well, he may have gotten in the last word tonight, but that was only one small battle. The war was just beginning.

To start your membership, simply complete and return the Free Book Certificate. You'll receive your Introductory Shipment of 3 FREE Zebra Contemporary Romances, you only pay $1.99 for shipping and handling. Then, each month you will receive the 3 newest Zebra Contemporary Romances. Each shipment will be yours to examine FREE for 10 days. If you decide to keep the books, you'll pay the preferred subscriber price (a savings of up to 20% off the cover price), plus shipping and handling. If you want us to stop sending books, just say the word... it's that simple.

If the FREE Book Certificate is missing, call 1-800-770-1963 to place your order.
Be sure to visit our website at www.kensingtonbooks.com.

FREE BOOK CERTIFICATE

Yes! Please send me 3 FREE Zebra Contemporary romance novels. I only pay $1.99 for shipping and handling. I understand that each month thereafter I will be able to preview 3 brand-new Contemporary Romances FREE for 10 days. Then, if I should decide to keep them, I will pay the money-saving preferred subscriber's price (that's a savings of up to 20% off the retail price), plus shipping and handling. I understand I am under no obligation to purchase any books, as explained on this card.

Name _____

Address _____ Apt. _____

City _____ State _____ Zip _____

Telephone (___) _____

Signature _____

(If under 18, parent or guardian must sign)

Offer limited to one per household and not to current subscribers. Terms, offer and prices subject to change. Orders subject to acceptance by Zebra Contemporary Book Club. Offer Valid in the U.S. only.

CN123A

Thank You!

lll..l..lll..u.llll.l.ll..l..l.l..ll.l..l.ll..lll..l

Zebra Contemporary Romance Book Club

Zebra Home Subscription Service, Inc.

P.O. Box 5214

Clifton , NJ 07015-5214

PLACE
STAMP
HERE

Ten

Kelly woke for the third time in bed in the hotel. Alone again.

Pouting, she decided she'd just about had enough of this. Two husbands in the hotel, both of whom would be more than happy to share her bed, and she had to sleep alone. Worse, she'd done it to herself. Today, she was going to have to announce a decision so she could sleep with *some*one. She didn't want to go to bed frustrated one more night.

Yes, she knew it was selfish, but she had put her life on hold for five years, especially the physical aspects. She hadn't realized how much she had given up until Chaz had showed her so clearly what she had been missing. She deserved to be a little selfish . . . didn't she?

Sighing, she got up and suddenly noticed a small oblong package on her desk. It must have been there last night, delivered while she was gone, but she had been too tired to notice. Curious, she picked it up and unwrapped it. It turned out to be a nine inch "muscle massager" and a pair of firecrackers. What in the world . . . ?

There was a note with it.

Dear Kelly,

Here's your gift, as requested. Simply use the vibrator in the accustomed manner. Then, at the appropriate time, stick the firecrackers in your ears and light them. Voilà! Mind-blowing sex.

Love, Scott

Kelly burst out laughing. It was so like her brother. But she wasn't quite reduced to that yet. And she didn't want anyone else to find it in her room, either.

Quickly, she wrapped up the vibrator and stowed it in the trash can in the bathroom then showered and dressed. Not knowing what was going to happen today, she put on casual slacks and an icy blue sweater. Now she was ready for anything the day might throw at her. She hoped.

A knock came at the door. Expecting it to be her breakfast, sent once more by a generous husband or brother, she opened it.

Well, she was half right. Her breakfast had arrived all right—a large tray of muffins, fruit, and coffee—but Chaz was carrying it.

"May I come in?" he asked with a plaintive expression.

Her heart went out to him. This self-imposed celibacy was hard on her, but it was equally hard on her husbands. The sooner she got this decision over with, the better. "Sure."

She opened the door wider and Chaz placed the tray on the desk, then gave her a sympathetic look. "You okay? Your mother didn't come back and rip you a new one?"

"No," Kelly said shaking her head ruefully. "Though

I imagine she'll be by later to, er, give me the benefit of her advice."

Chaz nodded. "As I thought. That's why I'm here— to make sure she doesn't hurt you too badly."

How sweet. She'd forgotten this protective side of Chaz. After five years of living without him and protecting herself, she certainly didn't need it, but she did like it. Wistfully, she thought of how nice it would be to share that with someone again. She was tired of carrying the burdens alone.

Aloud, she said, "That's very kind of you, Chaz. But not really necessary." Especially if he had ulterior motives for being alone in her room with her, which she suspected he did.

"It *is* necessary," he insisted. "For me, if not you." He crossed the room to put his arms around her, gently. "Though I had no intention of doing so, I left you alone for far too long. You had every right to expect me to be there for you, and I wasn't. I want to make that up to you . . . for the rest of my life."

Kelly blinked back tears as she leaned into the comfort of his embrace. "Oh, Chaz," she murmured thickly. Should she tell him her decision now? It was the perfect opening, and he had a right to know if she wanted to be around for the rest of his life or not.

She opened her mouth, but a knock came at the door.

Chaz squeezed her lightly. "Don't answer it. Pretend you're not here."

Kelly gave him an admonitory glance. "You know I have to. I don't want to be rude."

Chaz released her with a roll of his eyes. "Oh, yes. And heavens knows that's the worst that could happen."

Ignoring that little comment, Kelly peered out the peephole. This time she wasn't going to be taken by surprise. "It's Spencer," she said in consternation.

Chaz's face turned grim. "What does *he* want?"

"Probably the same thing you do." But she really didn't want to referee a contest between the two of them. "Come here," she said, pulling Chaz toward the closet. "Hide in here until he's gone."

Chaz balked, scowling. "Why? Are you ashamed of me?"

"No, but I shouldn't have let you in here alone with me when I haven't announced my decision yet. It's not fair to Spencer."

His expression arrested, Chaz said, "So you've made a decision?"

"Yes. But now isn't the time. I'll put Spencer off, then we can talk, okay?" She tried to push him into the closet, but he still resisted. "Or you can leave while I let Spencer know first."

"All right," Chaz conceded with a frown. "I'll stay. But I'm not hiding in that closet again. I don't like enclosed spaces, remember? That is, unless you come in with me. . . ."

Oh, yes. She remembered all too well. Feeling her face heat with that memory, Kelly veered away from the closet and opened the bathroom door. "Then stay in here. And be quiet."

"All right." He grabbed her by the arms and gave her a quick, fierce kiss. "But don't be long."

"I won't."

Straightening her hair and feeling harried when Spencer repeated his knock on the door, she opened it and smiled at him. It wasn't like Spencer to bother her.

"Sorry, I was . . ." She gestured vaguely at the bathroom.

He apparently took it as an invitation to enter, for he came in and looked around a little uncertainly.

"I really shouldn't let you in here alone," she said. "It's not fair to Chaz." Actually, it was more than fair, considering where Chaz was at the moment, but Spencer didn't have to know that.

He nodded. "That's what I wanted to talk to you about. How did it go, yesterday, with him? We lost you kind of early."

He looked so anxious, Kelly's heart went out to him. But, conscious of the possibility of Chaz listening in on the other side of the door in the bathroom, she said, "It was nice. Very different from my date with you, but nice."

"Better?"

"Different," she said firmly. So different that it was difficult to compare the two. As Scott had so succinctly put it, it was like the difference between elegance and excitement. But an excess of either wasn't good. Why couldn't she have a balance in her life?

I want both. And she deserved it, darn it.

"Did it help you make your decision?"

"Not really," she murmured honestly. She had already made her decision, but spending time with both men made her regret that a decision was even necessary.

"But you will make one?" he asked anxiously.

"Of course. In fact—"

Another knock came at the door. Glancing through the peephole, she said, "It's Scott."

She wavered for a moment. Scott obviously wanted

her to choose Chaz. If he saw Spencer in here, ostensibly alone with her, Scott might be sarcastic, or start extolling Chaz's virtues. And she just wasn't up to dealing with that.

Exasperated, she pulled Spencer toward the closet. "Hide in here for a few minutes, okay?"

Spencer looked at her as if she'd lost her mind. "Is that really necessary?"

"Yes, it is," she said, wishing someone would do what she asked without an argument for a change. "He won't leave if he knows you're here. Just give me a couple of minutes to get rid of him, then there's something I want to say to you."

His eyebrows rose. "You've made your decision, then?"

"Yes, but now's not the time." She shoved him into the closet. "Just stay here until I tell you to come out, okay?"

Though his face was set in disapproving lines, Spencer nevertheless complied with her request.

As she closed the closet door, Chaz opened the one to the bathroom. She stopped him with a frantic wave of her hand. "Not now," she mouthed.

Nodding, he disappeared back into the bathroom and closed the door.

Sighing, she opened the door to Scott and tried to keep him out in the hallway, but he breezed on past her.

"Mother might see me out there," he explained. "And I have no desire to meet with her again. I already spent several hours on the grill while you and Chaz were out playing yesterday."

"I'm sorry," Kelly said. "I didn't intend for you to catch the brunt of it." She hadn't wanted to catch it either, but with Mother, there wasn't exactly a choice. Someone had to fry.

Scott plopped down in a chair and snitched a handful of grapes. Waving one hand dismissively, he said, "Never mind. But it would put us all out of our misery if you would just announce your choice."

"I know," Kelly said softly, extremely conscious that both potential choices were no doubt listening as hard as they could from their hiding places. Lowering her voice, she said, "I plan to do that soon. But I have been wondering whether to tell them separately or together." Doing it only once had a great appeal, but . . .

"Separately, I think," Scott said. "You don't want one guy watching triumphantly while you crush the other one's hopes."

Yes, that's rather what she thought, too. "That makes sense."

"So," he said with a grin. "How'd you like your present?"

She rolled her eyes. "Very funny."

"Really? I thought it appropriate myself. And so very useful. . . ."

She couldn't help but chuckle. "Maybe, but—"

She broke off when yet another knock came at her door. She stared at it incredulously. *What is this, Grand Central Station?*

Scott popped the last grape into his mouth and frowned. "If that's Mother, I'm leaving. I've already had the pleasure of being interrogated once. It's your turn."

Kelly looked through the peephole and said, "It's not Mother, it's Candace."

Scott rose, tossing the grape stems into the trash can.

Grabbing his arm, Kelly tried to steer him toward the door, hoping to get rid of one person, at least.

But Scott wouldn't budge. "No, it's safer in here until Mother arrives. I'll just stay here."

"You can't do that," Kelly protested. "What if what Candace has to say to me is private?"

He shrugged. "What does it matter? You tell me everything anyway."

Well, almost everything. Right now, there was the small matter of two husbands hiding in her room. "I think you should go."

"No." His face brightened. "Tell you what—I'll just hide until you can get rid of her."

Kelly resisted the urge to roll her eyes. What an original idea.

She stopped him when he headed for the bathroom. "Not there." Though she was quite sure Scott would find the situation amusing if he discovered her husbands in hiding, she didn't feel like enlightening him right now. Besides, the explanations would be embarrassing, and Scott would never let her live it down.

Looking surprised, he asked, "Why not?"

"Because," she said lamely. When that didn't seem to deter him, she said, "I have . . . things in there." The only "thing" in there was Chaz, but she hoped her vagueness would make him think there were some mysterious feminine fripperies that he wouldn't want to see.

He shrugged. "Okay, the closet then."

He headed in that direction, but she grabbed his arm again. "No, not there."

"You have *things* in there, too?" Scott asked with a quirk of his eyebrow.

"No," she said, desperately searching for a reason

Scott would believe. She didn't want to have him discovering Spencer in the dark—she doubted they'd have as much fun as she and Chaz had. "But it's very dark and stuffy. Trust me—I spent some time there, remember?"

"Okay," Scott said in exasperation. "Then where?"

"Under the bed?"

He gave her a sardonic look. "I don't think so."

"Then . . ." She glanced around, looking for a spot. The drapes. Perfect. As another, more insistent, knock came at the door, she shoved him toward the curtains by the sliding glass door to the balcony. "If you must stay, then wait behind the drapes. And be quiet."

He grinned. "Like a mouse."

Once Scott was safely ensconced in his hiding place and she made sure both the closet and bathroom doors were firmly closed, Kelly opened the door to Candace. "Hello," she said politely. "Can I help you?"

Candace gave her a tentative smile. "Yes, I have something I want to ask you. Can I come in?"

It figured. Why did everyone object to having a nice conversation in the hallway, for heaven's sake? But Kelly couldn't think of a good reason to keep her boss waiting outside, beyond admitting she had three men hiding in her room, so she invited Candace in as graciously as she could.

Candace took the seat where Scott had been very recently, and squirmed a little.

Kelly sighed. If Candace was uncomfortable, that meant she was probably about to say something Kelly didn't want to hear. Unfortunately, three other sets of ears might hear it as well. "What can I do for you?" Kelly asked with a sigh.

Candace pleated her skirt with her fingers. "I was

just wondering . . . do you know much about Amalia Garcia?"

Now that was the last thing Kelly expected to come out of Candace's mouth. "No, I'm afraid I don't," she said stiffly. "You'll have to ask Chaz about her."

Looking even more uncomfortable, Candace waved a hand in apparent apology. "That's not what I meant. I just thought . . . she's so exotic. Different. Don't you think she'd make an interesting *Pizzazz* Girl?"

Amalia? The new *Pizzazz* Girl? Kelly felt herself tense. Interesting wasn't the right word. Annoying, maybe. Disagreeable. Even ridiculous. Especially since that meant Kelly would have to work with the woman. But she couldn't say all that to Candace, especially since her boss had kept Kelly on for so long, even though Spencer, the man Candace loved, was pursuing Kelly.

Not knowing what else to say, Kelly murmured, "I'm not sure she's . . . suitable."

Candace nodded as if she didn't care about the answer. Which meant that wasn't her real question. And the way her rear end was planted in that chair, it appeared she wasn't going to leave until she voiced her real concern.

With three impatient men hiding in various parts of the room, Kelly figured she needed to speed this up. She would just have to be blunt. "Why are you really here?"

Candace looked up in surprise. "Why, I didn't—" She broke off, appearing sheepish. "I was just wondering if you'd come to a decision yet. You see, I love—"

"Yes, I have," Kelly said quickly, not wanting Candace to embarrass herself by unknowingly admitting her love in front of Spencer.

"Oh, really?" Candace said in a tone she tried to keep casual. "Who have you decided on?"

Kelly felt sorry for the woman, but really couldn't reveal her choice yet. "I'm sorry," she said as gently as she could. "But I need to let them know first."

"Oh. Of course—" Candace began, then cut off when another knock came at the door.

This knock, however, was far more imperious than the others.

Mother. Kelly's nervousness ratcheted up a few notches.

"I'll just go. . . ." Candace said, and rose from the chair.

"No," Kelly said. "You have to hide." But where? She couldn't put Candace in with any of the three men, and she wouldn't go under the bed. Kelly was totally out of hiding places.

Wait, the chair—there was an upholstered club chair in the corner on the opposite side of the wall from where Scott was hiding. "Over here," she said. She pulled Candace toward the chair and pushed her down below it until her boss was on her hands and knees, well hidden. "Stay here," she whispered.

Giving her an incredulous look from her position around Kelly's knees, her publisher asked, "Why?"

Good question.

Feeling foolish, Kelly wailed to herself, *It seemed right at the time. . . .*

What had she been thinking? Obviously, she hadn't been thinking at all. But she couldn't admit that now or back out without looking like a fool.

More of a fool, she amended silently.

"Everyone else is doing it," she said lamely. It didn't seem to satisfy Candace, so she added, "It'll only be a minute. I'll get rid of whoever this is, then we can have a private conversation."

Yeah, right. Private. Like that would happen.

Kelly peered through the peephole again. As she'd guessed, it was her mother. She glanced around the room and was disconcerted to see three male faces peeking back at her from their various hiding places.

No, they couldn't discover each other *now*. She froze, not knowing what to do. "It's Mother," she said desperately, trying not to look at any one man.

The three faces vanished immediately.

Kelly relaxed and opened the door to her mother. "Why are you here?" she asked without preamble.

Grace Richmond raised her eyebrows. "Is that any way to greet your mother? Especially when I've only come to help? Aren't you going to let me in?"

It was a little crowded in there, but hell, why not? What was one more? Kelly opened the door wide. "But only for a minute. I need to find Chaz and Spencer and tell them of my decision."

As Kelly closed the door behind her, Grace asked, "So you've made one, then?"

Kelly nodded. To forestall the inevitable, she added, "But I'm going to tell them first—it's only fair."

"Of course," Grace said. "The sooner the better, so we can all get back to our normal lives."

"Good," Kelly said firmly. "I'm glad you understand." She opened the door once again and gestured toward it, hoping Mother would hasten her departure.

Grace paused. "But you are going to choose Spencer, aren't you?"

Exasperated, Kelly didn't bother to be polite. "I'm

not going to tell you before I tell him, for heaven's sake."

"I know, but—"

"And the longer you dawdle here, the longer it will take."

"Well," Grace said huffily. But she finally got the point, because she headed for the door.

And came face to face with Amalia, who had her hand upraised to knock on the door. To top it all off, Billings rounded the corner with a sour look on his face, heading directly toward her.

Kelly closed her eyes in disbelief. *What have I done to deserve this?*

When no answer was forthcoming, she opened her eyes again to see Grace's freezing gaze meet Amalia's hot searing one. Kelly was just surprised steam hadn't formed along the battle front.

"I think I'll just stay a little longer," Grace said.

Kelly grimaced. "That won't be necessary." Though she didn't know why she was turning down her mother's assistance. Mother was very skilled in handling people like this.

"Where is Chaz?" Amalia demanded with her hands on her hips. "I know you haf him."

Grace drew herself up to look down her nose at the dramatic woman. "Don't be ridiculous. My daughter and I are here alone."

"Ha," Amalia exclaimed. She tried to shove her way past, but Mother held her ground and Kelly held the door firm in her grasp.

But now Billings had arrived. "Is there a problem here?" he asked with a disapproving sniff. "We have had a few complaints about your party."

"Complaints?" Grace repeated, looking even more

haughty than the manager. Taking a step toward him, she said, "Then do be so good as to remove this . . ." She glanced down at Amalia and dismissed her with a searing glance. ". . . this person at once."

Amalia stamped her foot, seemingly oblivious to Grace's contempt. "I will not be remofed. You haf kidnapped my Chaz and I want him. I know he is in there." She peered inside past Grace's and Kelly's blocking bodies and said, "Yes, I see shoes."

She shoved past them so hard she almost knocked Grace off her feet. Rushing over to the drapes where she had apparently spotted Scott's feet, Amalia pulled the drapes aside with a dramatic flourish. "Aha!"

But disappointment filled her face when it was only Kelly's brother.

Never at a loss, Scott smiled at her, smoothed back his hair, and strolled out from behind the drapes as if it were a perfectly ordinary occurrence. "Thank you for inviting me to breakfast, Sis," he said, looking suave and debonair. "But I must really go now."

Grace gave Kelly a disapproving look, but thankfully kept her tongue still in front of Billings.

Scott halted for a moment, unholy amusement filling his eyes as he glanced behind the club chair. But, always the gallant knight, he asked, "Have you found your earring yet, Candace?"

Candace rose from the floor, looking sheepish and red-faced. Smoothing her skirt down then fingering her earlobe, she said, "Yes, I did. Er, thanks for asking."

Scott nodded politely, ignoring Amalia's narrowed suspicious expression and their mother's disapproving one. "Then perhaps we should go now. It's getting a little crowded in here."

Kelly almost whimpered. He had no idea. . . .

With insouciant ease, Scott put his hand at the small of Candace's back and steered her out from behind the chair. As he passed the desk, he plucked a muffin from the tray and offered a peach to Candace. "No need for us to starve," he said with a wicked grin.

Candace merely nodded and took the peach, though she seemed unable to meet anyone's eyes.

Great—there went any chance of advancement at *Pizzazz*. Kelly doubted Candace would forget this humiliation for a long time.

"Yes," Kelly said, her voice rising despite herself. "Maybe you should *all* go."

But trying to budge Amalia when she was on a mission seemed impossible. Though Scott and Candace left the room, Amalia made a beeline for the closet and rummaged through it.

"Aha!" she exclaimed once again. "I knew it. There is a man here." She reached in and hauled him out, looking disappointed once more when Spencer came blinking into the light.

Kelly cringed and raised a hand to hide her face but risked a glance at the two by the door. Mother was looking outraged and Billings's expression had turned to stone.

Spencer appeared a little ruffled, and when he saw four pairs of eyes staring at him, he didn't even try to explain. Instead, he just turned bright red and left without saying a word. Smart guy.

"You see?" Kelly said. "Chaz isn't here. Now, if you could please leave?" She needed to gather the few remaining shreds of her dignity about her.

"No," Amalia declared. "He is here, I know it." Then her gaze lit on the closed bathroom door. With another dramatic "Aha!" she yanked it open.

Chaz stood there calmly, zipping up his trousers. "The bathroom will be available in a moment," he said. "Can't you wait?"

An insane urge to laugh bubbled through Kelly, but the sight of Mother's and Billings's expressions cured that urge, fast.

"I knew it," Amalia said triumphantly with a glare at Kelly. "You haf been hiding him from me."

"Nonsense," Chaz said, buckling his belt. "I came for breakfast and needed to use the facilities, that's all."

Well, it was a really nice try, but Kelly didn't think the two in the doorway were buying it. In fact, her mother's expression promised retribution.

To add her bit to the confusion, Kelly gestured toward the tray. "Would you like some fruit?" she asked Chaz lamely.

Laughter filled his eyes for a moment, quickly stifled. "No, thank you. It's a bit crowded in here. I think I'll take my chances on the restaurant."

"Good," Amalia exclaimed. "I go with you."

By this point, Billings had stiffened so much, he resembled a marble statue. Deliberately not looking around the room, he addressed the air just above Kelly's head. "Are there any more . . . people in this room?"

Kelly smiled weakly. "No, I think that's it." She thought for a moment. Yes, that had to be it. No more hiding places were left.

"I should hope so," her mother said. Apparently, she just couldn't contain her indignation any longer. "What *were* you thinking?"

Giving Grace a sharklike smile, Chaz moved toward her and took her arm. "You aren't criticizing your daughter in public, now are you?" he murmured. Not giving her a chance to answer, he propelled her out into the hallway where Scott, Candace, and Spencer had stayed to watch the show with varying levels of disbelief on their faces. Naturally, as Chaz moved out the door, Amalia followed him.

That left only Billings. It was feeling kind of empty now, but Kelly wanted it emptier yet. She stepped toward the man, and as she expected, he edged backward into the hall, not wanting to be contaminated by her presence.

The hotel manager glared icily at all of them. "The Pourtales does not condone this sort of behavior—" he began, only to be interrupted by Chaz.

"What sort of behavior is that?" he asked. "Is there some law against people having breakfast together?"

Yeah, sure, that was all that was going on. And they played hide and seek just to whet their appetites.

Apparently reluctant to call him a liar, Billings said only, "We have had several complaints about the noise level and conduct of those in this hallway. I'm afraid we cannot countenance it any longer. If this goes on, I'm afraid we will have to ask you to leave."

Mother looked thoroughly affronted. "I've never been thrown out of a place in my life."

"There's a first time for everything," Scott said with a grin and a gleam in his eye.

Kelly wouldn't put it past him to do something outrageous right now, just to have the experience of seeing their mother tossed out on her can.

"It won't happen again," Kelly assured Billings quickly. "They're just all anxious for me to make a decision. Once I have, we'll all leave."

"And will you be making that decision soon?"

Billings asked in a tone that implied he hoped it would be very quickly.

"Actually, I've already made it."

He raised his eyebrows. "Would you be so kind, then, as to favor us with the result?"

"I, uh—" As Kelly stood in the doorway of her room, they all stared back at her with expectant expressions. But no matter how much they all wanted to know, this was *not* the way she was going to announce her choice.

And, damn it, they shouldn't expect it of her, either. Drawing herself up in righteous indignation, Kelly said, "I don't think so."

And closed the door firmly in their faces.

Eleven

Startled, Chaz laughed. It was so unexpected, so whimsical, so unlike the Kelly he remembered.

Grace gave him an incredulous look. "This is not funny."

"Oh, but it is," Chaz exclaimed. "Just like one of the old black-and-white comedies." The kind he and Kelly had loved to watch together.

Scott grinned back at him—the only other person in the hallway who got the joke. Kelly slamming the door in their faces was so perfect, so marvelously apt, exactly the right thing for the spunky ingenue to do at exactly the right time.

"I didn't know she had the guts," Chaz said in delight.

"Nonsense," Grace said. "It was cowardice."

Chaz couldn't let that misapprehension stand. "On the contrary. It took a great deal of courage for her and one hell of a lot of moxie to slam that door in our faces and break a lifetime of your conditioning."

Grace bristled, preparing for a comeback, but Billings stopped her with a gesture and a pained expression. "I beg your pardon, but could you please take this discussion somewhere more . . . private?"

"Fine," Chaz said. "I'm more than willing to leave."

Deuce frowned. "But I want to hear who Kelly chooses. And I assume the rest of us do as well."

His voice and expression implied that he wondered why Chaz didn't feel the same.

Chaz shrugged. It wasn't that he didn't care—he did, very much—but Kelly would choose her own time and her own way to tell them. And she'd certainly earned the right to do that. "We should all leave her alone for a little while. Let her get her bearings back." And recover from the embarrassment of being caught hiding four people in her room.

"*You'll* leave her alone until she makes a decision?" Deuce asked in dubious tones.

Chaz shrugged. "Sure, if that's what she wants." He wasn't about to tick her off now.

He turned to leave, but Amalia caught his arm. "Wait," she said with fire in her eyes. "What about us?"

Chaz shared an incredulous glance with Scott. Would this woman ever give up?

Of course not—he should know that by now. He spoke very slowly to her, as if to a two-year-old. "There is no us. There is you, and there is me, but there is no *us*. There never has been."

Confusion wrinkled her brow. "But we are to be married."

I don't believe this.

"That's not gonna happen. I will never marry you." For good measure, he added, "Ever."

She still didn't look convinced. Good Lord, what proof *would* she believe? Ah, he had it. Raising his arms to the heavens, he said, "May God strike me dead if I'm lying."

An expectant silence fell in the hallway and Amalia

even sneaked a glance upward. With her convent-school upbringing, she could do no less.

Chaz dropped his arms. "See? Nothing. I'm still alive. If God believes me, don't you think you could, too?"

Amalia's face held an odd expression compounded of confusion, frustration, and anger. "You, you—" she began, then broke off to fling her arms in the air and let loose a stream of Spanish. Good Lord, she looked like a younger, leaner version of Charro without the "coochie coochie." Turning on her heel, she stalked off, saying over her shoulder, "You haf not seen the last of me."

Chaz sighed. One down, five to go. "Scott, perhaps you would escort Grace to her room. . . ?"

Scott grimaced, but could obviously see the sense in removing his mother from the battlefield. With aplomb, he offered his arm to his mother and said, "A good idea. Let's give Kelly a couple of hours or so to calm down."

Grace glared at both of them for a moment, then took her son's arm with a sniff in Billings's direction. Chaz wasn't sure why she'd agreed to leave, but he wasn't about to question it.

As they departed, Chaz turned to Deuce and Candace. Deuce had a stubborn look about him, and Candace was obviously waffling, wondering if she should stay and stake her claim on Deuce or leave him alone.

Chaz sighed. "There's no sense hovering in the hallway. You might as well wait in the comfort of your room until Kelly decides to come out." And maybe if Candace was in that honeymoon suite with Deuce, he might discover some of *her* charms.

"And leave the field clear for you?" Deuce asked, glancing at Kelly's door.

That wasn't a bad idea, but it wasn't Chaz's intention. "Not at all," he said honestly. "I swear—I won't go near that door until she asks me to."

At Deuce's doubtful expression, Candace said, "I think you can trust him."

Chaz nodded. "You can. I never break my word." Giving Candace a significant glance, he added, "And didn't you have something you wanted to talk to him about?" If she was smart, she'd find something.

Confusion crossed her face for a moment, then determination replaced it. "Yes, I do." She took Deuce's arm and steered him in the opposite direction. "I think I may have found our *Pizzazz* Girl."

Deuce gave one uncertain glance over his shoulder, but allowed his boss to lead him away.

Good—that was taken care of.

"And do you have instructions for me?" Billings asked in a tone as dry as the Colorado air.

Smart-ass. "Yeah. Go back to work and lighten up."

Figuring that was as good an exit line as any, Chaz denied himself the pleasure of seeing Billings's reaction and strode off to his own room.

But once he was there, he didn't know what to do. He threw open the door to the balcony to let in some fresh air and help him feel less like a caged animal, but fifteen minutes of inactivity drove him nuts. Waiting wasn't his strong suit, and the only other thing he was interested in doing was wooing Kelly. But he had given his word not to bother her until she was ready.

Or had he? His gaze fell on the curtains billowing in from the balcony and he smiled slowly as he realized he'd only promised not to go near her *door*.

* * *

Candace led Spencer to his door and stood expectantly as he unlocked it, not giving him the opportunity to turn her away. Chaz had generously given her this opportunity to be alone with Spencer, and her mind raced as she wondered how best to take advantage of it.

Though Spencer ushered her into his room politely enough, she could tell he wasn't with her mentally. To keep his mind off Kelly, Candace repeated, "I think I may have found our *Pizzazz* Girl."

"That's nice," Spencer said in an abstracted tone. "Who?"

"Amalia Garcia. Don't you think she's striking?"

"I suppose."

Ignoring his indifference, Candace enthused, "She's a new face with a unique look, and her attitude is totally self-confident. I think the camera will love her. She's definitely got the pizzazz we've been looking for."

Good—she had his attention now. "Yes, I see what you mean," Spencer said slowly. "In fact, I thought the same thing when I first met her."

Candace beamed at him. She knew they were on the same wavelength. "Good. Should I approach her about a possible position?"

"I don't know," Spencer said in reluctant tones. "Kelly might not like it."

Who cared what Kelly wanted? Candace was the publisher of *Pizzazz*.

"Don't worry about that," Candace said, dismissing his concern with a wave of her hand. "They'd be working in totally different departments. Their paths will probably never cross."

Then again, if Amalia's presence was going to remind Kelly she was angry at Chaz, maybe it wasn't such a good idea. "Let's wait and see what happens," Candace suggested.

"All right."

Deftly, Candace turned the discussion to the magazine, trying to keep his mind off Kelly and remind him of how many things he and Candace had in common. Now, if only Kelly would do her part and make the right decision, Candace might have a chance.

Her ear pressed against the door to the hallway, Kelly couldn't believe what she'd heard. Chaz had stood up for her and, even more amazing, they'd all listened to him and left her alone. Though she was a bit embarrassed at her own impulsive action, it had felt incredibly liberating to break out of the stifling shell she had grown over the old Kelly . . . Chaz's Kelly. Spencer's Kelly would never dream of doing such a thing. So whose Kelly did she really want to be?

She shook her head, smiling ruefully. Was there really any choice?

A bit at loose ends, she sat down on the bed and tried to figure out what to do with the time Chaz had bought her. Unfortunately, nothing came to mind even after ten minutes of hard thinking.

Luckily, a knock at the door roused her from her introspection and, relieved to see it was Scott, Kelly let him in.

"Hi, Sis," he said as he breezed in, then made a big show of checking the bathroom and the closet.

"There's no one here but me," she said, half exasperated, half amused.

"You never know," he said with a grin as he checked behind the draperies, the chair, and even under the bed.

"I thought I was alone with you earlier. Imagine my surprise when I found you'd been harboring all sorts of strange characters here."

"Only two . . ." she said plaintively.

Scott raised his eyebrows. "I counted four."

"I meant two *before* you."

"I see. But hiding your two husbands . . ." He shook his head. "I didn't know you had it in you."

Neither had she. "There were . . . extenuating circumstances."

"I can imagine."

She bet he could. But she really didn't want to explain. "What do you want, Scott?"

"Nothing, really. But Chaz managed to convince everyone to wait until you were ready to announce your decision, and I'm just here to make sure they do."

"Oh, Scott." Who could ask for a better brother? "Thank you."

He gave her a hug. "You look a little frazzled. Why don't you get some rest while I stand guard? Unless you want some lunch?"

The way her stomach was churning? "I don't think I could eat anything right now."

"Then we'll have an early dinner and you can call them to your room one by one after that. How does that sound?"

She smiled at him. "Perfect. I'll let you know if I get hungry."

"Good." He gave her another hug, then left her alone in the room once more.

He was right—she was a little frazzled and had the beginnings of a headache. Maybe some rest would do her good.

She lay down on the bed, trying to clear her mind of

the embarrassment and looniness of the morning. She dozed off, and a few hours later, she woke to find her headache had disappeared and the sun had gone down.

She had just realized this when she heard a tapping sound. That was odd—it wasn't coming from the hallway door this time. Where . . . ? Surprised, she realized it was coming from the balcony door. Drawing back the drapes, she let out a startled gasp of laughter.

Unbelievably, Chaz stood on her balcony wearing a flowing white poet's shirt, a narrow black mask that just circled his eyes, a pencil-thin moustache, and tight black leather pants. He posed dramatically with his hands on his hips, a red rose clenched between his teeth, and devilry in his eyes. With the moon shining behind him, he was quite a sight.

Chuckling, she opened the door, letting in a cold breath of fresh air. "Errol Flynn, I presume? Or is it Douglas Fairbanks Jr.?" All he was missing was the rapier.

He whipped the rose from his teeth and offered it to her with a flourish. When she took it, he bowed deeply with one leg stretched out straight before him, and declared in a phony French accent, "No, it eez I, zee Courageous Corsair, zee greatest luh-vair in all zee world. I have come to steal you away to my boudoirrr."

He drew out the last word with a rolling of the "r"s, struck another dramatic pose with his hand curved above his head, and waggled his eyebrows at her.

Kelly giggled, delighted. And she had to admit his attire was very sexy. The tight pants left nothing to the imagination, accentuating his cute butt and molding to the front of his crotch, clearly delineating the fact that he was very glad to see her.

She smiled. He had played a few roles during their marriage, but this was a new one. Wondering if she should play along, she inhaled the sweet fragrance of the rose, and regarded him with amusement as she tried to suppress a smile. "I don't know. . . ."

He reared back in mock astonishment. "Can it be? No woman can resist zee Courageous Corsair." He held his hand out in an imperious gesture. "Come, fly with me."

She quirked an eyebrow at him. "How? Do you have wings?"

Clasping one hand to his chest, he declared, "Your beauty gives my heart wings, but I must confess I have a more mundane way of reaching zee ground." He gave the edge of the balcony a significant glance. "A rope."

She frowned. "A rope?"

"Yes. Fear not, lovely lady. I shall hold you tight and ne-vair let you go. You will be safe with me."

If only it were true. . . . Kelly smiled and decided to play along, for a little while at least. "But I can't fly away with a complete stranger. I have responsibilities here, a decision to announce."

He waved that away as if it were inconsequential. "It eez nothing," he said with a breezy snap of his fingers. "Your decision can wait. Our passion cannot." He held his hand out again. "Come wiz me and experience zee most sensual night of your life."

Her heart skipped a beat. *Oh, yes.* He was so tempting. Could she? "But . . . don't you want to hear my decision?"

He shrugged gracefully. "What eez that to zee Courageous Corsair? It eez as nozzing. You, me, cool sheets, and our hot bodies entwined togezzer. Zat eez all zat eez needed."

It sounded heavenly.

He moved toward her with feline grace and snatched up her hand, lifting it to his lips as he captured her gaze with his searing glance. The delicate pressure of his lips on the back of her hand was surprisingly sensuous and Kelly let out a small gasp as a thrill coursed through her.

Oh, my. He was awakening things in her that she'd thought long forgotten. Warm, sizzling things. She didn't want to analyze these feelings, didn't want to second guess how she should feel. She just wanted to do it.

Could she?

He backed away toward the balcony, still holding her hand, still holding her mesmerized with his heated gaze. "Come wiz me," he whispered in a low, sexy voice. "It will be an adventure."

Yes!

She let him lead her toward the balcony. "But what about my things?" she asked weakly, knowing she shouldn't go with him, yet secretly longing for him to talk her into it.

"Wiz me, you shall want for nothing," he promised in a persuasive tone. "Come, I shall supply everyzing you need . . . and more."

He tugged her, unresisting, into his arms. "But first, a small sample of what eez in store for you. . . ."

Enclosing her in a warm, erotic embrace, he kissed her.

It wasn't just any kiss. He put his full attention into it, into *her*, and swamped her senses with his sheer sensuality. She had heard the phrase "kissed senseless" before, but this was the first time she had ever experienced it.

She blamed it for allowing herself to be swept off

her feet. Somehow, she couldn't remember how, but the two of them made it down the rope, Kelly still clutching the rose he had given her, and into the central courtyard of the hotel.

He quirked a smile at her and grabbed her hand, then they dashed off together to a waiting cab at the side of the hotel, trying to minimize the amount of time spent in the cold night air.

The cab driver smirked at them as Chaz seated her in the back seat, but Chaz was undaunted. "To zee villa, Pierre," he declared.

"Whatever, dude," the driver said with a shake of his head.

But even the cabbie's attitude couldn't detract from the romance of the moment. Curling one arm around her shoulders to hold her close, Chaz cupped her cheek in his other hand and feathered soft kisses against her neck, then whispered sweet, erotic promises in her ear.

Kelly shivered in anticipation, hoping the drive wouldn't be very long. It wasn't, as soon the cab pulled up to a quaint bed-and-breakfast. Smoothly, Chaz paid off the cab driver and whisked her up to their room.

Inside, he had prepared the setting carefully. The fragrance of two dozen red roses, matching the one in her hand, filled the frilly, Victorian room, lit only by candlelight. The soft strains of romantic music lent a seductive atmosphere, drawing her even deeper into the mood he had created. Thoughtfully, he had even turned back the covers on the bed.

The bed. Her heart beat even faster as she thought about the possibilities. This room was made for seduction.

He watched her with an expectant expression and Kelly glanced ruefully down at her sweater and slacks.

She was the only jarring note in the room. "I'm not dressed for this," she murmured.

Chaz kissed her hand and gave her a soulful look. "You are beautiful to me no matter what you wear." He paused, then added with a grin, "But eef you wish to change, I have a surprise for you in zee bathroom."

Bathroom. Good idea. It would give her a chance to think for a moment, outside the boundaries of the spell Chaz had woven about her. "All right, I-I'll be right back."

He bowed extravagantly once more, saying, "Of course. I shall await your pleasure."

"O-okay," she squeaked, and scurried into the bathroom like a frightened mouse.

She closed the door and leaned against it, trying to catch her breath. But Chaz had been busy even in here. Small groupings of scattered candles provided the only illumination and soft fluffy towels lay invitingly by the tub with scented soaps and lotions. The lovely fragrance of lavender and musk scented the air.

As she took in the heady ambiance, Kelly realized she was leaning up against something soft and silky. She stepped back to take a look and realized that something was the garment Chaz had provided for her to wear—a slinky red charmeuse nightgown with a peignoir to match.

She fingered the silky material. Oddly enough, she had never owned a negligee like this. But, oh, how she wanted to. Quickly, before she could change her mind, she stripped off every bit of her boring street clothes and put on the daring red gown Chaz had chosen for her, then looked in the mirror.

Oh, my, is that me? The gown dipped low in the front, showing a generous expanse of cleavage, the bodice held up only by the whim of two tiny spaghetti straps. The silk hugged her breasts, lifting them suggestively, then skimmed down past her hips to fall in a puddle to the floor. Along the way, it hinted at peaks and valleys only too ready to be explored. And the sheer lace dressing gown that covered it added to the allure, making her cheeks look flushed with desire and her skin creamy and begging to be touched.

Wow, I look hot.

Immediately embarrassed by the thought, Kelly covered her burning face with her hands. That was something Chaz would say, not her.

And he was waiting, very patiently, outside. She wanted to join him, to see the look in his eyes when he saw her in this piece of seduction, but her mind screamed at her to wait. If she went to him, there would be no turning back, no changing her mind. Chaz had always been able to seduce her with a look and a kiss, and would probably always be able to do so. But was it worth it?

Life with Chaz was like a wild roller coaster ride, full of highs and lows. The highs were wonderfully thrilling, but the lows could be pretty darned low.

In contrast, life with Spencer would be more like a merry-go-round, nice and safe. There would be no high, thrilling peaks . . . but then again, he wouldn't make the bottom drop out of her stomach in the valleys either.

Chaz knocked softly on the door. "Zo, my sweet," he said, still using that silly French accent, "I am ready for you. Are you ready for me?"

Warmth swept over her entire body. Oh, she was more than ready. Chaz was so sexy, so charming, so . . . irresistible. She wavered, unwilling to commit herself to any course of action just yet.

Then Chaz spoke again, reverting to his normal tone of voice. "If you're not ready for this, honey, we can always go back to the hotel. Just say the word."

Gratitude and love made her speechless for a moment. His consideration decided her. To hell with merry-go-rounds. She had missed the thrill of the roller coaster. Smiling, she opened the door.

Chaz's thunderstruck expression was her reward, and it was easy to see his expression since he had gotten rid of the mask and the moustache, not to mention his shoes. "My God," he said reverently. "You're stunning."

Since he had forgotten to use the accent, it was very clear the words came from his heart. And that was the sexiest thing he'd done all day.

"What—" He cleared his throat and tried again. "What made you decide to come out?"

Grinning mischievously, she grasped his collar with both hands and pulled him toward her. "I figure you'll give me the ride of my life. . . ."

He looked a little startled. "Uh, it's been a very long time since I've done any . . . riding. I hope you don't expect too much."

Chaz, uncertain? Kelly laughed and brought his lips closer to hers. "But I have it on the best authority that you are the greatest lover in all the world."

His arms went around her. "Not me. That must have been some other guy. But I promise to do my best."

His soft kiss made her senses fizz and her head swim. Then he deepened the kiss, delving deep into her mouth as his caressing hands slid over the silk of her gown. It was as if he had concentrated his entire being on her. Right here, right now.

It was a heady sensation, feeling like the center of his universe, and a sudden rush of adrenaline cleared the dizziness from her head and sent prickles of awareness zinging along her nerves. The first rush of the wild ride had started.

Ohmigod, I forgot how wonderful this is. How wonderful Chaz is.

He slid his hands across the slick silk on her back and down to her buttocks where they rested for a moment, kneading her tender flesh. It felt incredibly erotic, and Kelly returned the favor, sliding her hands over the luxurious leather of his pants. She cupped his firm buttocks in both hands and squeezed. Oh, yeah, he had always had great buns.

As he inhaled sharply and thrust his hips against hers, she recalled that other parts of him weren't so shabby either. The thick ridge of his erection strained against her belly, just a little too high to give her any real satisfaction. She wanted—needed—him lower.

She raised to her tiptoes, trying to rub herself against where it would do the most good, but he was a little too tall. However, it did have the happy effect of bringing her breasts to his attention.

Continuing to knead her buttocks with one hand as he kissed his way down her neck, Chaz raised his other hand to one of her breasts and cupped her there while running the cool, silky material over her nipple with his thumb.

Oh, yes.

"More," she whispered as she hastily removed the lacy dressing gown and tossed it aside. It was just in the way.

"Happy to oblige," Chaz murmured against her neck and slid both thin straps of the nightgown down her shoulder to bare her breasts and gaze at her in admiration. "Damn, I'd almost forgotten how beautiful you are."

Impatiently, she let the straps slide off her arms, and the entire gown puddled to the floor, leaving her totally nude. She felt a little self-conscious. It had been so long since they were together this way and her body had changed over the years, not for the better. Was she still attractive to him?

But the look in his eyes gave her no doubt that she was. He led her over to the bed and lay her down, still gazing at her with the look of a starving man who had just come upon a plentiful feast.

But when he lowered himself to her side, he surprised her by laying his head softly between her breasts and hugging her tight. "God, I missed you."

It totally floored her. She had never seen Chaz so open and honest, so needy. A surge of longing suffused her, so intense it was almost painful. Tenderly, she smoothed his hair. "I missed you, too," she murmured. And she had. She had missed the fun and excitement of having him around, missed his silly humor, missed his lovemaking.

They stayed that way for a long moment, then Chaz nuzzled the curve of her breast and his tongue darted out to give her pebbled nipple a quick lick.

She gasped softly, surprised at how that small action had sent her back up to the next incline of the roller coaster. And when he took one breast into his mouth and suckled, she couldn't help but throw back her head and moan in pleasure. Ohmigod, that felt good. And it felt even better when he seemed to immerse himself in her, as he grasped her breasts in both hands and rolled his head back and forth between them sucking and licking and driving her crazy.

But Chaz was wearing too many clothes—she wanted skin against skin. "You, too," she whispered, and began to unbutton his shirt.

Quickly, he rose to finish the job and stripped his shirt off, revealing his familiar chest, tanned darker from the Amazonian sun than she had ever seen it.

God, she loved his chest. She leaned up against him. It was sprinkled with sun-lightened dark blond hair that curled against her nipples, bringing them to even tighter peaks.

But it was his pants she really wanted gone. She reached down and undid the top button of the beltless slacks, then unzipped them slowly. She hadn't seen an underwear line in those tight trousers and didn't want to catch any sensitive skin in the teeth of the zipper.

Her teeth, now, were a different story.

As she eased the zipper down, his erection sprang free and she grasped it, enjoying the feel of his hard shaft sheathed in silky soft skin. She leaned down to swipe her tongue across the tip and nip it with her teeth, but he gasped and pulled her away.

"No," he said in a tone full of regret. "If you do that, I'll explode here and now. I want this to last, this time."

"So do I," she said with a smile, and helped him peel the pants off the rest of the way. She paused and stared, puzzled. His entire body was darkly tanned, except for the area around his crotch. "What'd you do? Wear a thong?" she asked.

He shrugged. "I had no choice. My clothes rotted off after awhile and I had to go native."

Annoyance filled her as she realized Amalia had seen him in a Chippendale's outfit for many years. No wonder she was so bent on having him.

But that white area drew Kelly's attention again and

she smiled. Well, there was one part he had kept private, anyway. And it was all hers . . .

She reached out to take possession and gently kneaded his soft sacs in one hand while she drew her other hand over the length of his shaft. His moan of pleasure and the look of ecstasy on his face was her reward. But he didn't let her enjoy it for long.

Grabbing her around the waist, he tumbled them back to the bed and took one breast into his mouth as his hand delved between her legs. She was hot and wet, more than ready for him, and it was so good to feel his fingers inside her, rubbing the sensitive flesh that hadn't felt a man's touch in years.

The roller coaster took a breath-stealing surge up the next incline.

But when he found her throbbing secret nub, all it took was one slippery stroke of his finger to bring her rushing up over the top of the highest curve into the screaming sensory overload of a loop-the-loop, then plunging downward in spasming spirals of sheer sensation.

As the tremors gradually ceased, Kelly opened her eyes to see Chaz staring at her in a kind of awe. But she couldn't let him go any longer without taking that ride, either. Pushing him flat on his back, she swung her leg over his hips and eased herself down onto his thick shaft, sliding slowly all the way down to his base. Ah. A perfect tight fit that felt oh, so right.

She grinned as she saw Chaz's expression. He seemed so totally overwhelmed that he was unable to do anything but lie there and quiver helplessly with need.

But she had no such problem. Raising her hips just a little, she slid quickly back down again. Chaz gasped and jerked, thrusting his hips upward. But there was no place farther to go—he was sheathed to the hilt. God, it felt good to have him there, filling her fully and completely.

But she didn't want his ride to be too fast. Slowly, she tightened her muscles around him, wondering if she'd lost the knack over the years. Apparently not, for as she caressed him from the inside, he whimpered and clutched the bedclothes in both fists.

She did it again, raising and lowering herself a little this time, and he moaned even more. But when she did it the third time, the friction against her long-deprived sensitive flesh started her own coaster rolling again. *Oh, yes.*

Closing her eyes, she rode it and Chaz through ever-increasing peaks of sensation, cresting a little higher each time until Chaz lost control and grasped her hips to hold on tight. They thrusted frantically against each other until they burst over the top together, flying free for a pure moment of ecstasy until gravity pulled them down once more to ride the shuddering shockwaves to the end.

Gasping, Kelly collapsed on top of Chaz. The ride was over, but it had left her replete and totally drained. There was no way she could move under her own steam.

As if it took superhuman effort, Chaz slung one arm over her back, then flopped the other one on top of that. Squeezing her briefly, he said, "That was . . . That was . . ." He trailed off, evidently unable to find the words to describe what they had just shared.

"One hell of a ride," she muttered into his shoulder, still unable to move.

She felt him nod, and one of his arms fell limply back to his side. She knew exactly how he felt.

They lay there for a few minutes and Kelly sighed in

contentment. Shoving the rest of her worries out of her mind, she let herself just enjoy the moment. And Chaz.

But soon Chaz stirred and rolled them both to their sides, then kissed her softly on the mouth.

"Kelly? I have a question to ask you."

He sounded so tentative, so uncertain, that she had to open her eyes to see if his expression matched his tone. It did. "What is it?"

"I have to know. Who—who did you choose?"

His expression was so full of raw need that it touched something deep inside her. "Oh, Chaz," she said, caressing his face. "It's you. It was always you." No other decision felt right.

He let out a sigh and buried his face in her neck. Surprised, she stiffened for a moment. What was that wetness on her neck? Could it be tears?

Sighing, she cuddled him to her, regretting that she had made him wait, that she had let him suffer. She hadn't realized how much she really meant to him.

But still, there was one more thing she had to know. "So, you haven't done this with . . . anyone else?"

"No," he said, raising his head a little. "How can you ask that?" He paused, then added, "If you mean Garcia, that's just . . . sick. I'd rather make love to a python."

There was so much loathing in his voice, Kelly couldn't help but believe him.

"But have you been true to me?" he asked with a raised eyebrow.

There was a teasing note in his voice that she didn't quite understand. "What do you mean?"

"Well, while I was stuck hiding in the bathroom, I found something interesting in the trash. My competition?" he asked with a grin.

Mortified, Kelly said, "No, of course not. Just Scott's idea of a joke." One he would be very happy to hear had snowballed on her. She gave Chaz a hug. "Besides, no one and no thing could possibly compare with you."

Chaz smiled at her and caressed her check. "Right back atcha, honey."

She sighed happily and relaxed once more, reliving the wonderful sensations she'd just experienced. Wow— she was right about that roller coaster. The heights were incredible, higher than she'd ever gone before.

But a niggling doubt haunted her. What about the lows?

Candace watched, pleased, as Spencer and Amalia paced the hallway outside Kelly's door and Scott surveyed them all with a small smile on his face. Once more, Chaz had managed to spirit Kelly away from under Spencer's nose.

Inevitably, the elevator opened and disgorged another person to join the party—Kelly's mother. "What's going on?" Grace Richmond asked with a frown.

Spencer paused in his pacing to say, "Kelly is missing." Reluctantly he added, "And so is Chaz."

"Are you sure?" Grace asked.

"Yes," Spencer said, running a hand through his hair. "We've called them numerous times and knocked on their doors, even checked the whole hotel. They're gone."

"Do you think something has happened to them?" Grace asked in alarm.

Scott grinned. "Oh, I doubt it."

Grace scowled at him. "Then what can they be doing?"

His grin widened, turning almost lascivious. "I think that's obvious."

"Don't be crude," his mother said.

Candace was just glad someone had finally pointed out the obvious to Spencer. "They could be anywhere," she said. Doing just about anything.

At least, she hoped so.

Moving toward Spencer, she added, "There's nothing we can do about it until they return. Why don't we wait in our rooms where it's more comfortable?"

"All right," Spencer said in resignation. "We're not doing any good here."

He looked so dejected, Candace moved toward him to offer comfort. Laying a hand on his arm, she said, "I'm sorry you have to go through this."

"So am I," Spencer said absently. But as he did so, he rubbed her hand where it still lay on his arm, then squeezed it softly.

In gratitude? Candace's heart leapt in response. Maybe it was more than that. Maybe he cared for her more than he realized. . . .

Twelve

Chaz woke in Kelly's arms the next morning and lay there, just drinking in the moment as he stared down at his wife. She cuddled up against him, one arm curled over his chest and one leg thrown over his thighs. Bare skin to bare skin, just the way he liked it.

He smiled in remembrance. They had spent the night getting reacquainted the best way he knew how. And between bouts of lovemaking on the bed, in the tub, on the floor, he had shared a few stories of his captivity and learned a little more about what her life had been like while he was gone.

The whole experience was enlightening. He knew now that it was too late to get his comfortable old Kelly back, but he was coming to appreciate the advantages of this new, more confident, wife of his.

Pure contentment filled him, but he had no illusions that his good fortune was due to any action of his. Kelly's presence in his arms and his bed was a miracle, a great gift. If only he didn't screw it up. . . .

She stirred and he cuddled her close, murmuring, "Good morning."

She looked up at him and smiled, and it was as if the sun had burst from behind the clouds to share its glory.

His heart skipped a beat. *I'm the luckiest man in the world.*

"So," she said. "How is my Courageous Corsair this morning?"

He grinned back at her. "Zee Courageous Corsair eez . . . pooped out." He dropped the phony accent. "I don't even have enough 'courage' to move after what you did to me last night."

She sighed and laid her head on his shoulder. "I know what you mean. I'm a little sore myself. And hungry. . . ."

Those last two words sounded plaintive. And, learning that Kelly wanted something that was in his power to provide, Chaz found the ability to move. "All right. I can take a hint."

He got out of bed and pulled on his pants, grinning to himself at the way Kelly watched him with appreciative eyes. "I'll just go get breakfast."

"In *that* outfit?"

He glanced down at the leather pants. They *were* a little risqué. "I didn't bring anything else to wear."

She shook her head. "I don't think so. You might shock the other guests." She slid the sheet off and rolled out of bed. "Why don't I get breakfast instead? You don't want to give the little old ladies heart attacks."

It was his turn to watch appreciatively as she sauntered, looking a little self-conscious in her nudity, into the bathroom where she had left her clothes.

"Okay," he called in after her. Last night, his outfit had seemed like a good idea, but he could see where it might be a little over the top in the bright light of day. "But bring back a lot—I worked up quite an appetite."

She dressed and left, then was gone a little longer than he expected. She came back bearing a tray and an amused expression. As he opened the door for her, she asked, "What did you tell those people downstairs about us?"

"Oh, yeah. That. I kind of told them we were on our second honeymoon." He watched her closely for signs of anger, but she just laughed.

"No wonder they were so nice—and kept giving me more food."

The tray, piled high with a continental breakfast, looked heavy so he took it from her and put it on the small desk. "Looks great. Is this what took you so long?"

Closing the door behind her, she said, "No. I also called the hotel to let Scott know where we are so he doesn't call out the National Guard or something."

"Good idea." Chaz had thought about cluing her brother in the night before, but wasn't sure if Scott would go along with what amounted to kidnapping. Or it would have been, if Kelly hadn't been so eager to go along with him.

They settled in to eat and after a swallow of an incredibly light and flaky croissant, Chaz said, "I know you and your brother have always been close, but you seem even closer now than you were before."

She nodded. "Ever since I moved back in, Scott and I have kind of bonded together to deal with Mother."

Chaz felt a little guilty. Scott had said Kelly moved back home to save money so she could afford to search for Chaz. Back home to the dragon Chaz had rescued her from in the first place. "I'm sorry you had to do that, honey. If I could take back those missing years, I would."

"Oh, Chaz," she said with a misty smile. "Don't

worry about that. How could I not spend everything I had looking for you? I'm just glad you're alive."

Puzzled, he asked, "But I took out an insurance policy. That should have helped."

"Only if you were deceased. And since we didn't find a body, I couldn't put in a claim unless you were declared legally dead. I still haven't."

He was still confused. "Didn't your mother help out with the money situation?" She lived like a queen. Surely she could spare some cash for her daughter.

"She couldn't. I know it looks like she has a lot of money, but she doesn't really. I learned that when I moved back in. The house takes a lot of upkeep and the only reason she's been able to hold on to it is because Scott manages her money for her. Actually, having us there to share the expenses helped her, too."

Chaz frowned. He wanted to ask why Grace didn't just move into a smaller place and sell some of those antiques and jewels she had lying around the house, but he knew what the answer would be. Appearance was everything to Grace Richmond.

"So, will she be upset with you for leaving?" He didn't care how little money he and Kelly had—there was no way he was living in the same house with her mother.

"Of course not. She already accepted the fact that I was going to live with Spencer."

Yeah, Chaz could see where Mr. Elegant would be the apple of Gracie's eye. "But you're not going to live with him anymore," Chaz said, though it came out more like a question than he had intended it to. "You're going to live with me . . . right?"

Kelly smiled and caressed his cheek. "Of course. And Mother will just have to cope with that." She sighed. "It will be nice to have a home of our own again."

Now this was more like it—he loved Kelly in this dreamy planning sort of mode. Since they had both made considerable inroads on the contents of the tray, he dragged her back to bed to cuddle with him. Sighing contentedly, he asked, "What kind of place do you want?"

She snuggled up against him, laying her head on his shoulder. "Hmm, I don't know. I'd love to go back to our old apartment, but I doubt it's available."

"That would be nice," he agreed. They had been very happy there, and the place held many good memories.

"Maybe we can afford something a little nicer now. A condo, maybe, or a small house?"

"Do they pay you well, now that you're an editor?"

Her lips twisted in a rueful smile. "I'm not even sure I have a job after making Candace get down on all fours to hide from my mother." She splayed a hand across her face. "God, how embarrassing."

He squeezed her reassuringly. "I don't think you have to worry about that. Now that you've freed up Deuce, she'll probably be so grateful she'll give you a raise."

"Deuce?" she asked with a puzzled expression.

Oops. He waved a hand dismissively. "Just my little nickname for your . . . the guy who horned in on my territory. Never mind."

She shrugged. "Well, I'll be happy if I can just keep my current job. The money is better than what I made before I was promoted, but it's still not great. We can get by until you find a job."

He nodded absently and nuzzled her neck, loving the feel and the smell of her in his arms. "That shouldn't be a problem. Whatever you want, honey. Anything will seem like a palace with you . . . especially after what I've been living in the past few years."

Her arms tightened around him. "Oh, Chaz. I so want you to have everything you missed, to make up for lost time. What do you want in a house?"

"I told you—it doesn't really matter, so long as you're there. I just want a place of our own." Unlike the zoo of the last few days with people popping out of the woodwork every time he turned around.

Her arm tightened around him and she played with the hair on his chest. "Having a home is important to you, isn't it? Especially since you haven't had one in so long."

"Yes—it's one of the things that kept me going all that time, knowing you were here waiting for me." He sighed, remembering. "I had fantasies about returning to you and our old life together. I always loved coming home to you, and I always will."

Her hand stilled on his chest. "Always will?"

"Of course," he said, squeezing her tight. "Do you doubt it?"

"You mean, you're planning on leaving again?"

"Not anytime soon. But you said it yourself, I have to find a job. I've been making some inquiries and learned there's a dig in Turkey looking for someone with my skills. There's a rumor of precious artifacts there, and I'm sure I can find them."

"Turkey?" She sat up to stare down at him and he was surprised to see a spark of anger in her eyes. "Are you kidding?"

Uh-oh. It appeared he was on quicksand once again without quite realizing how he had gotten there. "No,

I'm not kidding. I can't live off you for the rest of my life. I need to earn my keep."

"By taking off and leaving me alone again?" Kelly asked with tears in her eyes. "I couldn't stand that, Chaz. I lost you once, and I don't ever want to go through that again."

"You wouldn't," he assured her. "Turkey is nothing like the Amazon."

"Yeah, right. Well, I may not know much about geography and world affairs, but I do know that part of the world is never quite stable. What if you get caught up in a war? What if you're captured again? What if you're *killed?*"

"Aw, honey, I won't be." He sat up and tried to give her a reassuring hug, but she shrugged him off.

"Don't you 'aw, honey' me. It's dangerous and you know it." She got up from the bed to pace in the small room. "Can't you do something else?"

"Like what?" he asked in trepidation. "This is the only thing I know how to do. I don't have any other skills, and with no recent job experience, who'd hire me?"

"Anyone would hire you, once you tell them the circumstances," she said in a cajoling tone.

"Hire me to do what? Flip burgers? I couldn't stand that." Cooped up in some greasy little joint, never seeing the sun, never experiencing the joy of a unique find? It sounded like hell. She couldn't really expect him to do that . . . could she?

"You wouldn't have to flip burgers," she said, her voice rising. "And the danger isn't all I'm worried about—I hate having you thousands of miles away. I'm sure there is something else you can do. Here."

He frowned. "But nothing I'd enjoy as much as what

I do now." He wouldn't ask her to give up a job she loved. How could she ask that of him?

Besides, it was more than just a job, it was a part of who he was. The adventure of traveling to new places, the excitement of a new find, the thrill of having his name in the history books. . . . He didn't want to give that up.

She crossed her arms and stared at him with a defiant expression. "I couldn't stand it if you left me again. I'm tired of worrying about you, tired of wondering if you're dead or alive. Chaz, I want you to stay in Denver."

He rose from the bed to face her. "Are you giving me an ultimatum?" he asked in disbelief.

She lifted her chin. "I suppose I am. It's your job or me. Which will it be?"

Stunned, he could do nothing but stare at her for a moment. Either choice was totally abhorrent. Either he stayed in Denver with Kelly at a boring, soul-stealing job, or he did the work he loved and lost his wife. And he knew homebody Kelly would never agree to go with him. Running a hand through his hair, he said, "How can you ask me to make this kind of choice?" It was a no-win situation.

Kelly threw up her hands in disgust. "You know what? Never mind. If you even have to stop and think about it, then the answer's plain. Your job is far more important to you than I am. Hell, you proved that when you stayed in the jungle after you were set free—just so you could find a few more baubles to add to your collection."

"That's not fair," he protested. "I needed those 'baubles' as you call them, to fulfill my contract. They weren't just some passing whim—they're what allowed me to earn my way home and give us enough cash to pay for a few months' living expenses. For both of us."

"No, they're what allowed you to continue playing Indiana Jones—your favorite role."

He shook his head, wondering where the hell he'd gone wrong and how he could possibly put it right. "That's not my favorite role," he corrected her softly. "My favorite role is playing Kelly Vincent's husband." The Courageous Corsair was kind of fun, too.

"I'm sorry, Chaz. I don't believe you." She wiped a tear away. "Just take me back to the hotel, okay?"

"Why?" he asked in alarm. Had he screwed up totally? Was she planning on going from his bed to Deuce's arms?

"Because I need time to think. Time without you."

God, that hurt. He didn't want her doing *any*thing without him. "But—"

"No buts, Chaz. You said last night that all I had to do was say the word and you would take me back to the hotel. Well, I'm saying it."

She had him there. He never went back on his word. Sighing, Chaz said, "All right." He finished dressing and called a cab, his heart leaden.

"It'll be here in a few minutes," he told her.

Apparently unable to keep still, Kelly was straightening the bed, cleaning up their breakfast, and generally tidying up. When she came to the red gown pooled in the floor, she hesitated, then fiercely balled it up and threw it in the trash.

God, why don't you throw my heart in there along with it? he wanted to ask, but Chaz knew better than to say it aloud. Instead, as she headed for the bathroom, he removed the negligee from the trash, smoothed it out, and folded it carefully, tucking it inside his voluminous shirt.

"What do you want with that?" she asked as she caught him at it.

"Memories. . . ." The remembrance of one perfect night with Kelly . . . before he had managed to fuck up the rest of his life.

Kelly sat in the cab, fuming as they headed back to the hotel. How could he do this to her again? The night before had been so wonderful, so special . . . but it was all fake. Even as he'd lavished her with attention, babbled on about how much he loved her, he was planning to leave her again.

But isn't he worth waiting for? a little voice asked.

Maybe, but he wasn't worth the pain of worrying, of wondering if he were dead or alive. And she would always worry. How could she not? He took huge risks, believing they had to be big to make the payoff even bigger.

In some ways, she admired him for that, but when the risk he was taking was with their marriage, she couldn't stand it. She wasn't willing to take the chance of losing him again. Not any more.

From the other side of the cab, Chaz asked, "What are you going to do?"

"I don't know," Kelly said in clipped tones. Right now, she was too angry to even think about the future.

"Have you changed your mind about choosing me?"

The little boy quality of his voice should have melted her heart, but all it did was tick her off more.

"*You* changed my mind for me." If he hadn't been so

insensitive, so dense, so idiotically *male*, she wouldn't
have to change her mind.

"What does that mean?"

The anxious tone in his voice made her realize what
he was really asking was if she was going to dump him
to take off with Spencer. But the way she felt, she
didn't care to clarify. Besides, she didn't know what
she was going to do yet. "That means you made me
change my mind about spending the rest of my life
with you."

There, let him figure that one out.

"You can't mean that," he protested.

"I do mean that. Besides, the way you live, the rest
of your life won't be very long anyway."

Chaz tried to scoot closer to her, but she gave him
a dirty look and he halted. It didn't stop him from
using a cajoling tone, however. "I'm sorry, honey. I
didn't mean to hurt you. I'll say anything, do anything,
if we can just stay together."

Kelly almost sneered. "Anything but give up your
job, you mean." When he couldn't answer that, she
added, "I'm sure you'd *say* anything. But would you
mean it?"

"Of course I would," he said, sounding wounded.

"Only until the next time an exciting job or rumor
of a new find comes up. Then you'll forget all about
me and jet off to some stupid dirty dig that doesn't
even have a proper *toilet*."

"What does the toilet have to do with anything?" he
asked in bewilderment.

"I don't know," she said in exasperation. "Maybe it
symbolizes the fate of our marriage."

"You can't mean that," Chaz repeated, shifting on

the seat so he could look her in the eye. "I love you and you love me. We can work this out. Somehow."

No, he was *not* going to sweet-talk her into going along with his plans for their life together. He had always been able to do it before, but this time she wouldn't let him. "Just be quiet, Chaz. I'm too angry to talk about this any more."

"You're not going to make any hasty decisions, are you?"

"I might if you don't keep your mouth shut."

He finally seemed to get the hint and kept quiet the rest of the short way back to the Pourtales. But she couldn't stop him from following her as she stalked across the lobby.

Chaz seemed to squirm a little as Billings raised his eyebrows at Chaz's attire and two gay men gazed with appreciation at his tight pants, but it only made him move faster as he and Kelly reached the elevator and rode up together, silently.

When they came out into the hallway of the third floor, Kelly spotted what was waiting for her and muttered, "Great. Just great."

Mother and Spencer seemed to be having an intense if genteel argument with Scott in the hallway while Candace and Amalia watched . . . along with half a dozen other hotel guests who lingered in the hallway or peeked out their doors.

Kelly would have ignored them all and locked herself in her room, but she suddenly remembered she didn't have a key. She had left it behind with all the contents of her purse the night before.

She hesitated, not knowing which was worse— going back downstairs to ask Billings for another key or asking one of the gang here to do it for her.

But Scott had spotted her then, or so she assumed from the look of intense relief that crossed his face. They all turned to see what he was looking at and Amalia made a beeline for Chaz.

"Where have you been?" Mother demanded.

"I've been so worried about you," Spencer said.

Amalia grabbed Chaz's arm. "There you are. I haf something *muy importante* to tell you."

"Sweet outfit," Scott said with raised eyebrows at Chaz. "Trying out for the ballet?"

And everyone else seemed determined to put their two cents worth in as well. The resulting babble made Kelly want to scream. "Quiet," she said in the firmest tone she could manage. When they all stared at her in surprise, she added, "Let's take this out of the hallway before we're all thrown out of here, shall we?"

"Like where?" Scott asked.

"Spencer's room?" Kelly suggested.

Chaz bristled. "Like hell—"

"Don't be ridiculous," Kelly said with exasperation. "The honeymoon suite is the biggest room on this floor. Or would you rather have everyone crammed in your room?"

She could tell he understood the logic, but still didn't like it. But since he didn't say anything, she took his silence for consent. "Spencer, if you would open the door?"

"Certainly," he said and hastened to do as she asked.

They all trooped into the honeymoon suite. Kelly would much rather have done without the presence of her mother, her boss, and Chaz's leech, but their stubborn expressions showed they weren't about to leave now.

Once they had all settled inside, Grace stared

haughtily at her daughter. "Where have you been? We've all been worried sick, and Scott would tell us nothing."

"Now, Mother, I'm sure he told you I was all right."

"Well, yes, but considering the company you were in," she said with a searing glance at Chaz, "I wasn't sure you were *safe*."

Kelly sighed but decided not to answer that bit of rudeness. "You don't need to know where I've been."

"But what have you been doing?" Candace asked in a half-fascinated, half-hopeful tone.

Kelly might as well come clean, though she really didn't care for the thought of airing her laundry—dirty or clean—in public. "I was getting to know Chaz better," she said with as much dignity as she could manage. "I thought we might have a reconciliation. Turns out I was wrong."

"Wait a minute," Chaz protested. "There was nothing to reconcile about—we weren't arguing."

But Spencer's expression had turned hopeful. "Does that mean. . . ?"

How could he ask? Surely he must realize she had spent the night with Chaz. How could he still want her after that?

And though she might be angry enough with Chaz to scratch him off her list of potential husbands, she knew that life with Spencer wouldn't be right either. She would always be comparing him to Chaz . . . unfavorably.

But she couldn't say that out loud and humiliate Spencer in front of everyone else. "It means I want to be alone."

A silence fell and Amalia tugged on Chaz's arm

again. "I haf something important to tell you," she persisted.

Chaz shrugged her off. "I don't want to hear it," he all but snarled at her.

A knock sounded at the door, and everyone looked around in surprise. The whole gang was there already—and none of them even in hiding. Who could it be?

Spencer opened the door to reveal Billings standing there rocking on his heels with a supercilious expression and his hands behind his back.

"What's the problem?" Chaz asked. "We're keeping the noise level down."

The manager inclined his head, silently acknowledging the truth of his words. "That isn't why I'm here."

"And why is that?" Chaz asked belligerently.

Kelly gave him a warning glance. It wouldn't do to anger the manager if they wanted to stay here any longer. But it appeared Chaz needed some outlet for his frustration, and Billings looked like a likely target.

Billings's expression didn't change one iota. "My maintenance staff found something odd this morning in Mrs. Preston's room."

"That's Mrs. *Vincent*," Chaz said with a menacing look.

"Stop it," Kelly said. Though Billings probably had some suspicions, he didn't know exactly what was going on with their little party, and she wanted to keep it that way.

Unfortunately, there was nothing she could do to stop Billings's revelation. He pulled a coil of rope from behind his back. "This was tied to Mrs., er, to the lady's balcony."

Kelly closed her eyes in disbelief as she felt the weight of everyone else's gaze on her. Great. Now they'd want her to explain that.

Billings continued inexorably. "My staff thought you might have chosen a unique way of avoiding paying your bill, but since your purse and all your belongings were still there, I concluded there might be a different need for the rope."

Grace stared at him, her mouth agape. "What in the world . . . ?"

Kelly snatched the coil out of Billings's hands and avoided looking at Chaz. No doubt he was wearing a big grin. In fact, she avoided looking at anyone else, to avoid the questions in their eyes. "Thank you," she said with as much dignity as she could manage and dropped the rope on a nearby chair. "I don't suppose you brought—"

Silently, Billings held up a key.

"Thank you," she repeated and snatched it out of his hand.

He might have made it off her black list if he had left it at that, but apparently, he couldn't. Bowing slightly, the assistant manager added, "Since you left so precipitously out the window, I thought you might be in need of a key to your room."

Annoyed by the gasps as the others suddenly realized what the rope was for, Kelly snapped, "And you didn't think I might have met with foul play?"

"Well, no," he said with a small smile. "You see, I remember seeing Mr. Vincent entering the hotel with that rope earlier."

Now she was in for it. But first, all eyes turned to Chaz, who just grinned.

"Surely you didn't climb down from the third floor on *that*," her mother said in horrified tones.

Kelly felt her cheeks flush with warmth as Scott unsuccessfully tried to stifle a chuckle. It did sound rather foolhardy now, but it had been rather exciting at the time.

Spencer turned to glare at Chaz. "You gave your word. You said you wouldn't go near her until she was ready."

"Not quite," Chaz drawled. "I said I wouldn't go near her *door*. The balcony is nowhere near the door."

Candace looked impressed by this odd bit of reasoning and Scott let out the laugh he'd been trying to suppress. "Damn, I wish I could've seen that. What'd you do? Swing in from your room like Tarzan, or climb up to the balcony like a human fly?"

"Climbed up," Chaz said with a twinkle in his eye. "But it wasn't easy."

Kelly rolled her eyes, but there was no stopping these two when they were on a roll.

"Oh?" Scott said in a delighted tone. "Do tell."

"Well, the trellis helped, but it's kind of difficult to climb in the dark with a mask on and a rose between your teeth."

"Not to mention those tight pants," Scott said with a laugh.

"Yeah. I'm afraid I may have startled the people on the second floor."

Candace smiled a little wistfully, but no one else seemed amused. Except perhaps Billings, in a smarmy sort of way. "Thank you," Kelly told the manager firmly and shut the door in his face.

"Tell me more," Scott urged Chaz.

Kelly glared at her brother. "No, I think that's

enough for one day. Now that I have my key, I'm going to my room."

"But you can't leave us like this," her mother protested. "Don't you have an announcement to make?"

"No." And Kelly had no intention of elaborating on that statement either.

"But I haf an announcement," Amalia said.

"What's that?" Scott asked with a grin. Obviously, he was the only one brave enough to ask the question.

"Chaz and I are to be married," Amalia declared brightly as if she hadn't said it a dozen times before.

Almost everyone in the room rolled their eyes.

"No, we are not," Chaz said firmly. "I told you. *God* told you. It ain't gonna happen. Can't you take a hint?"

"But we must be married," Amalia said in bewilderment. "I am with child." As they all stared at her in astonishment, she beamed at Chaz and clarified, "*Your* child."

Thirteen

Chaz stared at Amalia, stunned. What a whopper.

But before he could say anything, Kelly turned on him with fury in her eyes. "You said you loved only me. That you had never touched her."

"I didn't."

"Then how did she get pregnant?"

Chaz spread his arms helplessly. "Hey, I think we've established the fact that she's a pathological liar. Besides, I'm not the only man in the world, you know."

"Then who did the deed? One of your pygmy captors?" Kelly asked sarcastically, giving Amalia a scathing once-over. "Yeah, I can just see them trying to scale Mount Garcia."

There was a choke of laughter from Scott, and both Chaz and Kelly turned on him, saying simultaneously, "That's not funny."

Scott backed off with his arms raised and Chaz took a deep breath, then leapt into the fray again. "I don't know who got her pregnant. So far as I know, it was an immaculate conception."

Kelly sniffed. "Well, you're no Joseph and she's certainly no Virgin Mary."

Amalia shoved her hands on her hips and glared at Kelly. "But I was virgin, until Chaz." Then her expression turned sly and calculating. "It was the best night of our lives."

From Kelly's heightened color, that lie only made her burn hotter. If Chaz didn't do something soon, he was afraid she was going to explode. "No, honey," he reassured her. "That's impossible. Last night was the best night of my life."

"Ha," Kelly exclaimed. "So you admit you were with her."

Damn it, how had she gotten that idea? "No, I don't. I can't admit it, because I've *never* been with her. She's lying again."

Grace chose this moment to break into the conversation. "So what *did* happen last night?"

Chaz slanted a glance at Kelly, letting her choose how much to reveal.

Since all other eyes were on her as well, Kelly turned red. She muttered something about a roller coaster, but before anyone could ask her to repeat it, Amalia was stamping her foot again.

"I am *not* lying. I am pink," she declared.

Pink? They all looked at each other in equal incomprehension.

"What?" Chaz ventured, though he hoped he wouldn't be sorry he asked.

"The little line, she is pink."

Bewilderment was replaced by enlightenment on most of the expressions in the room. "You mean you took some sort of home pregnancy test?" Chaz asked, just to make sure he understood.

"Yes. We shall have a fine, healthy son."

Now, he was positive a home pregnancy test wouldn't show *that*. Good Lord, what universe did this woman live in? Because it sure wasn't the reality Chaz belonged to. "Those tests aren't totally accurate, you know." Were they?

"Oh, it is," she assured him. "Now you haf to marry me."

"Fine," Kelly said in exasperation. "Marry her. Anything to shut her up."

Not a chance. "But I don't want her—or some other man's illegitimate kid. If she's even pregnant at all."

"Of course I am," Amalia said in indignation. "Would I lie about that?"

"Of course you would," Chaz said in equal resentment. "You've lied about everything else."

Amalia pouted. "I am not lying."

Kelly still appeared skeptical, so Chaz said, "Look, I know. I'll take a paternity test. That'll prove I'm not the father."

Candace shook her head. "I don't think you can do that until after the baby's born."

"If there even is a baby," Chaz snapped back. And if there was, he couldn't wait for months to prove his innocence. He'd lose Kelly by then.

"You see," Amalia said in triumph. "You haf to marry me."

"No, I don't," Chaz snapped. "Besides, I'm already married, or have you all forgotten? I'm happily married to Kelly." And he wanted to keep it that way.

"Oh, pooh," Amalia said, waving away his eight-year marriage as if it were inconsequential. "We can fix that before the little one comes."

"But I don't want it fixed. I want Kelly, not you." Casting around for some way to make her believe him, he said, "Remember yesterday? Even God agreed with me."

But Amalia's expression turned smug. "I think

about that. God didn't strike you dead because He save you to be the father of my child. He forgives you. I forgive you." And the woman had the nerve to hold her arms out to him in absolution.

"No," Chaz said desperately. "There is no way you can prove I'm the father of that child or force me to marry you."

"Oh, yes there is," Amalia said with a smug smile.

"Like what?" None of this crap she was spouting would hold up in court.

"Juan and Gilbert."

"Huh?" She'd totally lost him . . . and everyone else in the room, too, if their expressions were any indication.

"My brothers," she explained. "They come all the way here to welcome you to the family. They wait by your door."

"Is this another lie?" Chaz asked suspiciously.

"No, look. You see."

When Chaz hesitated, Scott said, "Here, let me." He crossed to the door and opened it slightly to peer out.

"What do you see?" Chaz asked.

"Hmm, two big bruisers about seven feet tall with bulging muscles and a striking resemblance to Amalia." He paused, then added, "They look pissed."

Yeah, right. Chaz pushed Scott aside to look out for himself, then swore under his breath. Scott had been exaggerating, but only a little. And those two behemoths looked as if they wouldn't tolerate any disrespect to their sister. Now what?

"Juan, Gilbert," Amalia called through the partially open door.

Chaz closed it, fast. As soon as he did, he knew he

had made a mistake. He should have shoved Amalia out into the hallway with her brothers.

"How sweet," Kelly cooed. "A family reunion. Don't let us keep you from it."

Not funny. He glared at her, then at Amalia. "I don't suppose they'd listen to reason?"

Amalia shrugged. "They don't speak English very well."

And Chaz's Spanish was very rusty. While adequate for a dig, it wouldn't stretch to fake pregnancies and questionable virtue. He wouldn't trust Amalia to translate anything accurately, either. "What have you told them?" he asked.

"That you are the father of my child and refuse to marry me."

Chaz groaned and shut his eyes.

"You see?" Amalia said in triumph. "It is the right thing to do."

Oh, great. His choices were to marry Amalia or be beaten to a bloody pulp by her brothers, *then* be forced to marry her.

"Why don't you just do it, Chaz?" Kelly asked with a sigh.

Chaz regarded her in disbelief. She couldn't mean it. But she wasn't being sarcastic—she looked totally serious. "Why?"

"Because she'll hound you until you do."

No, that wasn't the question he'd asked. Not why should he marry Amalia, but why was Kelly saying such an awful thing? Unfortunately, the expression on her face said it all.

Shit. I've lost her.

* * *

Kelly knew she ought to feel bad when she saw the shock and despair settle over Chaz's features, but all she felt was numb. Let him have a taste of how it felt to have his world drop out from under him. Hell, let him marry the woman. He deserved the Latina man-eater after all he'd put Kelly through.

She wanted to believe him, she really did. But Amalia was so smug, so insistent, so damned glowing, how could Kelly not believe the woman? Especially since Chaz had conveniently left out the fact that he'd been imprisoned with her for five years. If he lied about that, he was probably lying about this, too. What man could resist such temptation for so long, especially when the temptation was so . . . persistent?

If only he hadn't lied about it, if only he'd told the truth, she might have been able to forgive him. But now she'd always remember that he'd made love to Amalia first, then to her.

Yuck. The thought of having shared any part of Chaz with that woman was revolting, but especially *that* part. Disgust shivered over her as she had the ir-rational feeling he might have somehow transferred Amalia cooties to her in the act of love.

I need a shower. Bad.

But amidst the anger and disgust, a little disap-pointment crept in, disappointment that it hadn't worked out. Last night had been so perfect that she had cherished the idea it might last forever. Fat chance. Her eyes narrowed as a sudden thought occurred to her. Had Chaz played the Courageous Corsair for Amalia, too? Had he charmed her with his romantic wiles?

The thought hurt, but Kelly had to admit it was un-likely. Amalia didn't need any encouragement.

A series of heavy thuds hit the door. The Garcia

brothers, no doubt. Amalia looked pleased, but Chaz was a little wary.

Well, Kelly was just pissed. There were more than enough people here to witness her humiliation. She didn't need any more. "I'll get it," she said through clenched teeth.

She stalked to the door and pulled it open. "What?" she demanded.

The brothers were just as big and beefy as Scott had described, but were better dressed than she expected. They stared down at her, then let out a spate of Spanish.

Kelly cut them off in midstream. She wasn't about to take any crap from anyone else, especially in a language she didn't understand. "Can't you see we have a situation here? You're not wanted. Go away."

Incomprehension was their only response.

Amalia came up behind her. "You can't say that to my brothers."

"Yes, I can. I just did."

Amalia seemed a little baffled by Kelly's logic. Kelly wasn't surprised. Obviously it didn't take much to confuse her poor little brain. To follow up on her advantage, Kelly added, "And if you don't like it, you can join them in the hall." One less person in the room would be a Good Thing.

"No," Amalia said, stomping her foot. "I stay here with Chaz."

"Fine," Kelly all but spat at her. "But your brothers stay outside. There's no room for them in here."

"No, they must meet Chaz," Amalia insisted.

"That's all right," Chaz said, holding his hands out in a warding-off gesture. "I can wait."

Of course he could, especially since the most likely

scenario was for the Garcia fists to meet Chaz's face. And she didn't want to be in the middle of a brawl in the bridal suite. "They stay outside," Kelly said firmly. "Take it or leave it."

Amalia frowned, but nodded in defeat.

Glaring at the beefy bookends, Kelly pointed to two chairs on the opposite wall and spoke in one-syllable words she hoped they could understand. "Sit. Stay."

Amalia added her bit by waving them toward the hall chairs with a few words of Spanish, and Kelly closed the door.

"Very good," Scott said. "And will you teach them to roll over and play dead next?"

"No," Kelly said, ignoring his untimely humor. "Next, I'm going to speak to Spencer." She'd put it off long enough.

As Scott sobered and they all turned to look at Spencer, Kelly added, "Privately. In fact, I'd appreciate it if you'd all leave."

"No way," Chaz exclaimed. "I'm not leaving you alone with *him*. Come on, Kelly. Give me another chance to prove I'm telling the truth."

She *so* didn't want to do this. Sighing, Kelly said, "Stop making assumptions."

"About what?"

"About everything, Chaz. About what I plan to say to Spencer, about you and me and our future together, about whether you even have the *right* to tell me what to do." She folded her arms and glared at him. "You don't."

"But—"

"I don't want to hear it. You gave up all rights to censure my actions when you slept with Amalia."

"But I *didn't* sleep with her," he said, exasperation strong in his voice.

"Tell that to her brothers." She turned to address the spectators. "In fact, you can all tell them—outside. Would you all please leave so I can talk to Spencer?"

Nobody moved.

"Okay, fine," Kelly said. Since she didn't intend to have this discussion in the hallway, she grabbed Spencer's hand and dragged him into the bathroom, then firmly closed and locked the door.

Inside, the luxurious accommodations were plenty big enough for their discussion, but they felt a little cold with all that pink and gray marble. Well, there was no help for it—she was just going to have to deal with it.

She glanced at Spencer's hopeful expression and took a deep breath. *God, this is hard.* "Spencer, I'm sorry it turned out this way."

He slumped against the marble vanity. "It's bad news, isn't it?"

But despite the dejection in his stance, he didn't look nearly as disappointed or despairing as Chaz. That should tell her she was doing the right thing, even if nothing else did. "I'm sorry, it wouldn't work. I don't love you as much as I loved Chaz."

"Loved? Past tense?" His spirits seemed to rise. "Does that mean you no longer love him?"

"I don't know." She had loved him so long, had worried about him for what seemed like forever. He was a part of her whether she liked it or not. Yes, she still loved him and nothing could change that. Except maybe distance. And time. "But I do know I can't live with him."

"Then stay with me," Spencer coaxed. "You could learn to love me. And I won't *ever* betray you."

Pain speared through her. Though she was certain he would never hurt her, she would never love Spencer the way she had loved Chaz. It wasn't fair to Spencer to pretend otherwise. She shook her head sadly. "It would never work. Besides, there is someone else who would love to be with you."

"Who?" Spencer asked in bewilderment.

"You know who," Kelly chided. "She's done some strange things the past couple of days, things that are out of character for her. And she didn't do them out of love for me."

Spencer shrugged. "Yes, I suppose I do know who you mean. But if you're not going to stay with Chaz, I might still have a chance with you. That's possible, isn't it?"

She hated to get his hopes up, but she didn't want to hurt him too much either. Especially since he looked so hopeful. "Anything's possible," she said gently. "But don't count on it. I'm not planning on changing my mind."

Spencer nodded thoughtfully. "Well, while I still have a chance, I'll wait for you. You're worth it."

He was very sweet, but she couldn't help but notice he'd said only that he'd wait for her, not that he'd fight for her. It only reinforced her decision to let Spencer go.

She leaned forward and kissed him on the cheek. "Don't wait too long. You deserve better than someone who doesn't love you. Think about Candace, okay?"

He just stared at her mutely, stubbornly.

Sighing, Kelly opened the bathroom door. It hadn't been easy but it had gone better than she expected.

Conversation ceased as soon as she opened the door and she felt the weight of everyone's gaze on her, silently asking what had just gone on in the bathroom.

In Chaz's case, hurt and despair went hand in hand with the unspoken question.

It's no one's business but mine, she wanted to scream at them. But she couldn't say that, and small talk was out of the question. A pregnant silence fell, which only ticked her off even more.

She was positively grateful when she heard a knock at the door. It gave focus to her anger. Kelly stalked across the room, preparing to give the Garcia brothers a piece of her mind whether they could understand it or not. She yanked open the door and froze as a flash went off in her face.

Blinking, she realized the flash was attached to a camera, which was attached to a reporter . . . one in a veritable sea of them, all surging toward her in an overwhelming wave, roaring out questions.

"Mrs. Vincent?"

"How do you feel about your husband coming back from the dead?"

"Will you answer a few questions?"

"Where has he been for the past five years?"

More flashes went off and Kelly finally unfroze long enough to slam the door in their faces. And throw the dead bolt. She turned to face the others and was surprised to see Chaz right behind her. Great—she was sure the pictures had captured both of them just perfectly.

Even worse, there went Kelly's only avenue of escape. Not to mention everyone else's. "Sorry, I thought it was Amalia's brothers." One of these days, she was going to have to learn to use the peephole.

Chaz shrugged. "Not your fault. Obviously, they already knew we were here."

"No," Kelly said with a shake of her head. "They only thought it. Now they know it." Sighing, she sat down on a nearby chair. "It looks like we're stuck here for awhile."

Her mother pierced her with a look. "Since we are, perhaps you would take a little time to explain yourself?"

"Explain what, Mom?" Kelly asked wearily. "You want me to bare my most intimate feelings in front of my publisher and Chaz's girlfriend? I don't think so."

"No," her mother said with a snooty tilt of her head. "But I think you owe it to us to let us know who you did choose." She cast a doubtful glance in Spencer's direction. "Apparently, Spencer and Charles know, so there's no sense in keeping us in suspense any longer."

Why not? "That's easy—I choose neither."

Her mother looked flabbergasted. "But—"

"It's not open for debate, Mother. I'm tired of this whole thing and I just want out. Is that so hard to understand?"

"No, it's not," Scott said and came over to give her a hug. "You deserve a break. What do you want to do?"

What she really wanted was to get out of here, but she could still hear the reporters out in the hallway, so that wasn't going to happen. She thought about it. "The first thing I need is a lawyer. I need to find out where I stand before I can do anything."

Scott nodded. "That makes sense. Would you like me to call Mr. Birnbaum?"

Kelly shook her head. Their family attorney was so old, she wasn't sure he could handle it. "This situation would probably shock him into a heart attack."

"So do you have someone else in mind?"

Well, there was one person. Kelly turned to her mother. "What about your boyfriend, Gerald Wainwright?" He had been pursuing her mother so hard the last few months, Kelly was sure he'd be willing to help. And though the portly attorney sometimes seemed more interested in his dinner than the law, he knew how to be discreet.

"He's not my *boy*friend," her mother said in indignation.

No, that term was too vulgar for her mother. "Your man friend then." And when her mother's expression didn't unfreeze, Kelly said, "Acquaintance. Whatever. Would you ask him to come?"

"I don't know. . . ." her mother hedged.

Kelly gave the door a significant glance. "Well, we can't exactly go to him, can we? Please, just call him. Don't try to explain the situation on the phone or you'll be at it all day. Just ask him to come. He'll do it for you." When her mother didn't move, Kelly added, "I can't do anything, one way or another, until this is resolved legally."

"Oh, all right," her mother said ungraciously and headed over to use the phone.

Kelly glanced around the room, taking in everyone's attitude. Chaz was surly, Amalia impatient, Spencer reserved, Candace hopeful, Grace annoyed, and Scott amused. Unfortunately, Kelly was stuck with the lot of them, *and* their emotions, until they figured a way out of this mess.

Great, just great.

Fourteen

Chaz glared at them all from his spot near the balcony, feeling the anger that had been simmering within him come to a boil. No matter what he said, Kelly seemed determined to believe the worst of him. Okay, he could understand that she might be a little ticked off that he had spent the past five years with Garcia, but she ought to believe him that nothing happened.

She needed to just get over it, tell him whatever he needed to do to fix it, and let them get on with their lives.

Unfortunately, she was being stubborn. He couldn't force her to believe him, and he didn't want to wait around until she finally decided to forgive him. For something he hadn't done, no less.

To hell with that. I want outta here.

Scott grinned. "Anyone care for a game of bridge?"

"Not funny," Chaz said with a growl.

"Hey, I was just trying to find a way to pass the time."

"Well, don't," Chaz snapped. He was sick of waiting. He headed for the door.

"What are you doing?" Kelly asked in alarm.

"I'm leaving."

She stepped in to block his path. "You can't."

"Why not? All I have to do is answer their questions and I'll be free to go. My fifteen minutes of fame—no big deal."

"But it *is* a big deal," she insisted. "They don't seem to realize the full impact of what's happened here and I'd like to keep it that way."

"Full impact?" What was she talking about?

Kelly rolled her eyes. "When they were yelling questions about me, there was one question that was conspicuously absent."

Chaz still didn't get it. He shook his head. "You're gonna have to spell it out for me."

"Ah, that question," Scott said in enlightened tones. "The one that goes, 'Are you a bigamist, Mrs. Vincent? Or is that Mrs. Preston?'"

Oh, *that* question.

Damn it, they were right. His escape now blocked, Chaz scowled. Only a total asshole would expose her to something like that. And in his current mood, he wasn't sure of his ability to keep the secret if they asked rude questions. But how long would he be stuck here?

He turned to Grace, who was finally off the phone. "So, is your boyfriend coming?"

She glared at him. "*Gerald* is more than happy to help, but he can't be here until tomorrow morning."

Shit. Spend the night with these people? No way. "I'm outta here," Chaz said before he even realized he'd spoken the words aloud.

"But I just told you why you can't leave," Kelly protested.

Chaz glanced around, feeling trapped in this damned frilly room, and looking for any means of escape. Then he spotted it. "Yes, I can," he said. He crossed to the chair by the door and snatched up the rope Billings had left. "With this."

Scott laughed. "Why not? You're still dressed for it."

Gee, thanks for reminding me. He glanced down. Changing clothes was yet another reason to get the hell out of this room, not to mention getting rid of the red negligee still hidden in his shirt. But that gave Chaz a plan. "I've got it all figured out." He glanced at Kelly. "Do you want to spend the night in this room until the reporters leave?"

"Not really."

And he sure as hell didn't want her in Deuce's clutches either. "Then we can make our escape while everyone else covers for us."

"I'm not sure what you mean," Kelly said hesitantly. "It's simple," Chaz said, running the rope through his hands. "You and I go down the rope, then two of these guys throw jackets over their heads and go out the door. The reporters will think it's you and me trying to avoid the cameras and follow them. They can lead them away from the third floor so all we have to do is sneak back in to go to our own rooms."

"We'll come back to the hotel?" Kelly asked uncertainly.

"Sure," Chaz said, warming to the plan. "They won't expect us to come back here, and you still need to stick around to wait for Gerald, right?" And Chaz had nowhere else to go at the moment.

"I guess so, but . . . who's going to pretend to be us?"

Chaz glanced around the room. "Scott can play me and . . ." He trailed off as he took in the female options. Gracie was out, and from the expression on

Candace's face, she didn't relish the idea either. "Uh, Amalia?"

Kelly looked pissed at the mere idea that Amalia could play her.

Amalia didn't look too happy about it, either. She crossed her arms and looked belligerent. "No. I will not leaf you alone with *her*."

"Would you rather I go out there and tell them she's my wife?" Chaz challenged.

Amalia pouted. "No."

"Then do this for me, please."

"Then you marry me?"

The whole room seemed to sigh in disgust as Amalia repeated her favorite mantra.

"I'll tell you what," Chaz said, prepared to deal. "If you can prove you are pregnant, then I'll consider it."

That seemed to stun everyone, which just made Chaz impatient. Did they think he was an idiot, fergawdsakes? This put the burden of proof on Amalia. Even if she was pregnant, which he sincerely doubted, he'd take all of half a second to "consider" marrying her.

He took advantage of the resulting silence to add, "Once Scott and Amalia have the reporters outside, all you have to do is refuse to answer any questions. They don't know who either of you are, so it shouldn't be a problem. Just pretend you wanted to leave the room without getting your picture in the papers. I'm sure Amalia's brothers will follow you, and once they realize their sister is being harassed by the press, they'll help you get rid of them."

"What about the rest of us?" Grace asked.

"Oh, stick a pillowcase over your head and run the

gauntlet," Chaz said carelessly. "They'll never know who you are."

"I'll do no such thing," Grace said, drawing herself up in indignation.

It was hard to believe this humorless woman had given birth to Kelly and Scott. Chaz sighed. "You won't need to. Once Scott and Amalia have drawn the reporters away, you and Candace can leave at your leisure. Even if some of the reporters do stick around or come back to this room, they don't know who any of you are. Just play dumb. It's me they want. And Kelly."

Scott nodded slowly. "That makes sense. I think it'll work, too." He grinned. "Hey, does that mean I get to wear your Zorro outfit?"

Much as Chaz would like to change clothes right now, he shook his head reluctantly. And he was *almost* sure Scott was kidding. "No, your denials will be more believable if you wear your own clothes."

Then, before anyone else could formulate any objections, Chaz grabbed the first two coats he could find and shoved them at Scott and Amalia. "Here." He went to look over the balcony. Good—no one was in the courtyard. Swiftly, he tied the rope to the railing. "Wait until we're safely down, then head out the door. Lead them out the south entrance, and we'll circle around to come in the north."

"Okay," Scott said, grinning like a fool. Chaz shook his head in disbelief. Scott was actually enjoying this.

"Come on, Kelly," Chaz said, determined not to lose momentum. "Let's go."

She glared at him, but headed toward the balcony.

"I'll go first," he said, "so I can catch you if you fall."

Her expression turned doubtful. "Fall?"

"Don't worry," he assured her. "It'll be easy. Just like last night, remember?"

"My memories of that part are a little hazy," she muttered with a wary glance over the edge.

Well, his weren't. He remembered how she had put her whole trust in him, had taken a leap of faith and jumped wholeheartedly into the adventure he had planned.

Too bad it hadn't lasted.

"You'll be fine. Unless you *want* to stay here. . . ?"

She glanced back at the roomful of people staring at her in varying forms of disbelief. "Okay, I'll do it."

Chaz quickly shimmied down the rope to the ground. Kelly, bless her, didn't even hesitate. She didn't need any help either, as she made it down easily.

She looked proud of herself, too, which surprised Chaz a little. He knew she could do anything she set her mind to, why didn't she?

A little breathless, Kelly looked at Chaz and her gaze sobered. "Are you really going to do it?"

"Do what?"

"Marry Amalia."

Anger rushed over him. How could she even ask such a question? "What do you care?" he snapped back at her. "You've just proved you wouldn't believe me, no matter what I say."

She looked taken aback, which just ticked him off even more. "C'mon," he said. "Let's get out of here." He strode off without a backward glance. Either she followed him or she didn't. At this point, he didn't care.

* * *

Candace peered down over the balcony. "They're down now," she told Spencer. And, amazingly, they were both safe. "You can untie the rope."

Spencer did, and nodded toward Scott. "Go ahead," he said. "They're leaving."

With a grin, Scott held Spencer's coat up over his head and instructed Amalia to do the same with Candace's. "Ready?" he asked the Latina, with a wicked grin.

"Yes," Amalia said, looking grim but determined.

"Okay," Scott said. "Candace, will you get the door? That way we won't have to worry about shutting it on the way out."

"Of course," Candace said. And she'd make sure she was behind it, far from any cameras. *Pizzazz* might not be able to weather the scandal if she was associated with this mess.

She opened the door and Scott and Amalia rushed out, holding the coats close against their faces. Candace quickly shut the door again, then couldn't resist a peek outside. "I don't believe it. The plan is actually working." The reporters all rushed off after the decoys, with Juan and Gilbert lumbering along in their wake.

She opened the door a little wider, cautiously. "They're all gone," she said in wonder.

"Good," Grace Richmond said and brushed past her. "I'm going to my own room before they decide to come back."

Candace said nothing as the haughty older woman left. Now, finally, Candace and Spencer were alone.

She closed the door and Spencer looked up in surprise from where he was coiling the rope. To prevent him from asking why she was still there, Candace said, "It looks like Chaz's plan is working."

"Yes," Spencer said with a grimace. "I hate to admit it, but he's very good at that sort of thing. Makes it hard to compete."

"Do you have to compete?" At his puzzled expression, she added in what she hoped was a nonchalant tone, "I mean, what did Kelly say to you in the bathroom?" Candace knew what Kelly had told them, but had she told Spencer anything different privately? He didn't seem upset. Did he think he still had a chance with her?

"The same thing she said to everyone else—she doesn't want either of us at the moment." He shrugged as if he didn't care, but she knew better.

"At the moment?" Candace didn't care for the sound of that.

"That's right," Spencer said with a grim smile. "That's how she feels now, but I'm not giving up hope. I've waited this long, I can wait a little longer."

Despair filled her. Couldn't he see it was hopeless? Couldn't he see that Candace loved him to distraction? But a little anger filtered through at his denseness. "Don't you think it's time to give up?"

"No. Why would I?"

She wanted to scream at him, but controlled her emotions firmly. "Well, it seems so . . . Pygmalion. You helped Kelly create herself in a new image, then fell in love with that image." As he seemed to ponder that, she added, "But who are you in love with? The real Kelly or the idealized version you created?"

He stared at her as if surprised she even had to ask. "I love the real Kelly, of course. I see her as she really is."

Candace sighed. She doubted that. No one seemed to know the real Kelly, least of all Kelly herself. But it was time for some plain talking. "You know it's obvious she loves Chaz. Even if she didn't, she feels an obligation to him. Once he showed back up in her life, I'm afraid you didn't have a chance."

Spencer slumped. "I know."

"Then why fight it? You know what the outcome will be."

"Because I hate to let him win at everything. The oh-so-charming Chaz Vincent has always been between us. The years of his captivity, she was always focused on finding him, always telling me how wonderful he was. And now that he's back, she sees his irresponsible ways as charming. And she thinks his theatrics—like climbing up to her balcony in some ridiculous costume—are romantic." He paused, his mouth set in an angry line. "It would serve him right if he were given a dose of his own medicine."

"What do you mean?" Spencer looked determined enough to do almost anything.

He gave her a look of surprise. "Nothing. Just that it would be nice if he were on the receiving end of some of his wild ideas for a change." Then a sudden calculating expression crossed his face.

Ignoring that, Candace returned to the subject that interested her the most. "So, if Kelly were out of the picture, would you see someone else?"

"Possibly," he said bitingly. "But I don't seem to be what women want. I'm not devil-may-care, flamboyant, or wicked."

"Not every man can be Chaz Vincent," Candace said. Then, her heart pounding in her chest, she decided to take a little risk. "But that isn't a bad thing, just different. You are handsome, elegant, suave, sophisticated. That's very sexy to some women."

That surprised him. "Sexy? You think so?"

"Very much so. Some women find that far more appealing." *Like me*, she wanted to add, but didn't have the courage. But she hoped her eyes conveyed the message she felt in her heart.

He nodded thoughtfully. "Maybe I should find such a woman then."

Finally. Candace tried not to let her exultation show as she said, "Yes, maybe you should."

Kelly had to hurry to keep up with Chaz's long strides. She sensed his mood had changed, but she didn't quite understand how. "What are you thinking, Chaz?" she said to his back.

No response, unless you counted a stiffening of his back and the fact that he picked up a little speed. She had to hurry even more to keep up with him. Okay, maybe he just wanted to get back in his room before the reporters spotted him again. She could understand that.

At least the view from this angle was really nice. No matter what she thought of Chaz's morals, she had to admit he was very sexy and had a cute butt, especially in those leather pants. But right now, even his butt looked taut and angry.

She followed him back into the hotel and up the stairs to the third floor. At the top of the stairs, she tried to catch her breath and spoke again. "What are you so ticked about? I'm the one you lied to."

Still no answer.

He peered out the stairwell door and must not have seen anyone, for he strode across the hall to his room. As he fished in his shirt for his wallet—it obviously wouldn't have fit in those tight pants—Kelly tapped him on the shoulder. "Hey, remember me? I want to talk to you."

He glared at her as he fit the key in the slot. "That's not what you said earlier."

"Well, I changed my mind." Especially since she wanted to know what the heck was going on in his. When he opened the door, she pushed her way in behind him. "And I'm not leaving until we talk."

He shut the door and bolted it. "Fine. Say what you have to say." He glared at her. "But I'm getting out of these clothes."

Now that he'd agreed to listen, she wasn't quite sure what to say. As she hesitated, he unbuttoned his shirt and pulled out the nightgown she had worn so briefly the night before, then dumped it on the floor.

She stared at the crumpled heap of red silk, feeling a shaft of pain pierce her. Why had he gathered it up so carefully this morning, only to discard it so callously now?

Okay, sure, she had done the same thing this morning. But she had been very angry, had felt betrayed by his eagerness to leave her again so quickly after he had finally come home. What right did he have to be angry at her?

Small feelings of guilt and doubt niggled at her. Chaz didn't normally get angry for no reason. Had she been too harsh with him?

His flowing white shirt hit the floor, landing on top of the red silk.

She glanced up to see Chaz glaring at her as he pulled a T-shirt down over his head. "Are you planning to feed me the same pap you gave Deuce? Well, save it."

There was that strange nickname again. "No, I just want to know why you're so angry."

"Do you have to ask?" he asked as he unbuttoned his pants.

"Yes," she said, swallowing hard and trying not to look at anything below his waist. "Explain it to me, Chaz."

His hands on his hips, Chaz leaned forward from the waist. "You want to know why? Fine. I'm angry that I came home to this stupid farce, that Garcia is a frigging clinging vine, that my wife is married to another man—"

"But—"

His raised voice rode over her protest like she hadn't even spoken. "And I'm totally pissed off that you don't believe a goddamned word I say."

"That's not true," she protested.

"Yes, it is. Garcia, who by the way hasn't lived in the real world for decades, makes up some little fantasy about me—and you believe her?"

"It sounded true. . . ."

"In what alternate universe?" he asked incredulously. He made an impatient gesture. "You know what? I think you were looking for a reason to punish me."

"What?" That didn't even make sense.

"Well, I'm no shrink, but even I can see that you haven't forgiven me for getting lost, for leaving you alone for so long. Rationalize it any way you want, it's obvious you're punishing me."

"I am not. I've been looking for you for five years. Why would I want to punish you once I finally found you?"

"Oh, I don't know. Maybe because you finally got your life just the way you like it? A good job, a wuss for a husband, and Mommy's approval? Well, you got it, babe. I hope you like it."

"But—" she began, only to cut her words short when Chaz turned his back on her, drew down the zipper and bent over to peel off his tight pants.

Her mouth dropped open as Chaz mooned her. Jeez, talk about body language. "Now that's just rude."

"You didn't think so last night," he said in biting tones as he rummaged in a drawer and pulled out some clothing. "I distinctly remember you admiring my bare ass." Then, unfortunately, he covered it with a pair of briefs.

"I don't want to talk about last night." Or his ass.

"Why not?" He jerked his jeans on and glared at her. "Remind you too much of what you'll be missing?"

Unfortunately, yes. "Last night was . . ." Wonderful, magical, romantic. It made what came afterward so much more disappointing.

"Was what?" he demanded. "Don't tell me you didn't enjoy it, because I know better."

Ignoring that, she drew herself up and said, "It was under false pretenses."

"What false pretenses?"

"I was under the impression that you were going to stay in this country."

He shook his head in disbelief. "You're as bad as Amalia."

Now there was an insult she couldn't ignore. Her eyes narrowed. "What do you mean by that?"

"You both live in fantasy worlds of your own imagining, where you're the queen of the world and everyone does exactly as you expect, no matter how much they hate it. There has to be some give and take in marriage, you know."

"I know. All I wanted was to spend some time with you, to live with you as husband and wife. Instead, you make plans to leave me at the first opportunity, without even consulting me. Where's the give and take there? That's not a marriage. That's a male version of heaven."

"What?"

"You know—come home to the compliant little wife, get your rocks off, then take off for something more exciting and adventurous." The truth of those words speared more pain through her heart. "I'd never be enough for you, would I, Chaz?"

"You're missing the point."

"Then tell me what it is."

He shook his head sadly. "The point is that you can't, you won't, trust me or forgive me."

There was a little truth in that, but . . . "Give me a reason to," she challenged.

He turned his back on her and started pulling more clothes from the drawer. "No, thanks. That's all I've been doing for the last few days, but it hasn't worked. I'm tired of it."

"So that's it? It's over, just like that?" And why did it make her want to cry?

Chaz stared at her in disbelief. "Isn't that what you said you wanted?"

"Yes, but . . ." Chaz had been fighting for her all along. Why was he giving up now? Then, as he stuffed some clothes into a backpack, she asked, "What are you doing?"

"Packing."

"I can see that. Why?"

He shrugged. "No reason to stay anymore. You've made that clear."

No, he couldn't leave again. Not when he had just gotten back. "You can't go now," she blurted out.

"Why not?"

"Because . . ." She searched for a reason to keep him here. "Because we don't know all the legal ramifications yet. You have to wait until we talk to Gerald, to see what our situation is in the eyes of the law." When he hesitated, she added, "It's only another twelve hours or so. Surely you can wait that long."

Chaz shook his head. "I can, but can the Garcia brothers?"

Oh. She'd forgotten about them. "Just stay in your room—they can't get to you then."

He gave a weary sigh and dropped the backpack on the bed. "Okay."

"You agree?" she asked in surprise. She hadn't thought it would be that easy.

He shrugged. "Why not? I don't want to argue anymore, and you're right. It won't hurt to wait a little longer."

Satisfied now that she had won at least a small concession, Kelly said, "I'll just go back to my room then."

"Wait a minute." Chaz crossed the room to peer out the peephole. "There's someone lingering in the hallway. Looks like a reporter."

She pushed him aside to look for herself. Darn it, he was right. "Do you mind if I stay a little longer, then?"

"You could try to make a break for it," Chaz said diffidently. "It's only one guy."

Ticked that he seemed so eager to get rid of her, Kelly peered out again. "That's true, but he has a camera and I'd rather not give him any more opportunities for unauthorized photos. Besides, he can't be sure we're here, or even which room we're in. Maybe he'll give up after a little while and go away."

Chaz shrugged. "Whatever. Stay if you want. I don't care."

Not exactly hospitable. But that didn't matter. For some strange reason, she was rather reluctant to leave. . . .

Fifteen

Not wanting to deal with the awkward silence, Chaz addressed another problem. "I'm hungry." Their continental breakfast seemed like ages ago, though it had only been a few hours.

A frown creased Kelly's brow. "What do you plan to do about it?"

"I thought I'd eat," he said dryly.

Kelly rolled her eyes. "You know what I mean."

Yeah, he was being difficult. So what? "We can order room service."

"But if they bring food to this room, the guy outside will suspect we're here, and we'll never get rid of him."

Annoyed, Chaz asked, "What do you suggest, then? All they have in this tiny fridge are some peanuts and snack stuff. That won't make a meal and they're not cheap."

"Maybe—"

The phone rang, interrupting her, and Chaz answered it.

"Hi, it's Scott. Say, that idea worked like a charm—"

Chaz interrupted him, asking, "Where are you?"

"Downstairs, in the lobby. Waiting for the reporters to clear out."

"Well, one of them came back up here and is lurking outside. Could you do us a favor and grab some burgers or something and bring them up to us? Kelly's here and she doesn't want anyone to know where we are."

"Sure," Scott said. "But won't he figure it out when I knock?"

Oh, that's right. Chaz thought a moment. "Don't knock, then. Just call from downstairs and we'll watch for you. Pretend you're putting your key in our door, and we'll open it. He won't know it's not your room."

"Okay," Scott said and they hung up.

"That was Scott," Chaz said, then added unnecessarily, "He's bringing us lunch."

"I heard," Kelly said.

And the awkward silence fell again. Chaz dropped into a chair while Kelly paced in the small confines of the room and looked out the peephole about every two minutes. After a half hour of that, he was ready to beg her to stop, but Scott finally called and they let him in as arranged.

Scott headed toward the desk with a bag that exuded the heavenly aroma of fries, but stopped abruptly and looked down at his feet. "Very nice," he said. "Tell me, does the red negligee go over or under the Zorro outfit?"

Damn it, Chaz had forgotten to pick the clothes up off the floor. He strode over and bundled them up, shoving them in a nearby drawer. "Neither," he said shortly. "They both came off at about the same time."

If he thought to disconcert Scott, he missed the mark, as was evident from Scott's smirk.

Kelly, though, looked a little embarrassed. "What did you bring us?" she asked, obviously trying to change the subject.

Scott offered her the large bag with the air of a man presenting her with precious jewels. "Burgers and fries as requested."

Good—man food. And lots of it. Chaz moved to clear off the desk.

"Did you bring anything to drink?" Kelly asked.

No complaints about the plebian food, he noticed. That was one thing Chaz had always liked about Kelly—she didn't share her mother's abhorrence of the common man's preferences.

"No, I was afraid the sight of three cups might tip off the guy in the hallway," Scott explained.

"No problem," Chaz said. "There are sodas in the fridge."

As they settled in to eat, Scott filled them in on what had happened. "It worked just the way you said it would," he said with a grin. "They chased us down the stairs and out the side door. I wasn't sure whether to keep on going or not, but one of them got the bright idea to grab Amalia's coat. He yanked it away from her, then another did the same to me."

Scott laughed. "They caught some of her hair in a button. You should have seen their faces when Amalia turned and started screeching at them."

"Did you tell them anything?" Kelly asked.

"Didn't need to. They obviously knew we weren't you guys, but they shouted a bunch of questions at us anyway. I just ignored them, but when one of the photographers was stupid enough to snap a shot of Amalia in full-tilt mode, one of her brothers broke the camera." Scott shook his head, smiling. "So the reporters yelled at them in English and they screamed back in Spanish. No one seemed to understand a word anyone else was saying. It was priceless."

"So, how'd you get away?" Chaz asked around a mouthful of fries.

"They got ticked off when Amalia called them *bastardos*—they understood *that* well enough—and surged forward. The Garcia brothers blocked them, and we were able to escape." Scott shook his head admiringly. "I tell ya, the Denver Broncos could sure use those guys."

"What happened to Amalia?" Chaz asked, hoping she hadn't decided to follow Scott.

"Oh, she was still raving as we came back into the hotel. One of the desk clerks made the mistake of asking her to lower her voice, and she lit into him. While she was still chewing him out, I got out of there."

"Good," Kelly declared. "Then they didn't get any more information from you."

"Not a word," Scott declared.

Chaz grinned. "Sounds like you enjoyed yourself."

"Yeah," Scott said. "I gotta hand it to you, Chaz. Life is never dull when you're around."

Too bad Kelly didn't feel the same way.

She wiped her mouth with a napkin and dropped the rest of her meal in the trash. "Do you think that trick would work again on the guy outside?" she asked Scott.

"No, he knows me now."

"And it would just confirm we're here," Chaz added.

Kelly sighed. "Then how am I going to get out of here?"

Scott glanced back and forth between them. "You really want out? After last night, I thought—"

Kelly cut him off with a gesture. "Yes, I want out."

But Chaz was beginning to wonder. Kelly had seemed awfully eager to get rid of him until he had gotten angry. Then she wouldn't leave him alone. What was going on?

And, he suddenly wondered, what would happen if they spent a little more time together, alone?

So when Scott gave him an inquiring look, Chaz shook his head slightly, trying to convey that he didn't want Kelly to leave.

Scott regarded him thoughtfully. "Well, you left the rope in Spencer's room, so that's out. Chaz is the man with the plans. You have any ideas on how to get her out without being spotted?"

"Sorry," Chaz said. "All tapped out. Besides, all we have to do is wait. Sooner or later he's gonna have to leave to get something to eat or go to the bathroom."

Scott nodded. "True."

"But what if he doesn't? I can't stay here all night," Kelly protested.

"Why not?" Scott asked. "It's a big bed and it's not like you haven't slept together before."

Was he under the impression he was helping? Chaz raised an eyebrow at Scott, who shrugged.

"This is different," Kelly insisted.

"How?" Scott asked.

"It just is. And we're not going to sleep together, so forget about it."

Scott shrugged. "Then maybe you can use the time to talk things out."

"We did that this morning," Kelly bit out. "That's why we're separating."

Damn, this was getting them nowhere. Chaz glared at Scott and gave another small shake of his head.

This time Scott seemed to get the hint, for he stood up and peered in the bag. "There's another burger and some fries left. Anyone want them?"

When Chaz and Kelly shook their heads, Scott rolled up the bag and said, "Okay, I'll take it, so it won't go to waste." Heading toward the door, he said, "Think it over, okay, Sis? You don't want to screw up the rest of your life with a bad decision."

Kelly just glared, so Scott shrugged and left.

Once the door closed, Kelly peered out the peephole again. "The reporter's still there." Then she gasped. "I don't believe it."

"What?"

She turned to stare at Chaz in disbelief. "Scott gave him the bag."

Chaz couldn't help but laugh.

"It's not funny."

Yes, it was. But all he said was, "Your brother has some strange methods of getting his own way."

"What do you mean?" Kelly demanded.

"Isn't it obvious? He wanted to make sure we'd be stuck here long enough to talk things out." Chaz gave her a considering look. "He has a point."

Kelly crossed her arms. "We have nothing further to say to each other."

Chaz sighed. This wasn't going to work. "Okay, maybe you're right."

She looked suspicious at his easy capitulation. "What does that mean?"

"You're right," he repeated. "I guess we've said it all." Besides, he was tired of arguing. Yawning, he headed for the bed.

"What are you doing?"

"Well, we didn't get much sleep last night, and I'm tired. The meal made me sleepy, too. I think I'll take a nap."

"What do you expect me to do?" she asked, her arms still crossed and her foot tapping impatiently.

He lay down on the bed and propped an arm under his head. "Whatever you want. Just do it quietly, okay? And please don't pace—you'll wear a hole in the rug."

"I'll just watch television then."

"I wouldn't advise it," Chaz said dryly. "The noise might alert the reporter that we're in here. "Why don't you lie down, too? You've got to be tired."

She ran a hand over her face. "Maybe I am, a little." She glanced dismissively at the bed, then gave the chair a considering look. "I'll use the chair."

"Come on," Chaz said impatiently. "That chair isn't comfortable enough to sleep in. All I'm suggesting is a little shut-eye. I'm too tired for anything else." That wasn't strictly true, but she needed to believe it or he'd never get any peace.

"Oh, all right," she said, in an ungracious tone.

Soon, they were both flat on their backs, at the outer limits of the king-sized bed, staring up at the ceiling. Chaz tried to relax, but the knowledge that Kelly was only a few feet away on a nice comfy bed made him stiffen in more ways than one.

Silent, unmoving, she seemed as tense as he was, and Chaz wondered what was going through her head. Was she yearning for him as much as he wanted her? Did she secretly want him to touch her, to cuddle her in his arms? Or was she waiting for him to make the mistake of touching her so she could lash out at him again?

Damn, if he could only read her mind. The stiffened posture of her body language said he'd draw back a bloody stump if he laid a single finger on her, but the fact that she had joined him on the bed hinted at mixed feelings. What should he do?

Indecision left him immobile and sleepless.

Aw, to hell with it. He really did need some sleep. With a sigh, Chaz resolved to catch a few winks and turned on his side, his back to her.

It seemed to be the right thing to do, for he could almost feel Kelly relax as she sighed, too, and turned her back on him.

Well, hell. Maybe he'd get lucky in his dreams.

Chaz woke slowly, feeling a little disoriented. It wasn't often he woke in a soft bed with an even softer woman in his arms. He lay cuddled up to Kelly spoon fashion, her back to his front, in a warm, comfortable position. *Is this a dream?*

Probably not. If this was one of *those* dreams, they'd both be naked. He took a deep breath and realized he could smell her distinctive fragrance of herbal shampoo and baby powder. That cinched it—he didn't usually notice scents in his dreams.

Unfortunately, he was becoming more awake by the moment. They must have slept quite a while, because it was dark outside. That made it seem all the cozier inside, here with Kelly. He cuddled closer, carefully, hoping she wouldn't wake and spoil the moment.

Relaxing, he opened his eyes and realized they were in the center of the huge bed. Somehow, they had both crossed the chasm between them to meet in the middle. He wished they could do the same with their marriage, but it seemed it was all or nothing with them, with neither willing to compromise.

Kelly stiffened a little, then relaxed. How odd. If

Chaz didn't know better, he'd swear she had just woken. Had she? Was she even now feeling the evidence of his desire against her backside? If so, why didn't she move? Say something?

He listened carefully. Her breathing had changed, so she must be awake, or at least on the verge of waking. Did she realize yet that it was Chaz holding her like this, as if they were meant to be together?

She let out a small sigh and snuggled closer until Chaz could almost hear the fierce pounding of her heart. Oh, she was awake all right, but for some reason, she was pretending she was still asleep.

Well, that was fine with him, if it let him continue holding her. Chaz nuzzled her neck and slid his hand up under her sweater to palm one of her breasts through her thin bra. He let out a sigh of contentment, hopefully making it sound like he was still asleep.

She didn't even move. What was she thinking now? Whatever it was, she didn't seem to object to his touch. He dared even more, moving his hand gently to fondle her breast. When she didn't object to that, he pressed his hips into her backside, rubbing himself against her, determined to enjoy this rare moment to the full.

God, that felt good. And she must agree, because she hadn't let out a peep of protest. In fact, judging by the hardness of her nipple and the soft sounds she was making, she was enjoying it just as much as he was.

Good. He wanted her to remember this, to remember what it was like between them. He wasn't very good with words, but this sort of communication was right up his alley. He'd just let his body do the talking for him, to remind her what she would be missing if she let him go.

They snuggled that way for a little while, and Chaz

was wondering if he was brave enough to move his hand lower and take it to the next step, when Kelly stirred. He held her tighter, unwilling to let her go, and hoping she wouldn't break the spell.

Unfortunately, she did. Pushing against his hands, she said, "Chaz? Wake up . . . let me go. I really have to go to the bathroom."

Chaz reluctantly released her. As he rolled away, he pretended he was only now waking up. He didn't need the pretense, but he suspected she did.

Cursing the fact that women had such tiny bladders, and that they had just lost the moment, he pounded his fists on the bed. Could he persuade her to join him again?

When she came out of the bathroom, he stretched his hand out on the bed and patted it invitingly with a raised eyebrow.

Kelly looked away, obviously uncomfortable. Ignoring his invitation, she peered out the peephole. "He's gone," she said softly. "I guess I should leave."

"You don't have to," Chaz said, equally as low. He didn't want to do anything to scare her away, and right now, it looked like she was wavering. Maybe she'd stay if he spoke gently and didn't spook her.

Still not looking at him, she added, "I've been wearing these clothes since yesterday. I really need to get out of them."

Not a problem. Take them off here.

But it wouldn't be smart to say that out loud just now, no matter how much he meant it. Luckily, there was more than one way to get what he wanted. "Want me to come with you?" When she shook her head, he added quickly, "Just to be sure no one is hiding, ready to jump out at you?"

"No, that's okay. Besides, even though the reporter is gone, one of Amalia's brothers is out there. And he's watching this door."

Damn, that messed things up. Okay, Chaz couldn't leave. So what could he say to make her stay? He rose from the bed. "Kelly, I . . ."

He hesitated, wishing someone would provide the perfect words to make everything all right between them.

Her gaze met his, and he sensed a hesitation in her. Should he ask her to stay? Or would she kick him in the teeth by rejecting him again? Would his request gain him everything he wanted . . . or only make things worse?

The moment stretched as he tried to decide and she waited for him to say something. But just as he was about to risk it all and ask her to stay, she looked away.

"I'd better go. I'll let you know when Gerald arrives in the morning."

And she was gone.

Chaz slumped back down on the bed. Damn, he'd had his chance and he blew it. Now all he could do was hope their short moments of bliss would help her realize they were meant to be together.

He killed the hours as best he could, with room service, television, and sleep, but it wasn't easy. He tried not to dwell on what the lawyer might have to say, but it was tough not to wonder if the man would convince Kelly that Chaz's death certificate meant that their marriage was equally lifeless.

But when he finally heard a knock on the door the next morning, all he felt was relief that the waiting was finally over.

Unfortunately, it was Amalia waiting for him, all

decked out in a tight black dress that showed her figure to its best advantage. Now *that* was calculated to piss Kelly off. "What?" he asked warily.

"They send me to get you. The lawyer, he is here."

Why would they send Amalia? Then he saw Juan and Gilbert lurking across the hall and realized she was probably the only one who could call them to heel. He hesitated for a moment, not putting it past her to concoct a plan to kidnap him, but a quick glance down the hall showed the door to the honeymoon suite was open and Scott was beckoning to him. Shrugging, Chaz followed her to the room.

He glanced around the suite and noticed the whole gang was there again, plus one. Chaz moved to stand by Kelly, who, in plain slacks and a silk blouse, looked far sexier than Amalia, and muttered, "Do they all have to be here?" At least Juan and Gilbert had been stationed outside to ward off any reporters who might show up.

Kelly gave an apologetic shrug. "They all insisted. And since they've been in it since the beginning, I figured they deserved to be here now, too."

Maybe, but Chaz was getting tired of having an audience to some of the most important moments of his life. "Okay, let's get on with it."

Gerald Wainwright looked around the room in perplexity. "I don't understand," he said to Kelly's mother. "Why are all these people here? Are they involved in your legal problem?"

"It's not my legal problem. It's my daughter's." Grace waved a hand dismissively. "Someone else can explain."

Scott stepped forward and opened his mouth, but Kelly stopped him with a dirty look and a hand on his chest. Chaz couldn't blame her. No telling what the story would be when Scott finished with it.

"I'll explain," Kelly said firmly. "And all of these people have a stake in the outcome . . . sort of. At any rate, they're all aware of the problem."

"What *is* the problem?" the attorney asked.

"Well, I married my first husband, Chaz, eight years ago. He was lost in the Amazon for five years and we never found him, so I had him declared dead, then married Spencer a few days ago."

Chaz nodded in agreement. It wasn't as entertaining as Scott would have made it, but it was succinct and factual.

"Yes, I'm aware of that," Gerald said. "But I don't see the problem. I'm sure Mr. Birnbaum made sure everything was legal—he's a stickler for these things."

"Well the thing is," Kelly said. "Chaz isn't dead. He's very much alive. In fact, he's standing over there."

She nodded in his direction and Chaz gave the lawyer a little wave. Scott snorted.

"You're her first husband?" Gerald asked.

"That's me," Chaz said cheerily. And if he had his way, he'd be her only husband.

"I see," Gerald said faintly. Turning to Kelly, he asked, "Do you have proof of all these . . . proceedings?"

"Yes, I do." She pulled a large manila envelope from a nearby dresser and handed it to him. "I thought I might need it at the wedding or the funeral, just in case . . . someone . . . challenged me."

She threw Chaz an apologetic glance and he nodded reassuringly. By "someone" he knew she meant a member of his family. He was just surprised they hadn't made some kind of stink—it was their favorite hobby.

Everyone watched intently while Gerald perused the documents. "Everything seems in order here," he finally said.

"But what does it mean?" Kelly asked. "Am I a . . . bigamist?"

"No, no, of course not," he reassured her. "Since Mr. Vincent is deceased in the eyes of the law, your marriage to Mr. Preston is quite legal. I'm sure you are in no danger of being convicted of bigamy."

Kelly and Deuce looked relieved, but Chaz was confused. "Where does that leave me? Obviously, I'm not dead, no matter what that paper says."

"Of course not," Gerald said a bit pompously. "I think it will be quite easy to establish the fact that you're alive."

"No," Chaz declared impatiently. "I mean, where does that leave my marriage to Kelly? We were married eight years ago," he shot a glare at Deuce, "*long* before her second marriage, and we were never divorced. Doesn't that marriage take precedence?"

Gerald fiddled with the papers. "Well, er, I'm not quite sure. I've never actually heard of such a situation."

"Guess, then," Chaz said with narrowed eyes.

"Well, at first blush, I'd have to say that your marriage was dissolved when you were officially declared . . . deceased."

Damn it, that wasn't what he wanted to hear. "Are you sure?"

"No, I already said I wasn't," Gerald said huffily. "I haven't had a chance to research it yet. And I'm not certain there are any legal precedents."

"So maybe you're wrong?" Chaz persisted.

"That's quite possible," the attorney said. "I'll know more when I have time to check it out." He glanced at Kelly. "May I keep these papers awhile?"

"Yes, of course," Kelly said. But she wouldn't meet Chaz's eyes.

"Look at the bright side," Scott said. "At least Kelly's not a bigamist."

"Not in the eyes of the law," Chaz shot back. "But the eyes of the world are another matter." She might still be vilified in print, no matter what the courts said.

Kelly held a hand to her mouth as the implications evidently sank in. "Oh, no. He's right."

"Well, I can do nothing about that," Gerald said. "But in order to advise you further, I need to know which husband you intend to . . . keep."

Yes, that was the million-dollar question, wasn't it?

All eyes turned to Kelly. She raised her chin and looked only at the lawyer. "Neither."

Chaz bit back a swear word. Wrong answer.

Gerald nodded in what he probably intended as knowing wisdom, but it came across as bafflement struggling with surprise. "I see. Well, then, a simple divorce should take care of the second marriage."

"Annulment," Chaz corrected him. "It wasn't consummated." He wanted to make that very clear.

"Er, I'm not sure there are grounds for annulment under Colorado law," the lawyer said, beginning to look uncomfortable. But at Chaz's glare, he added quickly, "And I'll have to research to determine if anything needs to be done to dissolve the first marriage beyond what has already been done."

Chaz glanced at Kelly, hoping she would disabuse the attorney of the notion that she wanted to be parted from him, but she said nothing. Aw, hell. Was this it? Was their marriage over, kayoed by a technicality?

Amalia moved forward eagerly. "Now Chaz can marry me, yes?"

"I'm not sure of that," Gerald repeated. But, obviously puzzled, he asked, "Who are you?"

"The mother of his child," she said brightly.

Chaz just let his head drop into his hands and moaned.

"I see," Gerald said primly. "That complicates things. However, I shall endeavor to do my utmost to get this cleared up before the baby is born. Er, when would that be?" he asked, staring at Amalia's flat stomach.

"Never," Chaz said, annoyed that he had to explain this again. "She's not pregnant, and I'm not marrying her. I'm still married to Kelly." He added that last fiercely, as if by willing hard enough he could make it so.

Amalia narrowed her eyes. "But you said you marry me if I help you."

"No," he corrected her. "I said I'd consider it if you could prove you're pregnant."

"Okay," Amalia said brightly. "I prove it."

"How?"

"A simple home pregnancy test can confirm it in a few minutes," Kelly put in diffidently.

Now that was interesting. All of a sudden Kelly was giving him the benefit of the doubt? "All right," Chaz said, wondering what he was letting himself in for. "But I want another witness, to make sure she's telling the truth."

He glanced around at the possible candidates. It should be a woman, to make sure Amalia was the one who actually peed on the stick, or whatever she had to do. Kelly and Grace were out, for obvious reasons. "Candace, will you be my witness . . . and let us all know how it comes out?"

"Of course," Candace said.

Chaz didn't know why she was being so helpful, but he didn't care. From the interest on Kelly's face, at least his wife would stick around long enough to hear the results.

His spirits rose. Once Kelly learned Amalia had lied about being pregnant, maybe she'd stay even longer so they could kiss and make up.

Then a horrifying thought struck him. That is, if the test showed what he expected. What if it didn't? What if Amalia was pregnant with another man's child?

Sixteen

A niggle of doubt tickled Kelly's conscience. If Chaz was so insistent on the pregnancy test, could it be because he knew he was right?

Maybe. Then again, Amalia was equally as insistent that she was carrying his child. Who should Kelly believe?

Well, it didn't matter. The results of the pregnancy test should clear that question up. But . . . then what? If Chaz was telling the truth, did that mean Kelly should reconsider her decision?

She shook her head in disbelief. She'd flip-flopped back and forth so much lately, she felt like a damned pancake. Never mind. She was too confused to even think about all that now. She'd just wait and see how she felt when the results were known. But one thing was for sure. She had to stop being wishy-washy and make a damned decision.

Candace stood and glanced at her watch. "I doubt the hotel gift store has a pregnancy test, so it'll take me a little time to find a drugstore and get back here and perform the test with Amalia. Shall we meet back here in about an hour?"

Chaz nodded. "Good idea."

"Why don't you come with me?" Candace said to

Amalia. And she must have taken pity on Chaz, for she added, "Your brothers can come, too."

Amalia pouted. "No. They must watch Chaz so he not get away."

Somehow, with the mere lift of an eyebrow, Candace managed to give the impression that Amalia's suggestion was absurd. "You needn't worry about that. Chaz is as interested in the outcome of this test as everyone else." She glanced at Chaz and when he nodded, Candace added, "I promise he'll be here when we get back."

"That's right," Chaz said and headed for the door. "I'll be in my room. Call me when you get back."

He opened the door but halted abruptly when he came face-to-face with Amalia's brothers. "Explain it to them," he said curtly.

Amalia did so with poor grace as she and Candace exited and the brothers followed.

Once Chaz headed off to his room, Kelly didn't see any reason to stick around, so she left as well.

"Can I come with you?" Scott called after her.

"Sure." It would help pass the time.

As Kelly and her brother settled themselves in her room to wait, Scott smiled and asked, "So, which way do you want this to go?"

"What do you mean?"

"Do you want her to be pregnant or not?"

"How can you ask that?" Kelly said in disbelief. "Why would I want her to be pregnant?"

"Because if she is, that would mean you're right about Chaz. Or would it?"

Confused, Kelly said, "I don't understand what you're getting at."

Scott shrugged. "It doesn't really matter what the

test shows, does it? Even if she is pregnant, there's no proof that Chaz is the father."

"True, but—"

"And if she's not pregnant, that's no guarantee that Chaz didn't sleep with her."

She hadn't thought about it that way. "You're right." Her shoulders slumped. Either way, she still wouldn't have conclusive answers.

"Which means you still have a decision to make."

"No, I already made it."

Scott shook his head. "Not really. That was a knee-jerk reaction. I know it seemed like a good idea at the time to renounce both of them, but is that what you really want? To spend the rest of your life alone?"

Kelly lifted her chin. "What makes you think I'd be alone?"

His mouth quirked in a sad smile. "I don't really, but it's hard enough finding one person in a lifetime who seems like the perfect mate. You found two. Do you want to tempt fate by trying for a third?"

He had a point, but she hadn't expected her carefree brother to espouse such a view. Was he lonely? She had concentrated so much on herself over the past few years, she didn't really know how her brother's love life was going. "Maybe not."

He grinned, his uncharacteristic melancholy suddenly wiped away. "Besides, you've already trained these two husbands. It'd be a shame to have to start all over again with a new one."

Kelly laughed at the thought of training Chaz to do anything. "What do you suggest?"

He pondered for a moment. "Can I assume Spencer is out of the running?"

"Yes, I don't really love him. And I told him so."

"Do you love Chaz?"

She hesitated. That was the crux of the matter, wasn't it? "Yes, but I don't know if I can live with him."

"Why not?"

That's right—Scott didn't know. "Chaz is planning to leave for Turkey right away." Her mouth twisted in a grimace. "But he waited to drop that little bombshell until after we made love and I was naked in his arms."

Scott winced. "Too much information, Sis."

"Well, you asked. See why I'm so upset?"

"Can't you work it out somehow?"

"No. He won't stay here and look for another job, and I can't go through losing him again." She gave Scott a pleading look. "You know better than anyone what I went through. I can't spend my life waiting for him, never knowing if he'll come home or not."

Scott nodded thoughtfully. "That is a problem. But I see why he doesn't want to stay."

"What?" She stared at him in disbelief. "I thought you were on my side."

"I am, always, but I can see his side, too."

"What side?"

"You know Chaz is a thrill seeker. He's never going to be happy with a nine-to-five job. If he stays, he'll be bored out of his skull and miserable."

Scott didn't get it. "If he loves me, he'll stay and work it out."

"If you love him, you'll let him go," Scott countered.

"Hell, he's going anyway. I can't stop him."

"You're at a standstill, then."

"Yes, that's what I've been trying to tell you. You're

very glib, but the fact is, I'm not enough incentive for him to stay here." And that still hurt.

"No, I think it's the opposite," Scott said softly. "I think you're too much for him."

She scowled at him. "That might sound good, but it doesn't make sense."

Scott shrugged. "What I mean is, if he stayed, he would try to please you, but he'd be so miserable, he wouldn't be able to do that, and that would hurt him. It's obvious the man adores you."

"Is it?" she asked in a small voice. "I haven't seen much evidence of it."

"Yeah, right. Pull the other one. What do you call the fact that he dressed up like a make-believe character and climbed up three stories to romance you? Sounds like love to me."

"Well, maybe." He had tried awfully hard, hadn't he? Could Scott be right?

"Hell, even Amalia sees it or she wouldn't have had to call in her personal bodyguards to keep him away from you."

She hadn't looked at it that way. . . .

"You have to decide if you believe him or not."

"I've tried to believe him, I really have," Kelly protested. "But how could he have resisted Amalia for five years? Just look at her."

"I have. And I'm sick of her after only a few days. Can you imagine what five years with that woman would do to a man? I'm surprised he's sane. Hell, I'm surprised he's still heterosexual."

"But—"

"And any man who loves you as much as Chaz obviously does wouldn't give a piece of work like that a second look."

"You really think so?" And why did she sound so damned needy when she asked that?

"Of course I do," he said in exasperation. "Think about it. When he was with you, did he ever stray? Or even look at another woman?"

"No. . . ."

"Then why would you assume he did with Amalia? People don't change that much."

She hesitated, unable to answer his question, especially since he had a good point.

"Why are you so willing to believe the worst of him?" Scott persisted.

"I don't know." Kelly paused, thinking. Had she taken his love for granted? Was she being too harsh? "Chaz says I'm punishing him for being gone so long."

"Are you?"

She'd thought it absurd when Chaz said it, but there could be a kernel of truth there. "Maybe."

"Then don't you think he's been punished enough?"

She couldn't think straight. Too many things were floating around in her head. Unlike the White Queen in *Alice in Wonderland,* Kelly couldn't believe six impossible things before breakfast, let alone a dozen conflicting ideas.

But one thing was clear. Scott was right. Chaz was a very honorable man. And if that was true, she had to believe Chaz was innocent of everything Amalia had accused him of.

Relief filled her. Of course he was. If Kelly had been thinking clearly, she never would have doubted him.

"Okay," she admitted. "So I believe Chaz is telling the truth. So what? That still doesn't change the fact that he's leaving me again."

"Then give him a reason to stay."

"I did the other night. Several times. Hell, it was the best sex of our lives. If that doesn't make him stay, what will?"

Scott held his hands out in a warding gesture. "I *so* don't want to know this."

"He's leaving," she said again, more firmly. "And it'll break my heart."

"Then give him another reason to stay," he repeated.

"Like what? Pretend I'm pregnant like Amalia did? Even if I was willing to lie like that, which I'm not, it's way too early to tell." Besides, she was on birth control because of her wedding to Spencer.

"No, I mean help him find something else here to interest him. A fun job."

"Like what?"

"I don't know. Something dangerous like testing parachutes, or teaching people to bungee jump . . . or working at the post office. Something that would satisfy his desire for adventure but still keep him here."

"I'd still be scared to death he'd kill himself," she protested.

"Well, maybe. But at least he'd be here, and happy. Which would you rather have? Chaz in Turkey where you have no idea what kind of danger he might be in . . . or Chaz here in a known danger?"

"I'd rather not have him in danger at all," she snapped. That was the whole problem. "It's the waiting and worrying that kills me. The not knowing."

"And if he stayed here in a boring job just because you asked it of him, would you love the man he would become?"

Damn Scott—he was right. Chaz wouldn't be the man she loved if he weren't impulsive, flamboyant, larger-than-life. If he lost that, he wouldn't be himself anymore. And she would miss that terribly.

For the first time in the past few days, she was absolutely certain about something. She wanted Chaz in her life, no matter what. They'd find some way to work it out together. They had to.

Now she just had to find Chaz and convince him.

As Candace drove back to the hotel with all three Garcias in her car, she marveled at the difference in them. She had thought she would feel uneasy with the large men around, but once Chaz was out of the picture, they relaxed and became more human.

As the two men joked and teased their little sister, whom they clearly adored, it became obvious the family was very close. It went quite a ways toward explaining why they were so adamant about Amalia getting married, even if the man she wanted didn't want her. And finding her alive after her five years of imprisonment probably made them a little overprotective as well.

Their demeanor changed as they came back to the hotel and headed back upstairs, where the brothers became stern sentries of their sister's virtue once more. And when Spencer let Candace and Amalia into the suite, the Garcia brothers automatically took up positions outside the door without even being asked.

"Sorry," Candace said to Spencer with an apologetic smile. "But can we use your bathroom for this?" Candace was reluctant to let any of this madness into her room. Besides, everyone was returning to his room to learn the results of the test anyway.

"Of course," Spencer said. "I'll just, uh, go . . ." He

waved vaguely in the vicinity of the open door to the hallway.

"It's all right," Candace said in amusement. "You don't have to help."

He turned red. "I didn't think . . ." Shaking his head and giving Amalia's brothers a speculative glance, he said, "Never mind. I just need to get some . . . uh, shaving cream from downstairs. I'll be right back."

Candace followed Amalia into the bathroom, but luckily, she seemed to recognize what was necessary and did it without Candace having to explain. A little uncomfortable with the situation, Candace turned her back and busied herself with reading the box while Amalia followed the instructions.

When she finished, Candace said, "Okay, now we need to wait a few minutes." They waited in an uncomfortable silence while Candace wondered what to say to Amalia if the test turned out negative, which she rather suspected it would. When time was finally up, Candace said, "Let's check it."

Amalia picked up the tester and handed it to Candace, beaming. "See, I am pink."

Surprised, Candace looked at it, then patted Amalia's hand. "Yes, there is one pink line, but that doesn't mean you're pregnant."

"Why not?"

Candace showed her the box. "See? You must have two pink lines, to form a plus sign. You're not pregnant, Amalia."

Amalia frowned, but she didn't seem terribly disappointed or surprised.

"I think you knew that all along, didn't you?" Candace asked gently.

Amalia shrugged and wouldn't meet her gaze.

"Why did you say you were?" Candace asked. What had it gained her?

Amalia sighed. "You don't understand."

"Can you explain it to me?"

"Why?" she asked, pouting.

"I'd like to understand." Candace needed to know if lying was a way of life for this woman or if she had a good reason for what she'd done.

When Amalia hesitated, Candace added, "I don't want to judge you, I just want to know why you said you were pregnant." To know if she could trust her enough to hire her.

Amalia sank down on the edge of the tub and ran her hands through her long tangle of hair, her expression somber. "I come home after five years with Chaz in the jungle, and you know the first question my mother ask me?"

"What?"

"She ask me when do we get married." Amalia threw her hands in the air. "What can I say? I know she is right. I live with him for many years, we should marry."

"But it doesn't work that way in our culture," Candace said gently.

"But my mother, she not understand that. It is a matter of honor. Honor for me. Honor for my family."

"But there is no honor in breaking up another woman's marriage. You can see Chaz loves his wife. Can't you give him up?"

Amalia shook her head. "I cannot go home without a husband. My mother throw me out."

"Don't you have a job that would help you live on your own?" Surely she wasn't totally dependent upon her family.

"No. My brother Francisco get me the guide job to work with him. I hate that job. All the time work in the jungle." She made a face. "I never go back there again. I must marry Chaz."

Candace was beginning to comprehend a little more. Amalia did have a good reason for insisting on marriage, at least in her mind. No wonder she'd pursued Chaz so assiduously. "Do you want to go home?"

Amalia shrugged. "I haf no choice."

"But what if I gave you a choice? What if I offered you a job here, in Colorado?"

Amalia eyed her suspiciously. "What kind of job?"

"One where you would wear lovely clothes, make lots of money, and have your picture in magazines all over the world."

"Such a job . . . it is possible?"

"Yes, it is. I'm the publisher for *Pizzazz*, and we're looking for a young woman to represent our magazine, someone who is the essence of *Pizzazz*."

"What is this . . . pizzazz?"

"It is what you have—excitement, a zest for living, a love for the finer things in life."

"I can get a visa?" Amalia asked doubtfully.

"Yes, of course. Who knows, you might become a supermodel."

Amalia's eyes widened—that word she knew. To entice her even more, Candace added, "Why, you might become so famous you could even hire your brothers as bodyguards."

"Oh, no," Amalia said. "Juan is a teacher at the university and Gilbert owns three *restaurantes*. They would not like to be my bodyguards."

Candace blinked. That would teach her to judge on appearances. "Well, will you think about the job? If you take it, you'll have men fawning all over you. You won't need Chaz." Or her mother's approval.

"I think about it," Amalia said, the wheels already seeming to turn in her head.

Good. Maybe the lure of the job would get her mind off Chaz, so he could reunite with Kelly and free Spencer. Candace patted Amalia's hand. "I'm glad to hear it because I just heard a knock. It sounds like the others are arriving and I'll need to tell them the truth." She checked her watch. They were a little early.

Amalia sighed. "Yes, I see. Is okay if I go now?" She averted her gaze, looking uncomfortable. "I need to be alone for awhile."

She probably didn't want to face the embarrassment when Candace explained the results of the test. "Of course. I'll explain for you."

Candace opened the door and Amalia breezed out as Kelly and her brother entered.

Kelly glanced around, looking worried. "Have you seen Chaz? I called his room but he didn't answer."

"No, you're the first to arrive."

"Where are the bookends?" Scott asked.

"Juan and Gilbert?" Candace asked, not sure if that's what he meant. When he nodded, she said, "They were outside the door when I arrived."

"Well, they're not there now," Scott said with a frown. "Do you suppose they had to chase some reporters off?"

"I don't think so—we didn't hear or see anything."

The door opened and they all turned to stare at Spencer who was just now returning . . . empty-handed. His expression was a little odd, too. He looked as if he'd been up to something. A suspicion struck her. "Where's the shaving cream?"

"Shaving cream?" Spencer looked baffled for a moment, then uncomfortable. "They, er, didn't have any."

He was a horrible liar. But if he hadn't left to get shaving cream, what had he left for? Candace covered her mouth as the implications became clear. "Oh, no, what have you done?"

Seventeen

Kelly stared at Candace in puzzlement. What did she suspect? Did it have something to do with Chaz and the Garcia brothers being missing?

Uh-oh. With sudden apprehension, Kelly repeated Candace's question. "What have you done, Spencer?"

He lifted his chin. "Chaz Vincent isn't the only man who can develop a plan and follow it through," he said in a sulky tone.

"What plan?"

Instead of answering the question, Spencer said, "He deserved it after what he did to you."

"He didn't do anything," Kelly said. "And even if he did, he's been punished enough. What did you *do*?" Then the pieces clicked into place. "You speak Spanish, don't you? I remember hearing you speak it on the phone at the office."

"A little."

"You talked to Amalia's brothers, didn't you?" she persisted, taking a threatening step toward him as Candace and Scott watched in apprehension.

He took a step back, looking wary. "You weren't supposed to find out yet."

"When was I supposed to find out? When they found Chaz's body?"

Spencer scowled. "Don't be melodramatic. All I did was tell them Amalia was pregnant and Chaz was leaving town."

Fury rose within her. "That's all? That's the worst possible thing you could have done."

"It isn't as bad as you think. They just went to have a little . . . discussion with him in his room."

"That doesn't make sense. Chaz wouldn't open the door to them. Unless . . ." Her eyes narrowed as she moved even closer. "You persuaded him to open the door and *you* let them in. Didn't you?"

"Well, they needed an interpreter . . ."

Rage filled her and before she could even think about what she was doing, she slapped him.

Shocked silence filled the room and Spencer stared at her with his hand to his cheek. "I can't believe you did that."

"And I can't believe you left Chaz to their mercy. If they hurt him, I'm going to do a whole lot worse than that to you."

Scott came to stand by her side, his face grim. "And I'll help her."

"No, it's all right," Candace said in a conciliating tone. "I had a long talk with Amalia. They're not what you think. They're educated men. Civilized. I'm sure they won't hurt Chaz."

"They think Chaz has dishonored their sister," Kelly snapped back. "Even civilized men resort to violence in such circumstances."

"They didn't hurt him," Spencer said. "Well, only a little when he struggled. They tied him to a chair and Juan went to get a priest."

It wasn't until Spencer took several steps backward that Kelly realized she had taken a number of menacing paces toward him. "You mean you allowed them to tie up Chaz? A man who has been held captive in very primitive circumstances for the past five years? A man who just escaped his horrible prison? How could you be so unfeeling?"

"Me?" Spencer said. "What about him? He stole my wife."

Men.

Kelly rolled her eyes, unable to believe this. "I was *his* wife first," Kelly reminded him curtly. "And so far as I'm concerned, I still am." No longer feeling sorry for Spencer, she looked him up and down with scorn, adding, "It looks like I made the right choice."

There. That should kill any hopes he had of them ever making a go of it. Not to mention the slap.

Candace patted Spencer's arm consolingly, but he didn't look like a man who had just been spurned. He looked self-righteous and offended.

Well, Kelly didn't care how he felt. She had to get Chaz out of this mess. But first, she needed to know how things stood. Turning to Candace, she asked, "Is Amalia pregnant?"

"No."

"Thank goodness." That would make it a little easier to extricate Chaz.

"That's why she left," Candace added. "So she wouldn't be embarrassed when I told you. She had a good reason—"

"I don't want to hear it," Kelly said dismissively. "Do you know where she is?"

"No, but I had the impression she was leaving the hotel."

Great—the one time Kelly really needed the woman, she was missing. Grabbing Spencer's arm,

Kelly towed him out the door, saying, "Come on, you're going to fix this."

Mother arrived then, with Gerald in tow. "What's the meaning of this?" she asked in outraged tones.

"None of your business," Kelly said, her fury allowing her to say things she would normally never say to her stiff-necked mother. "Back off."

But of course Mother wouldn't bow out simply because Kelly asked her to. Grace followed as Kelly dragged Spencer to Chaz's door where a belligerent Garcia brother glared down at her, his arms folded. The fact that everyone had followed to watch the show probably wouldn't help her case, but she had to try anyway.

"Tell him Amalia's not pregnant," Kelly insisted.

Spencer did so, in halting Spanish. A short conversation ensued.

When Spencer paused, Kelly asked, "What did he say?"

"Gilbert doesn't believe me. He says you are forcing me to tell him lies."

Kelly rolled her eyes. Gilbert had an exaggerated opinion of her influence on Spencer. "Tell him that's why Amalia isn't here. She was so embarrassed by being caught in a lie that she's gone into hiding."

"I'll try," Spencer said hesitantly. "But my Spanish isn't very good." He held another short conversation with Gilbert, then said, "He says the reason she left is because of shame, that a priest will fix everything."

This was getting them nowhere. Kelly took a determined step forward and tried to push past Gilbert, but it was like trying to move a slab of granite. She stopped trying, realizing that, even if she could get past him, she didn't have a key to get in the room. Either he or Juan must have it, and she doubted they'd let her frisk them.

"This isn't working," Scott said, stating the obvious. "We'll just have to wait until Amalia returns so she can tell him the truth."

"But what if Juan returns first?"

"Well, they still have to find Amalia," Scott said reasonably. "Or the priest won't do them any good. We'll just have to wait."

"I can't wait. I have to help him get free," Kelly insisted. Chaz had hated being confined in the closet. Imagine how he was feeling now that he was tied up and couldn't get free.

Grace made an impatient gesture. "Oh, for heaven's sake. Just leave Charles there until they return. He'll be fine."

"He'll be fine?" Kelly repeated incredulously. "He's tied to a chair, beaten, imprisoned in his room, and probably terrified of what's going to happen to him. What if they did that to you? Would you think it's fine then?"

"Don't be ridiculous," her mother said in distinctly huffy tones.

"Well, I'm not going to just leave him there," Kelly said.

"It won't really hurt him," Grace said. "And I'm sure Charles is used to this sort of thing. There's nothing you can do."

Wrong. There had to be something she could do. Chaz needed her, and she was determined to free him. It was a matter of honor.

How ironic. That's exactly what Chaz would say.

Her mind raced. But what could she do? What would *Chaz* do in a situation like this?

A slow smile spread across her face. The very thing. Grabbing Spencer's arm, she hauled him back to his room. "Open up."

He did as she asked and she glanced around swiftly until she found the rope on the chair where Spencer had left it, then grabbed it.

"What are you going to do with *that*?" her mother asked.

"Hang Spencer," Kelly said shortly.

Spencer took a step back, his hand to his throat, and Candace laid a protective arm about his waist.

Kelly rolled her eyes. "Sheesh, it was a joke." Though Spencer deserved it after what he'd done to Chaz.

Spencer scowled. "You're beginning to act more and more like Chaz."

She was certain he meant it as an insult but said, "Thank you," just to annoy him. She'd much rather be like adventurous Chaz than stuffy Spencer. Why hadn't she realized that sooner?

"What are you really going to do with that rope?" Grace repeated.

"I don't think I'll tell you." Kelly had no intention of arguing about what she had planned.

Grace crossed her arms. "Well, whatever it is, I'm not going to let you do it. I'm sure it's dangerous."

As a matter of fact, it was. "You can't stop me." She pulled her brother aside. "Scott, will you help me with this?" she whispered.

"Sure." He eyed the rope doubtfully. "What do you have planned?"

"I'll have to find a way to rescue Chaz from the outside since I can't get past Gilbert from the inside."

"Want me to help?"

"The best way you can help is to stay here and guard

these idiots," Kelly said, exasperated. "Make sure Mother doesn't try to follow me and make a scene, and that Spencer doesn't make things worse by talking to Gilbert or Juan. Can you do that?"

"Okay, if that's what you want. Are you sure you don't want my help with the rope?" he asked plaintively.

She grinned at him. "I know I gave you the hardest job, but I really do need you to do this for me, Scott. I wouldn't ask if it wasn't important."

He sighed. "I know that. But be careful."

"I will," she promised him. Now that she'd decided she wanted to spend the rest of her life with Chaz, she wanted him to know as soon as possible.

Clutching the rope tightly, she headed for the door. When she did, Mother and Spencer moved toward her with determination in their faces. She didn't know if they were trying to stop her or simply talk to her, but she didn't care. Ducking behind Scott, she opened the door and was thankful he moved to block anyone from following her. Good. He had her back covered. Now to rescue Chaz.

As Kelly headed out the door, Candace wanted to scream in triumph. Not that she would actually do such a thing in public, but it was very tempting at this moment. Surely Kelly's slap had changed Spencer's mind about her.

Grace glared at her son. "Move, Scott. I must stop Kelly from doing anything foolish."

Scott shook his head. "Sorry, but I can't do that. Kelly's right. She has to do this—for her sake and Chaz's—and I'm not going to let you or anyone else stop her." He even folded his arms and glared at his mother, evidently doing his best to look like an immovable rock.

It must have worked, for Grace made a small huff of impatience and stalked off to sit in a corner of the room.

Catching Candace's eye, Scott made a small encouraging movement of his head in Spencer's direction. Yes, an excellent idea.

Pulling Spencer aside so the others couldn't hear them, Candace asked in her most sympathetic tones, "Why did you do it, Spencer?"

He shrugged, but didn't hide the guilty look on his face. "I forgot about his captivity," he admitted. "I just wanted him to know what it felt like to be on the losing end."

"That's perfectly understandable," Candace said soothingly. And she knew Spencer's actions were totally uncharacteristic of him. If he hadn't been pushed so far, he would have never done such a thing. But she had to make sure he realized the truth. "So . . . you realize it's over now?"

Rubbing a hand over the place where Kelly had slapped him, he said, "Yes. You were right."

Finally! "I was?" All too human, Candace couldn't help but want him to elaborate.

"Yes, I realize that now. It *was* a Pygmalion sort of thing. I created Kelly in a new image and fell in love with that image."

"But the image wasn't the real Kelly," Candace prompted softly.

"No, that's obvious," Spencer said with a roll of his eyes. "These past few days have shown that clearly. She isn't the Kelly I thought I knew . . . and I don't much care for the person she's really become."

Relief and exultation warred for dominance within Candace. It was about time. "So, you won't be too upset that I've invited Amalia to be our new *Pizzazz* Girl?"

"No, of course not. I think it's a wise business decision."

"What about Kelly?" Candace asked, probing.

"That is a problem. It will be hard for me—and Amalia—to work with her after this."

"Yes, of course," Candace agreed. Not to mention the fact that Kelly might just be too much temptation for Spencer if she decided not to stay with Chaz.

It was obvious Kelly and Chaz loved each other, but weren't able to work out their differences for some reason. Candace suspected it was because Kelly was too complacent, too comfortable in her current life and didn't want to leave it for an uncertain future with Chaz. Well, maybe Kelly just needed a little shaking up to make the right decision.

Taking a deep breath, Candace ventured, "What if Kelly was no longer at *Pizzazz?*"

Spencer stared at her in surprise. "I wouldn't want you to fire her for my sake."

"Not for your sake." For *mine*. But she added, "I think it would be best for everyone concerned if Kelly found a position elsewhere."

Spencer smiled at her and curled his hand in hers. "You might be right."

Her heart beating faster at the feel of his hand in hers, Candace knew she was right. But would Kelly feel the same?

Spencer frowned. "But you know, I really do feel bad about Vincent. I'd like to explain the situation to Gilbert."

Candace glanced apprehensively at Scott. "I'm not sure he'll let you."

"Maybe," Spencer said. "But I have to try."

Out in the hallway, Kelly glanced down at her clothing. Her blouse and slacks were okay, but the pumps had to go. Quickly, she ran to her room, trying to keep the rope hidden from Gilbert's sight, and changed into the cross-trainers Chaz had bought her.

Now what? Saying she needed to rescue Chaz from the outside was all well and good, but how was she going to do it? She moved out to the balcony where the wind gusted cold and strong. Chaz's room was two doors down the hall, and Candace's room was between them. Could she just cross from one to the other?

She leaned out and visually measured the distance between the balconies. The balconies were each about ten feet wide, but there had to be at least twenty feet between them. Too far to leap across, and even though she could attach one end of the rope to her balcony, how could she attach it to Candace's, then Chaz's? That wouldn't work. She'd just have to follow Chaz's example and climb up the trellis.

Sighing, she came back inside, shutting the door against the wind, and shrugged on the down vest. Stuffing the rope beneath the vest to hide it, she headed out the door.

Good. No one in the hallway but Gilbert. She hurried down the stairs and out the north entrance to reach the courtyard. No one was there, either, which was going to make it easier. No wonder—it was too cold to be outside today.

She glanced up at the balconies and realized she

didn't know which room was his. Cursing her lack of foresight, she wished she had tied a scarf to her balcony or something so she could know which room was which. And she didn't have time to go back to the room. Juan could return at any moment, and who knew what Amalia's brothers would do then?

She could figure this out. Mentally, she visualized the third floor hallway. Easy—Chaz's room was four doors from the end. So, all she had to do was count three floors up from the bottom and four balconies over from the end. *Got it.*

Moving to the proper section of the wall, she glanced up and gulped. That was a long way up. What if she fell?

I won't fall, she told herself sternly. *I can't. Chaz needs me.*

But she sure wished she had a grappling hook. Then all she'd have to do was toss it up and let it catch on the balcony and climb up the rope.

Well, no sense wishing for what she didn't have and couldn't find. She'd just have to climb the trellis.

She moved closer to examine it. It was wooden, painted white, and the interlocking slats formed small openings about six inches square—just right for a foothold. Each trellis section was about ten feet wide and they were laid side by side so they covered the entire width and height of the building.

Grabbing the wooden slats, she gave the structure a shake. It was securely fastened to the outside wall, but it moved more than she cared for. Would it hold her weight?

Well, if it held Chaz the other night, it should hold her today. And though there was some kind of vine growing on it, thank heavens it didn't have thorns. She could do this. All she had to do was make sure she stayed in the center of the trellis where the slats were strongest.

She snapped her vest closed and slung the coil of rope crossways across her body. There, that should hold it securely. Raking her windblown hair out of her face, she placed her right foot tentatively on one of the slats and leaned her weight on it. It held.

Grabbing the trellis in both hands, she put her other foot on it. The structure bowed out a little, but still held. She took another hesitant step upward, then another. So far, so good. She made her cautious way upward, stepping carefully around the slippery leaves.

About ten feet up, the wind gusted, blowing her hair in her face and making the trellis sway. Kelly immediately hugged the wall and felt like emulating the leaves that trembled around her. It was so cold, and she didn't have the training for this.

Why am I doing this again?

Oh yeah, to rescue Chaz. She froze in place. Maybe Mother was right. Maybe this was too dangerous. Chaz was in no immediate peril, but Kelly was. It might be better just to go back inside and see what happened.

Coward.

I can live with that.

Disgust filled her. No, she couldn't. For five long years, she hadn't given up on Chaz, had believed and hoped he was alive, even when everyone else had given up on him. Giving up now that he was finally back home would be a total cop-out, a denial of everything she believed in. Chaz would never give up on her, and she owed it to him to do the same for him.

More resolute now, she turned her gaze up toward her goal and headed toward it with a single-minded determination. Luckily, the vertical sections overlapped so she didn't have to worry about the weak parts at the top and bottom. Though her hands and face were freezing and it wasn't as easy as it looked to find secure footholds, she finally made it to the third floor balcony.

Tentatively, she reached out with her right foot and placed it on the floor of the balcony from the outside. Then she moved her right hand, her left hand, and her left foot to the balcony. Carefully, she swung herself over and dropped to the floor.

Made it!

The thought exhilarated her. She'd done it, she'd actually done it. She hugged herself and hunkered down out of the wind for a moment, sticking her hands in her armpits to warm them.

It took a minute or so before the shakiness passed and her knees didn't feel so weak, then she rose to her feet to peer in through the sliding glass door. Where was Chaz?

She couldn't see him. All she saw were some clothes on the bed. Women's clothes.

That stupefied her for a moment. Why would they put women's clothes in Chaz's room? Then the truth dawned on Kelly. Those were her boss's clothes, and her boss's luggage against the wall.

This wasn't Chaz's room. It was Candace's.

Kelly sagged in disbelief. How could she have made such a mistake? She glanced over at the other balconies. Yes, this was the fourth from the end, so how . . . ?

Her mind raced, giving her the answer. The first balcony was farther away from the end than it should have been. So, the room on the end either didn't have one . . . or the balcony was on the other wall, facing another direction.

Of course. Why didn't she realize that earlier? That meant Chaz's room was the next one over. Now what?

More time had passed than she had anticipated, and she couldn't waste any more. She glanced down and shivered when she realized how far up she'd come. She couldn't go down again, then back up to the other balcony. There was no time, and in this weather, she'd probably freeze to death before she made it. They'd find her lifeless body, frozen like an icicle to the trellis, the vines twining greedily around her.

She shook the image from her mind. *That's not helpful.*

She'd just have to go across the wall. She couldn't use the rope, of course, but she could cross the trellis to the other balcony the same way she had climbed up—hand over foot.

She took a deep breath and looked over at her new goal. Okay, it was only twenty feet. She had climbed much farther to get here. She could do this.

She *had* to do this.

Taking a deep breath, she swung her leg over the railing and once more found a secure foothold. *Just don't look down.*

Carefully, she resumed her precarious perch on the trellis and took a tentative step to the left. Unfortunately, Kelly soon learned that going sideways was more difficult than going up. She had to take a wide step left, then pull her right side over to her left. It was a lot slower going.

And as she neared the side of this ten-foot section halfway across, the trellis bowed out more, leaving her feeling very nervous, especially since it was hard to see where the edge was around the leaves.

She reached out to the left and grabbed a slat. It broke in her hand.

With a small scream, Kelly flailed for a secure hold and reached out blindly, grabbing another slat in desperation. It held.

Adrenaline pumped through her body, and her heart rate and fear revved up along with it. *I can't do this.*

She clung to the trellis as the lifeline it truly was. *I must do this.*

What had happened? Why did it break? Realizing she must have grabbed the piece on the very end of this section, Kelly relaxed a little. Okay, she just had to make sure she didn't put her weight on the edges.

Carefully, she reached out with her left foot, not quite as far as she had reached with her hand, and stepped down. The slat broke.

Her left foot floundered in the air for a moment as she sagged on the trellis. When she finally found purchase with her foot, she made the mistake of looking down. Three stories down . . .

She closed her eyes and dizziness assailed her. *Ohmigod, ohmigod, ohmigod. I'm going to die.*

But as her freezing fingers still clung to the wood and the dizziness abated, her fear receded as well. No, she had made it this far and she was *not* going to die, damn it. She was going to finish crossing this wall, rescue Chaz, and live happily ever after.

If she survived this, she would deserve it.

Okay, all she had to do was avoid the weak part where the two trellis sections joined together. It was a risk, but a calculated one. Carefully, she inched over square by square toward the edge. When she was sure she was at the limit of the safe part, she tightened the grip on her right hand and foot, and leaned out as far as she could to grab the other section in her left hand. It didn't break. *Yes!*

So far, so good.

With great care, she moved her left foot over just as far. It held, too, though the way the sections leaned out in her face made her stifle another scream. Both sections would break loose if she wasn't careful. Quickly, she brought her right hand and foot to join the left. The swaying stopped and she breathed a sigh of relief.

From there, the rest of the way seemed positively easy. After what seemed like eons, she finally dropped into the balcony. *Safe.*

Relief, elation, and satisfaction filled her. She had pitted herself against an incredible obstacle and survived. Not just survived—she had triumphed. Adrenaline gave one final surge and subsided. No wonder Chaz loved this feeling—it was quite a rush. Hell, it was rather fun, too, even the scary parts.

But it wasn't over yet. She still had to get Chaz out. She had taken so long. Was he still there? Was this even his room?

She looked inside, and intense relief filled her as she saw the back of Chaz's head. As Spencer said, he was tied to a chair—she could see the ropes.

She tried the door and, for once, luck was on her side. Thank heavens for Chaz's habit of leaving windows and doors open.

She slid the glass door open and Chaz swiveled his head around to stare at her, his eyes wide above the gag in his mouth and the bruise on his cheek. *Ohmigod. Poor Chaz.* He made a few noises around the gag and she held a finger to her lips. She didn't want Gilbert to hear them and give the game away. Not after everything she had gone through to get here.

She hurried toward Chaz and worked at the knots holding his arms to the chair until he was free. Finally. The thrill of success zinged through her.

He immediately reached up and pulled off the gag and, wild-eyed, threw it away as if it were a deadly snake. Jumping up, he rubbed fiercely at his arms where the rope had been. Good heavens, he was trembling. She had been right to rescue him.

"What are you doing here?" he asked in a fierce whisper.

"Saving you," she whispered back. What did it look like?

He looked annoyed. What? Did he think only men could be heroes? Well, she'd done a great job all by herself, thankyouverymuch.

"Why?" he asked insistently.

Strange question. "Because I realized I love you, and I want to spend the rest of my life with you." She smiled, anticipating his reaction.

She got one all right, but it wasn't what she expected. "That's a switch." His eyes narrowed. "Why? Because you learned Amalia wasn't pregnant with my child?"

She stared at him in surprise for a moment, wondering why he was so angry. Then again, he'd been beaten and tied up, not knowing what was going to happen to him. That was bound to make anyone a little cranky. Deciding to give him the benefit of the doubt, she said, "True, Amalia's not pregnant, but—"

"*Now* you believe me?" He shook his head sadly. "Why couldn't you trust me before, when it really counted?"

Damn. This wasn't going at all like she'd planned.

Eighteen

Chaz watched the shock settle on Kelly's features as he waited for her answer. She looked glorious. Red-cheeked and windblown from her exertions, she was nowhere near her mother's ideal of the perfect daughter.

But she was awfully close to being the perfect wife. He couldn't believe she'd climbed the wall. The fact that she would actually risk her life to rescue him made the blood thrill in his veins.

But he also couldn't get over the disappointment that she had to have outside confirmation that he was telling the truth first.

"But I do trust you," she said in a rush. "I was coming to tell you that when I found out you were tied up. That's when I learned Amalia wasn't pregnant—after, not before."

Chaz frowned. Could she be telling the truth?

"I swear it," Kelly said fervently. "Just ask Scott—he'll tell you."

"So why am I still being held prisoner here?"

"I guess Amalia was embarrassed at being caught in a lie. She's disappeared and her brothers won't believe that she's not pregnant. One of them went for a priest to marry you two."

"A priest?" Chaz repeated incredulously. So that was their plan. "That's ridiculous. Even if they could find a priest to go along with this stupid plan, it wouldn't be legal." And didn't they need a marriage license, not to mention Chaz's consent?

"Well, it might be. Remember, Gerald thinks we're no longer legally married."

"What do *you* think?"

Kelly made an impatient gesture. "I think we need to get out of here before they return." She lifted the rope coil off over her head. "We can talk about this later."

"No," Chaz said. "I want to talk about it now." Who knew if they'd have private time again later?

"Well, at least tie the rope to the balcony, okay? So it will be ready if we need it?"

"All right." As he secured the rope, Chaz asked, "If Amalia's test didn't make you change your mind, what did?"

"Something Scott said."

"What?"

"He made me realize that you were right and I was wrong. I guess I *was* punishing you, subconsciously."

"That's it?" She believed her brother but not her husband?

"That, and the fact that I realize you're an honorable man, and that means you wouldn't even look at another woman while you're married to me. I was wrong to suspect you of cheating on me. I know you'd never do that. I just forgot it for a while."

Chaz sighed in relief, not realizing how much tension had been in his shoulders until he let go of it. So she did understand.

Kelly moved closer. "I've missed you terribly, and I

don't want to go through the rest of my life without you. Can't we work this out?"

"I don't know. . . ." Their goals seemed so distant from each other. "Do you think we can find a solution that won't tear one of us apart?"

"I don't know either," Kelly said. "But I'm willing to try. How about you?"

A sudden noise at the door caught Chaz's attention. Someone was using his stolen key to come in the door. Bad timing. Quickly, he moved toward the door. Gilbert looked up in surprise to see him loose, and Chaz took advantage of the situation. Rushing forward, he lowered his head and slammed his shoulder into the large man's stomach.

When Amalia's brother landed on his butt in the hallway gasping for breath, Chaz saw Juan talking animatedly to a priest behind him, and Scott trying to restrain Deuce.

Deuce. This was all his fault. "You sonuvabitch," Chaz yelled. "You did this to me."

Scott let go of Deuce who turned a surprised face to Chaz. "Wait. I didn't—"

But Chaz did. Not waiting to hear what Deuce had to say, he punched him, full in the face. Deuce went down for the count, falling over Gilbert and knocking Juan and the priest over as he did so.

"And he scores!" Scott yelled, raising his arms in jubilation.

Chaz let out a choke of laughter but didn't stick around to see how the downed men would react. Instead, he slammed the door shut and threw the bolt. Damn, that felt good. He'd been wanting to do that for a long time.

"Come on," he said to Kelly as he heard a body hit

the door. "I don't know if these doors are built to withstand that kind of abuse. We'll talk later."

Kelly wasted no time in going over the side with him. For the third time, they climbed down a rope together.

At the bottom, Kelly asked, "What now?"

"I have no idea," Chaz admitted. "This was your plan."

Two men emerged into the courtyard. "Hey," one of them called. "Are you Chaz Vincent?"

Reporters. In answer, Chaz grabbed Kelly's hand and ran in the opposite direction. He risked a glance back. Damn, just as he thought. They were chasing him and Chaz had no idea where he was going.

"Maybe we can catch a cab out front," Kelly yelled.

"Good idea." But as he rounded the corner, he spotted three other men moving toward them from the opposite direction. When their eyes widened and one pointed at him, babbling excitedly, it didn't take a genius to realize they were reporters, too.

Quickly, Chaz made a ninety-degree turn and, still towing Kelly, dashed into the side door of the hotel. They'd just have to go through the lobby and catch a cab out front that way.

But he came to an abrupt halt when he reached the lobby. Damn. It was mobbed with people. And, oddly enough, he knew most of them.

They must have caught some fast elevators. Scott was arguing angrily with his mother and her boyfriend, Amalia and Deuce were talking excitedly with Candace, the Garcia brothers each had a firm grip on one arm of the shell-shocked priest, two policemen and three reporters were talking to Billings, and cameramen and openmouthed spectators were milling everywhere.

Ah hell, just when he wanted most to be alone with Kelly.

Kelly almost screamed in disappointment. Just when she wanted most to be alone with Chaz. She followed Chaz's example and tried to hide her face and edge around the crowd, but the five reporters from outside caught up to them.

Cameras flashed and reporters shouted questions at them. Kelly threw up her hands to shield her face, but when the entire crowd surged in their direction, she got separated from Chaz as the reporters and cameramen surrounded him.

With some vague idea of grabbing a cab and trying to rescue him anyway, she tried to fight her way free of the mob again, but was stopped by Billings.

He drew himself up stiffer than she had ever seen him and stared down his nose at her. "This is totally unacceptable," he said in freezing tones. "The Pourtales cannot condone this sort of conduct. You seem to be the catalyst for this appalling behavior. I insist you leave at once."

"You're evicting me?" she asked in disbelief. But none of this was her fault.

"Yes," he said with obvious relish. "You have one hour to pack your things and leave, or I will have the police escort you out."

"Fine," Kelly spat out. "I will be more than happy to leave your establishment. *And* to let people know how badly you've treated me." Placing her hands on her hips, she glared up at him. "It's a big mistake to piss me off, buddy. I work for *Pizzazz* magazine, you know."

It didn't seem to impress Billings. He just sniffed and stalked off.

"Actually," Candace said at her elbow, "that's what I'd like to talk to you about."

"What?" Kelly asked, trying to hide her exasperation. Couldn't Candace see this was not the time to talk shop? Reporters had cornered Chaz and he seemed to have given in and was holding a press conference. She wanted to know what he was saying.

The publisher nodded at Amalia who stood beside her with a smug smile on her face. "I've just hired our *Pizzazz* Girl."

"Her?" Kelly couldn't believe it. Candace had actually hired the bimbo? Trying to keep a reasonable tone, Kelly said, "I'm not sure I could work with her after what she's done the past few days."

Candace nodded sympathetically. "I understand. And I want you to understand that I appreciate the fact that you have released Spencer from any obligation."

Kelly glanced at her erstwhile second husband who was standing just out of earshot, watching them uncomfortably with a growing shiner under his right eye. "Well, we still have to get the annulment. But I take it he has finally seen the light?"

Candace smiled sadly. "Yes, I think he has. We have a date scheduled for tomorrow night."

So why the long face? "Good for you. I hope everything works out between the two of you." Now, if only she could do the same for herself and Chaz.

"So do I. And that's why it's so difficult for me to say this."

"What?" Kelly asked in an abstracted tone, trying to catch sight of Chaz.

"I'm going to have to let you go."

That got her full attention. "You're what?" She couldn't have heard right.

"I'm letting you go," Candace said.

Kelly knew that hiding business would get her into trouble. "I'm sorry I made you hide. It was stupid of me, but I—"

"That's not it," Candace said, interrupting. "But considering your antipathy toward our new *Pizzazz* Girl, and the fact that you and your husband used physical violence against one of our editors, I don't see how I can keep you on."

"Let me get this straight. You're firing me?" Just so Kelly wouldn't tempt her new boyfriend?

"Yes," Candace said, though she had the grace to look uncomfortable. "I just don't think it would be appropriate for you to continue working at *Pizzazz*." She gestured at the mob scene around them. "And I really don't want the magazine associated with this . . . situation."

Stunned, Kelly just stood there as Candace joined Spencer and linked elbows with him. *Ohmigod, what now?* Kelly was having a hard time taking it all in.

Chaz. She needed Chaz. She turned blindly to find him.

What she got was her mother.

"You have a lot to answer for, young lady," Grace said.

"Not now, Mother," Kelly said wearily.

Grace sniffed. "This scene is totally unacceptable. You're a disgrace to the Richmond name. Don't bother to come home. You're not welcome there anymore." Without waiting for a reply, she turned and left.

What did she mean by that? Kelly tried to follow

her, but a policeman stepped into her path. "Excuse me," she said, but the large young man didn't budge.

Staring impassively down at her, he asked, "Are you Kelly Richmond?"

"I was—that's my maiden name." What was this about?

"A.K.A. Kelly Vincent?"

"Yes."

"A.K.A. Kelly Preston?"

Uh oh. She held her hands out in supplication. "Yes, but I can explain."

He snapped cuffs on her outstretched wrists. "You can explain down at the police station where you'll be charged with bigamy."

She listened in a daze as he recited her rights. She was under arrest for bigamy? But how did they find out? Who had notified them? Not that many people knew. She glanced around wildly and her gaze settled on Billings, who looked all too smug.

That was how. He must have guessed.

As her world crumbled around her, Kelly let her face fall into her braceleted hands and tried not to sob. *Ohmigod, what do I do now?*

A shocked exclamation brought her head up. "What's going on here?" Chaz demanded, glancing at the cuffs.

Kelly glanced around wildly, hoping none of the reporters had followed him to witness her humiliation. But he must have given the reporters what they wanted, for they were all leaving the lobby, talking busily on their cell phones.

Kelly sniffled, trying not to cry. "I've been evicted, fired, disowned, and arre-rested," Kelly wailed. Then, seeing the horror on Chaz's face, a bit of hope filtered through. Blinking back tears, she said, "But the situation could be wo-orse."

Confusion plain on his face, Chaz asked in disbelief, "How?"

Kelly felt her lower lip tremble. "You could tell me you're leaving me again." And her heart stopped as she waited for his response.

Chaz's heart almost stopped at the hope in her eyes. She did love him. And, he suddenly realized, he'd been punishing her just as much as she had been punishing him. He didn't need Scott to confirm that Kelly was telling the truth about trusting him. As he'd told her brother only a few days ago, Kelly was the most honorable woman he knew. Of course she was telling the truth.

"Oh, honey," he said. "I love you. We can work this out." He tried to hug her, but the handcuffs got in his way.

He glanced at the young cop. "Are the cuffs necessary? She's not exactly a dangerous criminal."

The cop colored. "With the bigamy charge, her eviction notice, and the disorderly conduct of this unruly crowd, I thought it prudent."

Chaz scowled at him. *Lord save me from overzealous rookies.* "Well, she's not guilty of bigamy. Wait here, and I can prove it to you."

The cop stiffened. "I'm not sure I can do that, sir."

"You will if you don't want to be slapped with a charge for false arrest. That wouldn't look very good on your record, now would it?"

The rookie swallowed hard, but managed to keep his dignity. "I'm willing to hear what you have to say."

"Good—there's a lawyer here who can explain it to you."

Chaz quickly rounded up Gerald and sicced him on the rookie with instructions to get Kelly released immediately. It should be easy enough—Gerald had all the evidence on him to prove Kelly wasn't a bigamist.

While Gerald was doing that, Chaz spoke quickly to Billings, Kelly's mother, Candace, and Amalia in turn. By the time he returned to Kelly, the rookie had been joined by a stern-faced older cop who was releasing Kelly from the handcuffs.

"You're free to go, ma'am," the rookie said, chagrined. "I'm sorry for the misunderstanding." Glancing at the older cop, he added, "Really sorry."

Kelly just nodded and threw her arms around Gerald's neck. "Thank you so much."

Gerald patted her awkwardly on the back as the cops left. "It was nothing, my dear. You gave me all the necessary evidence."

She beamed at him. "But I couldn't have explained it nearly as well as you did." Turning to Chaz, she said, "He was wonderful. He spouted legalese at them until they finally gave up."

Chaz clapped him on the back. "Thanks for your help. We appreciate it."

"No problem, no problem," Gerald said. Then, apparently embarrassed at being thanked, he hurried away.

And suddenly Chaz's arms were full of Kelly. "Thank you, too," she said with an effusive hug. "Being arrested would have put the cap on a truly horrible day. Thank you for finding Gerald for me."

"It was the least I could do," Chaz murmured, reluctantly letting her go as she pulled back.

"But where did you go?"

"I thought I'd check to see if I could do anything about your other problems as well."

Looking surprised, she asked, "Were you able to?"

"Well, Billings backed down after I explained the situation and I . . . persuaded him to give you a little more time."

Kelly grinned. "And just what form did this persuasion take?"

Chaz shrugged. "I found out that *he* called the reporters and the police. And I told him if he didn't want his superiors to know that this hubbub is all his fault, he might want to treat you a little better. You can stay as long as you like."

Kelly laughed. "Well, the sooner I'm out of this place, the better. But . . . do I have a place to go home to?"

"If you mean will your mother let you in the house, yes." Chaz grimaced. "She was upset at the possible stain on the family name, but Scott and I convinced her that everything will be fine. You can go home . . . if you still want to." Though why anyone would *choose* to live with Grace Richmond was beyond him.

"And my job?"

"I'm afraid I couldn't help you there. You've burned too many bridges. With Amalia and Deuce both working there, Candace just isn't willing to risk the potential confrontations that might ensue. She has promised to give you good references, though."

"Well, that's something anyway," Kelly said with a sigh.

"You're not too disappointed?" he asked in surprise. "I thought you loved your job."

"Not really. It was a way to pay the bills and they treated me well, but I didn't love it."

"That's good," Chaz said in relief. "After what we did to Deuce, I don't think either of them will ever forgive us." He gazed down at her with a grin. "Scott told me what happened earlier. Did you really slap Deuce?"

Kelly grimaced. "Yes, but I'm not proud of it. I was just so angry at him for letting Amalia's brothers tie you up. I'm afraid I lost my temper."

Chaz found it heartening that Kelly had been angry enough for his sake to hit someone. Especially when that someone was Deuce. "Speaking of Amalia, she also explained the truth to her brothers so they're no longer after me . . . and they've released that poor priest."

"It was that easy?"

He shrugged. "As far as her brothers are concerned, what Amalia wants, Amalia gets. And thank God she doesn't want me anymore. The thought of being a supermodel is far more tempting."

Kelly laughed. "So we're both free now."

"Yes." Chaz reached out to stroke her arms. "But I don't want to be free of you. Not now. Not ever."

He knew that now. Whatever it took to keep Kelly in his life, he'd do it. He couldn't leave her alone after so many bad things had happened to her—bad things that he was responsible for. "I'll cancel that job in Turkey. Staying here with you is more important

"Oh, Chaz." Moisture pooled in Kelly's eyes. "We're quite a pair, aren't we? What are we going to do? Neither one of us has a job."

"We can find one," he said. "No problem."

"But will you be happy staying here with me?"

"Of course," he said firmly, trying not to let his doubt show in his voice. He wasn't entirely sure what he could do, but he'd try his best to make it work.

Laying a hand on the side of his face, Kelly said, "Oh, Chaz. I can't do that to you. Nothing you find here can equal the thrill of the job you have now."

"The thrill of being with you will just have to do," he said with a smile.

Kelly sighed. "You do know what to say to make me feel better, but I would hate to take that away from you. After experiencing it myself, climbing up and down those balconies, I now know why you crave it so much."

"You enjoyed that?" he asked incredulously, his hope suddenly rising.

"Yes." Kelly shook her head. "It's amazing, but I've never felt so alive, so exhilarated as I did today. The past few days, really, ever since you came back. I cracked my shell wide open."

"Then come with me," he urged.

"What?"

"I had no idea you enjoyed this sort of thing. Why don't you come with me to the dig in Turkey? You can experience the thrill of discovery along with me."

Kelly's eyes widened. "Can I do that? Will they let me?"

"Sure, why not?" Chaz said, ebullience lending his heart wings. "They always need extra people for administrative work, to assist the archaeologists, stuff like that. Even the most mundane job on a dig can be pretty exciting at times. What do you say?"

"That's perfect," Kelly exclaimed. "I'd love to go with you. And this way, I won't have to worry about you all the time. I'll know exactly what danger you'll be in."

"Yep, you'll be right there alongside me, sharing it with me." He grinned, ecstatic as he realized all his dreams were about to come true. "But there's one thing we have to clear up first."

"What's that?" Kelly asked, looking apprehensive.

"I want to make sure we're legal first. Will you marry me . . . again?"

Kelly threw her arms around him. "Of course, silly." She gave him a fervent kiss and grinned. "You always were my favorite husband."

Dear Reader,

I hope you enjoyed *My Favorite Husband*. As the name implies, the book was inspired by the movie *My Favorite Wife*—the version starring Cary Grant and Irene Dunn, to be specific. But, to make it my own, I switched the roles of the hero and heroine. And, though the premise is the same, the rest of it is my own offbeat take on the story.

The character of Scott Richmond, Kelly's brother, wasn't intended to be in the original story, but I had to have someone for my heroine to talk to, so he chimed in, then wouldn't leave. As a result, I had to promise him a book of his own. If you love Scott as much as I do, watch for his story in my next book, tentatively titled *Caught in the Act*, coming out in January 2005.

But you can't blame the "muscle massager" joke on Scott. My critique group insisted I use it after it was perpetrated on me by my brother and his wife. One of these days, I'll get even with them for it.

I love to hear from my readers—you can find me on the web at http://www.pammc.com or write to me at PO Box 648, Divide, CO 80814.

Pam McCutcheon

Discover the Thrill of
Romance With

Kat Martin

__Hot Rain
0-8217-6935-9   **$6.99**US/**$8.99**CAN

Allie Parker is in the wrong place—at the worst possible time . . . Her
only ally is mysterious Jake Dawson, who warns her that she must play
the role of his reluctant bedmate . . . if she wants to stay alive. Now, as
Alice places her trust—and herself—in the hands of a total stranger, she
wonders if this desperate gamble will be her last . . .

__The Secret
0-8217-6798-4   **$6.99**US/**$8.99**CAN

Kat Rollins moved to Montana looking to change her life, not find
another man like Chance McLain, with a sexy smile of empty heart.
Chance can't ignore the desire he feels for her—or the suspicion that
somebody wants her to leave Lost Peak . . .

__The Dream
0-8217-6568-X   **$6.99**US/**$8.50**CAN

Genny Austin is convinced that her nightmares are visions of another
life she lived long ago. Jack Brennan is having nightmares, too, but his
are real. In the shadows of dreams lurks a terrible truth, and only by
unlocking the past will Genny be free to love at last. . .

__Silent Rose
0-8217-6281-8   **$6.99**US/**$8.50**CAN

When best-selling author Devon James checks into a bed-and-breakfast
in Connecticut, she only hopes to put the spark back into her
relationship with her fiancé. But what she experiences at the Stafford
Inn changes her life forever . . .

Available Wherever Books Are Sold!

Visit our website at **www.kensingtonbooks.com**.